DOMINION
OF
DARKNESS

DELEYNA MARR

DELEYNA MARR

Heart Ally Books, LLC
Camano Island, Washington

Cover art: Deranged Doctor Designs

Published by:
Heart Ally Books, LLC
26910 92nd Ave NW C5-406, Stanwood, WA 98292
Published on Camano Island, WA, USA
www.heartallybooks.com

ISBN-13: (epub) 978-1-63107-021-1
ISBN-13: (paperback) 978-1-63107-020-4
Library of Congress Control Number: 2018932436
11 10 9 8 7 6 5 4 3 2

for Mark,

the love of my life

and my children

who keep life delightful!

Even

Westridge

Crossroads

River Crossing

North Thread

Weaver's Knot

Bright Range

Platted River

Kar

Southern Thread

Pelage

Soul's Rest

Azure Lake

Blue River

Dayspring
Castle

King's Grange

River Gleam

Springvale

Aurora

Aurora Territory

Glimmer

Rum Mines

Amity Strand

Summer

Beacon

N

Chapter 1

Awakening

Nian

Nian hated climbing this mountain. The old wizard pulled his flowing cape closer against the cold and tied his horse to a tree. He cursed the Shadows for choosing such a remote spot for his wife's tomb.

With a deep sigh that was more a growl, Nian tackled the long climb. He hadn't needed a lantern on this trail for years, having become so accustomed to walking it in darkness that it held little danger for him. Besides, no cliff could inflict near the damage his own shortsightedness had caused.

By the Light! When had this trail become so long? It hadn't seemed so far when he was young and in love. He'd bounded up the mountain then, unfazed by the pre-dawn cold. He'd come often at first, over forty years ago. Hopeful, until he learned that the enchantment could only be broken by the first Light of spring. Then the grueling hike became soul wrenching, with nothing but despair awaiting him at the summit. Now he trudged up the side of the mountain just before dawn on the bitter last night of winter.

He paused against a tree to catch his breath and watched his exhale turn to mist and drift away to nothingness. Someday soon, maybe the Master would allow him the same escape.

He'd been such a fool in his youth, oblivious to the tortures of time. The enchantment had seemed the perfect escape. Asleep together in the tomb, they would have become nothing more than a tragic tale. Two lovers buried on their wedding day. All would believe they'd taken their lives to avoid the King's rule.

When they awakened, they would have fled to the northern kingdom where their past could not follow. They would have been free to build a new life together.

The mountain cave should have been the first point on their journey to freedom, not an endless prison for his love.

Fool that he'd been, Nian hadn't imagined he would awaken before Elainya. Hadn't imagined growing old without her. Hadn't imagined being sent to betray her.

He hadn't imagined the consequences of trusting a demon.

The Shadow Lord had played on Nian's naive passion and trapped them both. Elainya in her endless sleep, Nian in a life of servitude. Would this never end?

The horizon showed the faintest tinge of the rapidly approaching dawn. A bird greeted the light with a song until it sensed his approach and flew away with a chirp of fear.

Nian forced himself to walk faster, although he couldn't fathom why. This dawn would be just like all the others he'd spent in the cave over the years—years when love and longing had powered his steps. Duty dragged him to watch over her, but duty had been replaced by dread.

Now he came only because he had no choice.

The wind moaned in the valley below, giving voice to his unspoken dread.

He was old—too old to be chasing after maidens, bewitching or bewitched. And she was young, beautifully young—too young to want the old man he'd become.

A faint light crept over the eastern mountains just as he reached the cave. He pushed through the overhanging brambles, pulled the vines aside, and allowed the first Light of spring into the cave. Elainya was still there, of course, as was the latest in the succession of her feline guardians, this one little more than a furry kitten.

Elainya had not changed since she was placed here over eighty years ago. Nian stood next to the slab and allowed himself a moment to dream of what their lives could have been like. Frozen in her last moment of purity, she was an unchanging reminder of what he'd lost, the embodiment of youthful stupidity, innocence, and ignorance. Impetuous. Rash. Elainya represented all that he had come to abhor.

The Light skittered along the floor, causing spiders and mice to run deeper into the shadows. Nian glanced down at the ray. Just like it had on each one of the more than forty occasions he'd witnessed this moment, the Light would note her waiting presence and then move on down the mountain to work its magic elsewhere, abandoning Nian to his regret.

Today, however, the Light hesitated...lingered. It seemed almost playful. As if it intended to stay.

The cave began to pulse with warmth, and Nian stepped into the shadows to watch the ray gather strength, afraid even to hope. The Light wavered over an empty stone slab, highlighting tiny particles of dust dancing to the echoes of music long silenced. Nian recognized the song the musicians had been playing down the hall when he had cast the spell. His wedding song. His wedding gift to his wife.

The presence within the sunbeam focused on him, and his pulse quickened. He knew what the Shadow Lord would do to someone he hated. How would the Light respond?

He drew a ragged breath. "I am here as the Shadow Lord's representative," he said. *My right. My duty.*

Accepting his presence, the Light moved on to the slab where Elainya lay.

Its glow passed through her long white veil and caressed the delicate curves of her body. She was gowned in fine white linen with golden filaments that entranced the Light.

This was ... new.

The ray raced along the flowing gown, pausing on the jewel set into the hilt of a knife hung at her side. The sapphire was so deep that the Light disappeared briefly and then pulled itself away.

Nian watched, transfixed, stunned by the sheer power. The Light wove its way up her gown to the pale hands crossed over her heart.

Here it paused again. The wedding ring had taken him months of work, carefully forging the gold to hold the two stones: a blue sapphire for Elainya, and a blood-red ruby for himself. The Light shunned the ruby and danced within the sapphire.

The ray flickered on the gilt embroidery of her bodice and traced a gold ribbon woven into her long, brown braid. The veil could not hide Elainya's beauty. Nian barely dared to breathe.

The Light was fighting against the spell. Bringing her back to life.

The cave was full of Light now, shoving aside the shadows that had held Elainya captive for eighty years. "Finally, she is ours," the shadows seemed to whisper. "Ours!"

The veil over her face stirred. A finger twitched.

An icy shiver trembled through him. This was Light magic, pure magic, more powerful than anything he could summon.

Soon his master would possess that power. Elainya would awaken at last.

Elainya.

He looked down at the age-lined hand he'd unconsciously lifted toward her body. She expected to wake to the embrace of her lover. Instead, she would shrink from the scratch of a stranger's grizzled beard, the gnarled fingers. The enshrouding shadows that owned his soul.

Her husband was dead, devoured by the curse of time.

He felt the familiar shadow's presence beside him but did not turn. For this moment, Elainya was a creature of Light. In his master's presence, he dared not acknowledge the beauty he saw before him. She seemed frail and young and innocent—too innocent for what lay ahead.

And he couldn't save her.

The Shadow Lord had come, and the woman he had once loved was waking. Nian had to play his part.

Color returned to her lips. Her eyes opened with a piercing blue glow that reminded him of the gems she wore. Elainya's eyes widened and the ray vanished.

Only a dim haze remained in the cave. Nian stepped to her side and gently removed the dust-laden veil that had enshrouded her. He longed to touch her, but he didn't dare, lest she feel the darkness within him. He stepped back, leaving her to struggle upright on her own.

The shadows massed and swirled, reclaiming the cave, and filling it with laughter that rang like thousands of calling gulls. Nian cringed and took another step backwards.

This would not do. He was the Shadow Lord's representative. He was here to greet Elainya on behalf of his master, not to fear her. She wasn't even aware of who she was yet.

As the laughter intensified, she began to cry. The sight of her tears gave him the strength he lacked.

Nian stepped out of the shadows, with all of the power of the Shadow Lord drawn about him like the black cape he wore. "Be silent!" he ordered, and the laughter ceased. He inclined his head slightly in her direction. "I apologize, my dear. They have no manners."

The slight tremble in her shoulders claimed his attention until his eyes met hers.

"Thank you." Her voice was a dry whisper, weak from ages of silence.

Why hadn't he thought to bring her some water? He fumbled with the flask on his belt and held it for her to take a sip.

She choked on the potent spirits. "I'm a Draska. I can't drink that."

"I have nothing else to offer you. It isn't poison." He took a long drink, grateful for the strength that warmed his blood. "I am also Draska."

She looked him over from his gray hair to the gnarled hands that returned the flask to its carrying pouch. He saw the echoes of Light magic sparkle and die in those twin sapphires. She stared at his face for a long moment. "I do not know you."

He wiped a drop of ale from his lips.

"You would not. You've been asleep for a long time. I come from the North, from Solitude. My name is Nian. I have been sent by the Shadow Lord to greet you and welcome you to your new life."

She looked at her surroundings and found herself nose to nose with a spider that hung from the ceiling. With a squeak, she jerked away and fell off the bier to land in a heap of rumpled finery on the floor.

Nian frowned. He was not handling this well. Of course, the girl would be disoriented. Probably in pain as well, but as a healer, she'd be able to mask that.

He stepped to her aid. "Let me help you up, Elainya."

"No. I'm fine. Just startled." She refused the hand he offered and pulled herself up, using the marble slab for balance. The tactile contact with the real world seemed to strengthen her.

She focused on him and then swept the room with her gaze. For a moment, her eyes closed. When they opened, she stared with determination at the other bier. Her movements were stiff, but her gaze never left her goal as she staggered across the cave. She placed her hands on the stone, and all hope that the greeting would go smoothly vanished.

"Dren. Where is Dren?" She reacted as if the stone had burned her. She traced a line in the deep dust that covered the slab.

"Drenil will never be far from you. Right now, you need food and rest. There will be plenty of time to answer your questions. If you will come with me, I will explain everything."

"No. You'll explain now."

At that moment, the gray kitten placed itself between her feet and faced Nian with a spit and a hiss, every inch of fur standing straight out from its body. He looked from the snarling kitten to the willful young woman and suppressed a laugh. "You will not give me orders, girl."

"You come from the Shadow Lord, you said?"

"My master, and now yours as well."

"I am no one's servant."

"You met only once, long ago. You may remember a traveler that came to the castle shortly before your wedding. He assisted in your escape."

He would have sworn she could not be any paler than when she lay sleeping, but now the blood drained from her face and she collapsed against the marble. Her voice was weak, barely reaching his ears. "Lord Fenshad was the Shadow Lord?"

As if conjured by her naming, the shadows in the room swirled and took corporeal form. Nian stepped back, gladly surrendering the meeting to his master.

He hadn't felt like such an inept since his own first meeting with the master. Remembering that meeting, his eyes took in the girl's proud stance, and fear clutched at his heart. She would show proper deference, wouldn't she?

Nian hadn't. He'd had no idea of the torture the master could invoke with only a twist of his sadistic lips.

The Shadow Lord never aged, having no actual body. Nian had seen him use this favored appearance to enchant women over the years: handsome, eyes dark and deceptively kind. But those black circles of mystery had no effect on Elainya at that moment.

"Where is my husband?" She stepped toward the master as if she could be a threat to him.

The cave walls rumbled ominously, causing a shower of dirt to fall near the entrance.

Nian badly wanted to be elsewhere. He couldn't just stand by and watch, though. "My lord, she's very young."

"Not too young to show respect," the master growled.

"She has not regained her wits. Please, my lord, let me take her to Aurora. I'll explain everything to her there. Give her time, and she will honor you for the gifts you have bestowed." He was sweating, the effort of confronting the master draining him more than the long early-morning hike.

The kitten leapt onto the slab and crouched behind the girl.

Elainya gathered the kitten to her chest, tucking its head under her chin.

The shaking of the cave stopped and the Shadow Lord turned to scrutinize Nian. For a moment, the master was silent. An echo of the pain of his own waking brushed the corners of Nian's mind. He prepared himself for the torment and was startled when the master withdrew.

"Nian, you are a sentimental old fool. Still, you have served me well and ask very little. I will grant you the"—he paused and spread his hands in mock graciousness—"kindness you request. But get your apprentice under control before my generosity is exhausted." The master's tone was amused. Playful. Feral.

Nian bowed. "Thank you, my lord. I will not fail you."

With a swirl of shadow and leaves, the body of the master dissolved, but his presence still ruled the cave.

Nian took a moment to focus his thoughts.

Elainya glared at him in a silence he doubted would last very long. She held the squirming kitten close, its frantic struggles to escape a contrast to her stillness.

"Come outside." Nian left the dank cave and breathed deeply of the clean air.

Elainya followed, her movements stiff. "Why do I feel like I should be grateful?"

"Because you're a young fool who was just spared an extremely painful lesson. Never question the master."

She set the kitten down and it bounded into the forest. He watched the girl take in her surroundings. There was a desperation to her searching that touched his heart. Of course she would be looking for Drenil. How Dren had wanted to be here!

They stood on an outcropping, with the entire world seemingly spread before them. His eyes followed a distant bird as it searched for easy prey. "I knew him, long ago. Drenil was a brave man. He saved my life."

"Was?"

In the brief silence that followed, Nian was sure he could count her heartbeats. Two, three. Four. "Drenil died over forty years ago, Elainya."

She fell as if invisible strings holding her upright had suddenly been cut. She wrapped her arms around her knees and trembled, silent only for a moment. "No!" she screamed. "I don't believe you." The circling bird darted upward and flew to quieter hunting.

"I'm sorry. He asked me to watch for your wakening, and I have been here faithfully ever since."

"We were married in the Draska tradition. I'm a healer. I know about the linking of souls. He can't be dead, because I am alive."

"The Shadow Lord was present at your wedding, presided over your linking. Even though you didn't know who he was at the time, nevertheless his presence controlled the outcome." Her eyes were unfocused, her breath coming in short, shallow gasps. "You were entranced when Drenil died."

Elainya drifted back to the present, nailing him with a stony gaze. "Thus you escaped sharing his death," he lied.

"I can remedy that," she said. She drew her knife faster than he would have thought possible.

The Shadow Lord's spell immobilized her. Nian could see her muscles straining to complete the killing stroke she'd intended, but the master's power was something she could not escape.

Nian knelt down in front of her, grateful that the master felt no need to do more than demonstrate her weakness. He gently took the knife from the girl's hand.

"No, you can't. You made a bargain. The Shadow Lord would provide you with a new life, in exchange for your service."

"I made that bargain with a traveler. He would get us to safety and then we would help him with a land deal he was working on. That was all." Her tone reminded Nian of a lynx he had once trapped in a canyon during a hunt. Not a safe animal to turn his back on, even if he was a Draska.

"It's time to help, but first you must learn to show the master proper respect." He transferred her knife to his left hand and looked into the depths of her eyes, willing his words to reach deep into her soul. "You cannot fight him, Elainya. Service can be a blessing. He has given you great gifts you do not even know of yet. He asks little, but you must not defy him. Do you understand?"

He tried to project a sense of danger into her mind but found her thoughts too full of confusion for clarity. She wasn't rational.

By the Light, he hoped the spell hadn't left her damaged permanently. He gripped her shoulder hard enough to leave a bruise and forced her to meet his gaze. Forced her to see the meaning of the words he didn't dare speak aloud. "Elainya, do you understand?" he asked.

"Yes," she whispered. He felt the master release his hold on the girl, and she lowered her hands.

"Good. We will go to Aurora, then, so I can see to your training." His worn-out knees trembled as he stood, and he reached toward the rock face for support.

In his moment of instability, Elainya stood and dashed into the forest, leaving him alone on the ridge, holding her knife, feeling like a fool. The master took form beside him. He gazed after the girl like a starving raptor.

"My lord, forgive me."

The Shadow Lord laughed and the shadows danced around him. "Nothing to forgive, Nian. Leave her to me for now. I want to let her get this rebellion out of her system. I'll enjoy teaching her that obedience is the smart path. Go back to your duties. She'll return to your side as surely as day follows night."

Nian bowed and headed back down the mountain. If he were lucky, Elainya would fall off a cliff. An accidental death would be a kindness.

Elainya

There is no pain in freezing, only in thawing.

My body ached and throbbed, at last forcing me to stop my headlong rush into the woods.

Drenil was dead.

The thought echoed through my heart, threatened to overwhelm me. I'd been allowed to escape. The demon would be watching. Observing. Waiting. This was not the time for mourning. I blinked the tears away.

There was a bend in the path, giving me an unhindered view across the valley and up the mountain to where the castle stood in the distance. The once-familiar view was breathtaking. The castle still dominated the golden dawn, the sharp-edged stonework in better repair than I remembered. The eastern watchtower was new, added in the years I'd lost. Where the pass opened out further down the mountain, the town had grown. New walls added another layer of fortification. Why add walls in a land renowned for peace?

The air smelled of cold night rains and earth ripped from its winter slumber by eager farmers. It was spring. Above everything, Sun's Apex shone with first light, reflected off its untouchable snow-covered peaks.

The kitten I'd seen earlier in the cave crept out of the bushes. I picked it up and ruffled its silky fur. It looked almost like the companion cat I'd kept with me at the castle, only this one was much younger, its mental voice not developed yet. I sensed excitement and playfulness as its tiny blue eyes met mine.

I looked southward for the morning fires of Aurora, but saw only the ancient Draska forests. I longed to fall into my mother's arms and let her stroke the pain away, but she had been dead for many years. How many, I had no way to know.

Her death had left the opening that I had filled in the King's court. At least she had not witnessed what a fool I'd been.

For the briefest moment as I wrestled with the Shadow Lord's spell, I thought I'd felt Dren's touch. That brief contact with Dren was a comfort, as thready as the terrified beating of my heart. Now it was gone, sealed off behind walls of stone.

I took a deep breath and let the fear wash over and past me. Useless distraction. At least I remembered that much of my training.

I petted the kitten and my ring sparkled, the ruby glowing still with the warmth of a vow. I caressed this small piece of my past's puzzle before taking a hesitant step. Somewhere, Drenil was alive. I had to believe that. Maybe everything the wizard had said was a lie.

The Lord of Darkness wanted me to go to Aurora in obedience. So that was the one place I could not go. I'd fled the castle yesterday and years ago. I could seek shelter at the castle. The Shadow Lord would not expect me to return there.

There had to be a way out of this bargain. If not, then I would just have to arrange a convenient death.

Chapter 2

An Introduction of Sorts

Elainya

How unprepared I was for waking! I would arrive at the castle unannounced, a beggar in a dress that looked like a burial shroud. The hem was dirty, the skirt shredded by clinging vines before I was halfway down the overgrown mountain path. The thin sandals I wore did little to spare my feet from stones that hid beneath decaying leaves.

My furry companion pounced upon a trailing thread and I turned to pull off the string. "You are not helping."

His antics did nothing to improve my appearance but did distract me whenever I started to panic.

He scurried off to chase a bug.

I might survive in the wilds, but this gown would not. I could make a new dress, something woolen and strong enough to withstand a walk in the woods, if I had time and materials. There was gold in the pouch I wore, but who would sell to a ghost?

Some Draska were good with illusion spells, but I'd never mastered the technique. As a healer, I'd never needed such trickery.

The budding trees warned of the cold nights of early spring; I would need shelter before nightfall. No mirage could provide me with warmth.

Food was what I needed first. I felt like I hadn't eaten in years and laughed, realizing I hadn't. I paused at a small stream and drank, trying to convince my stomach that this was enough. The kitten batted at some fresh water-fronds in a patch of sunlight, and we munched on them, pretending the bitter strands were filling.

"You're supposed to be a cat."

The kitten blinked up at me with pale blue eyes.

"You could catch a fish."

It looked at the water and then back at me.

"So, you are related to Lyricat, aren't you?"

I scratched it behind the ears as it purred up against my foot. Its ancestor had been my constant companion, a gift from my mother. More a friend than a pet, Lyricat had communicated her thoughts as clearly to me as if she'd been able to speak. I wondered if this ball of fluff could be taught the knack of thought-speech.

"Don't worry, little one. You'll grow big enough to catch those fish some day."

I tried to ignore the increasingly forceful sense of intrusion into my mind. The distant mental touch was back. If it was Drenil, he had changed since I'd last been with him.

The touch increased, urging me to obey the Shadow Lord. While the cat might not be able to communicate through mind-speech, someone else clearly could.

At last, I spoke out loud, my voice startling several birds from the trees. "Whoever you are, make your own choices, not mine."

The cat looked around in confusion. My intruder acquiesced, and I had a mental image of shrugging shoulders that felt both familiar and strange.

Nian

Nian could feel her plotting, trying to escape the Shadow Lord. His late breakfast lost its flavor. He stood up from his impromptu camp at the bottom of the hill and untied his stallion from the shelter where the horse had waited. He mounted Singe in a move that was slowed by age. He slapped the horse with the reins and it lunged into a gallop.

The girl was impossible. The Shadow Lord couldn't possibly expect him to train her; she was as wild and unruly as his stallion on a bad day. He'd already trained a perfectly good replacement. To start over with Elainya would be insane. He was too old for such nonsense. Rebellion was best left to the young.

He quickly altered his mood, bringing his mind back into submission to his master. He slowed the horse and calmed his outward appearance.

His thoughts had bordered on disobedience. If the master wanted her trained, of course, he would train her. He'd learned that lesson long ago. His mouth tasted like ash.

That lesson he would not forget.

Elainya would learn soon enough. He shut her out of his consciousness so he could return to the castle in peace.

Elainya

I choked on a mouthful of greens and looked down at the ring on my hand...a bonding ring. Yet here I was, alone, forty years after my husband had supposedly died. It had to be a lie. Dren had to be alive.

The remaining leaves of my breakfast fell from my hand.

I had to find a way to escape the Shadow Lord. Anger overwhelmed sense. Let the demon do what he wanted, I would not do his bidding. All I wanted was a chance for revenge. Grandmother Nala had warned me that demons always had a plan in their dealings with humans. Some day the Shadow Lord would reveal his plan to me, and then I would work to thwart it. That thought gave me hope.

The day was bright and lovely, but strange in its silence. Why weren't the birds singing? Nervous, I pulled myself up and resumed my walk, stiff from even the brief pause. I glanced at the kitten, who seemed determined to follow me, and picked up the gray ball of fluff.

I looked into the innocent young eyes. "No. You aren't old enough to talk yet, are you, cat? I doubt the birds are even afraid of you, you little terror." I put him up on my shoulder and enjoyed the way he snuggled his wet nose under my ear. "Terror. That would be a good name for you." He purred in response.

I could find help in Aurora, but I was too stubborn to go where the demon directed. Let him kill me. As long as he left me freedom of movement, I'd move in the opposite direction.

The path had deteriorated to a faint animal track, choked by the budding shoots of cling-vines and nut trees. I struggled towards the castle, trying to think of some way to explain my presence.

Nothing larger than a rabbit had passed this way in years. I'd avoided the main paths, keeping out of Nian's way. He'd most likely be on his way back to Aurora, but I didn't want to take any chance of his finding me. The light in the forest was tricky, revealing hazards where there were none and concealing real ones. In a patch of sunlight, I tripped over a vine and went sprawling in the dirt, scratching my face on a stray branch. A faint tearing sound accompanied my fall.

I rose up onto my elbows to survey the damage. Brushing the dirt from my face, I was glad to see there wasn't any blood.

Sitting up further, I looked at my tattered dress. Instead of white, it was now a mottled brown with flecks of green. I rearranged the bodice to cover some of the worst tears in the fragile shift. At this rate, I would arrive at the castle dressed in leaves. Terror backed away from me, refusing to climb back onto my shoulder after his tumble.

A scream, quickly stifled, erupted from a thicket off to my right. I got to my feet and crept through the trees to a point where I could peer into the clearing without being seen.

Judging by her clothing, the source of the scream was a peasant. Her dark hair hung loosely to her waist, the brown cloth that had covered it now grasped by a lanky young man, dressed in hunting finery of reds and yellows. He removed his mouth from hers and leered. "Scream again and I'll do that some more...."

She looked around in panic, but her wild eyes could not see me through the bushes. A hound barked nearby. She gasped. Her face grew ashen, but she did not scream again. The only people nearby would be friends of the youth.

"What have you caught, Jeiwan?" A voice called from somewhere nearby.

"A plump young rabbit—enough for all of us." The youth plucked at the laces of the girl's bodice with his knife like a cat playing with a mouse. She tried to pull away but was held by an iron grip on her slender arm. The desperation in her eyes dragged me into the clearing.

"I may be unfamiliar with your customs, but where I'm from, a knight does not court a lady with a knife." I forced my voice to sound calm.

He started at my sudden appearance from the bushes, then laughed. "I'm no knight, nor is she a lady." He raised his voice. "Come see what I've caught now! Some sort of tree spirit."

I could imagine how I looked to him, a tattered madwoman daring to challenge an armed man. Self-consciously, I ran my hand over my hair, pausing to remove a bright green leaf. So much for appearances.

"Let the girl go," I said.

"I'm not through with her yet."

"Yes, you are." At least my voice did not waver.

He focused his attention on me and shoved the girl to the ground. Terrified, she looked from one to the other of us but did not move to escape. His eyes roamed up and down my body and his face twisted into a predatory leer. "You'd rather I tended to you first? That can be arranged."

The moment he turned towards me slowed to an eternity. I noticed the beginnings of his first beard. He was too young for such behavior. He reminded me of the show cocks I'd seen at market, bright feathers puffed up with pride. My anger boiled over despite his youth.

"Oh, be still." I let a hint of my power reach out to control him. To my shock, he fell as if I'd struck a physical blow. Two others entered the clearing following a pair of small hounds. I pulled the girl to her feet and shoved her towards the hidden path I'd just left. "Run," I ordered.

She was out of sight before the newcomers recovered from the shock of seeing their leader lying unmoving amidst a patch of bright purple wildflowers, his shirt clashing madly with the surrounding forest.

The kitten was no where to be seen.

Jeiwan's two companions were dressed in browns and greens for camouflage. One was tall, the other even younger than Jeiwan. The tall one kept his eyes on me while he knelt beside the unconscious boy, joining with the dogs in examining their master. One of the dogs began a mournful howl. I waited to see what they would do, allowing the girl time to escape. He nudged the quiet form and shivered.

He stood to his feet with exaggerated slowness, empty hands outstretched. "You've killed Jeiwan." The younger boy was looking anywhere other than at me.

"I have killed no one. He's just asleep," I moved closer to help. Why had he fallen like that?

"Please, don't come any closer," he begged. His right hand was open, fingers spread in the warding symbol of Light.

Did he expect me to vanish like a shadow? While I could escape, I didn't want them chasing after the girl. Besides, this was a chance to get into the castle, even if it wasn't a good one.

"I'm a healer. I can't help him if you won't let me touch him," I pointed out.

The younger boy was now staring just over my right shoulder. Perhaps there was something wrong with him. Too late, I realized my mistake.

I heard a snap behind me and was plunged into darkness.

Nian

In one instant the distraction of Elainya's presence was gone. He stopped the horse and turned around as if by looking he could find her. How could she just vanish?

He held Singe to a tight reign. Where could he look? She wasn't asleep, he would be able to sense her then. The horse snorted his desire to continue towards home.

Unconscious? Not dead. The Shadow Lord wouldn't let her die. Had she defied the demon? Had the master taken her somewhere for training?

He would have known, wouldn't he? Nian shook his head in frustration. No, there'd been no sense of pain, just the sudden silence.

With a stiff twist, he dismounted and tied Singe's reign to a branch. Sunlight dappled the path back the way he'd just traveled, while ahead, the way led into a denser portion of forest. Perhaps he should turn back and look for her, but where to look? He would need direction.

He stood beneath a huge oak and let his head fall forward. With a deep breath for focus, he straightened and looked toward the darkest shadow at the edge of the clearing. "My lord?"

The shadows swirled and Lord Fenshad appeared, leaning casually against a tree, a rakish smile on his face. "Nian, you worry too much."

"She is injured?"

"No. She managed to get herself knocked on the head, but no permanent damage has been done. She's being brought to the castle."

"The castle?" What would it be like for her, returning to a place that in her mind she'd only just left?

"Of course. I said I wanted you to train her. She can try to run, but wherever she goes—there you will be waiting for her. How long do you think it will take her to stop running?"

"It may take a while."

The master laughed. "True. And won't it be amusing to see what she tries next?"

"My lord, I'm not a young man. Jauer is trained. Can't he...?"

"No, Nian. I do not want Jauer. I've told you that before." The Shadow Lord straightened and walked slowly across the clearing. "I do not mind you training him if that amuses you, but he will not serve my purposes. I need Elainya, and I need you." He paused, his deep eyes holding Nian's. "You were a delight when you were young."

The master brushed his hand lightly over Nian's cheek. "I enjoyed training you."

The deceptively gentle hand rested on Nian's shoulder. He suppressed a shudder and swallowed to regain his voice, but no words would come.

"Why didn't you ever try to run away, Nian?"

Nian looked deeply into the demon's eyes. "Because, my lord, I have always known there was nowhere to run."

Fenshad laughed. "How wise you are, and how respectful. With you it is always, 'my lord.'"

"Yes, my lord."

"How long has it been, Nian, since you last spoke to me with disrespect?"

Nian did not move away from that lingering touch, but he felt his throat grow dry at the memory. "Thirty-seven years, and one summer season, my lord."

"Such long and faithful service deserves some form of reward." He ran his hands down Nian's shoulders. "You're right, you are too old to be chasing around after Elainya. Your joints ache, don't they?"

Oh, how they ached! "Yes, my lord."

"I could make you young again. You'd be more than a match for your young apprentice then."

Nian didn't dare to breathe at the hope he felt stirring in his heart. He tried to hide his reaction, but he knew the moment the master saw the flicker behind his eyes, because the demon's smile grew raptorial as he leapt upon that faint hope. "No, no, of course not. It won't work to have you young. She needs to respect you. What I can do, however, is to remove those aches."

Fenshad gripped Nian's shoulders until they popped, sending a sharp pain through his shoulders and down his spine.

The lightning bolt of agony rippled down his legs and out through his feet. The Shadow Lord released his hold and stepped away.

Nian staggered and managed to catch himself upon the tree.

"There now. How does that feel?" the demon asked.

"I don't know." Was it a trick? He mentally searched through his body looking for any hidden surprises the demon might have planted. "The pain is gone."

The demon paused to check the fingernails of one hand, flicking away a speck of dust. "I suppose I could train her my-self...." The master ran a hand over his hair. "Yes. She would be entertaining. Would you rather I had her taken elsewhere? I could relieve you of the...burden of her presence."

"No, my lord!" Nian brought his voice under control. "I un-derstand. I will do as you wish." The old aches were gone. He felt energetic, able to move and dance. "Thank you."

The master smiled, but his eyes were cold. "Don't question me again, Nian."

"No, my lord."

Nian bowed his head for a long moment, and when he looked up, the demon was gone. Elainya's return was making him careless, rash. With a steadying breath, he mounted Singe and rode to the castle to wait for Elainya.

Elainya

I came to with my eyes covered by some form of blindfold, and my hands securely tied in front of me. A filthy rag had been shoved into my mouth, and then tied roughly behind my head, snagging my hair and pulling uncomfortably. The rag tasted of sweat and dirt. I gagged.

"That's too tight, you're choking her." The voice came from my right and held the high-pitched tones of youth.

My head was dropped unceremoniously into a pile of leaves. "Of course, Joln, I suppose you'd rather she used her magic on us all. I'm sure she'll be more comfortable after we're dead."

I recognized the voice of the taller youth. "She spoke to him, but she also looked at him. There's no telling whether her magic lies in her hands, her eyes, or her voice. I'm not taking any chances."

A third voice, presumably my unseen attacker, intervened. "Kreig is right. We cannot take any chances with a person of her persuasion. We will take her to the king."

I felt a hand testing the gag. The cloth loosened a bit. "Still, I do not think we need to be cruel about it. After all, knowing Jeiwan, she was probably provoked."

Kreig snorted. "Well, I'm not carrying her. She can walk."

I felt gentle hands under my elbows. "Are you awake? I regret the necessity to restrain you, but surely you understand our position."

I nodded carefully, and winced when the gag pulled out another strand of hair. This third companion at least had manners. He lifted me to my feet. "She is light as a feather!"

"That's fine, Tromas," Kreig said. "If you find her so light, go ahead and carry her. I've got my hands full with Jeiwan."

I felt myself lifted over Tromas' shoulder. With a cheerful whistle to the dogs, my captors set off.

I took a deep breath, tried to dispel the dizziness that surrounded me, and choked again on the foul rag. I let my senses wander over the ache in my head. No permanent damage, at least. My natural talent sped the healing.

Something had heightened my abilities. I could feel the power coursing through my blood even now, washing away the sense of weakness. Could I escape? Possibly, but then where would that leave me? At least this way I would get inside the castle. Perhaps I could still salvage the situation, as long as I remained calm.

Who knew what I might be capable of now? I didn't want to hurt anyone...else, I thought guiltily. Knowing that I could escape if I wanted to was some comfort.

Maybe whatever I'd done to Jeiwan was somehow a result of being out of touch with my body since I'd wakened from the spell. I'd felt awkward and unbalanced. Maybe my abilities were out of kilter... or maybe they'd been changed by my pact with the

demon. What had that magician said? Something about gifts....
I shivered.

The three companions were silent as they walked on, and
I tried to figure out how far we were from town. My captor
smelled of forest and wood smoke. He didn't smell as if he'd
been sleeping rough. He might have eaten breakfast at a camp
in the woods, though. I didn't remember it being far from the
cave to the castle. My stomach growled loudly at the thought of
food.

"This woman is starving!" Tromas' voice laughed as I was
jounced along. "Do we have anything she can eat? No wonder
she's so light."

"What are you planning to do, untie her?"

"I have some rolls in my pack," Joln's young voice offered.

Tromas stopped and set me gently on my feet. "Well, witch,
we have a problem. I would like to feed you, but my companions
fear you will put a spell on us all if I remove your gag. Is that
true?"

I shook my head, trying to seem trustworthy.

"Oh, yeah. I'm sure she'll be telling you the truth!" Kreig's
voice dripped with sarcasm. "She said she didn't kill Jeiwan, and
I saw her do it with my own eyes."

There was silence for a brief moment. "Well, will you swear
by...whatever it is you consider holy...will you swear that you will
do us no harm?"

"Swear that you won't talk!" Joln added.

I nodded, wondering how I was supposed to swear if
I couldn't speak. Tromas' hands fumbled with the gag. He muttered as he tried to pull my hair aside, and I winced. My cheeks
felt raw. "This was far too tight."

I felt a knife blade along the base of my skull and froze.

"Do not fear. I will not hurt you." The gag came away with
a sudden slice, and I spat it out, gasping for air not tainted with
sweat.

"You cut my handkerchief!" complained Kreig.

"It was impossible to remove otherwise."

"Now what do you plan on gagging her with?"

"Her word. She seems honorable. We will leave it off."

A hard bit of roll was placed into my tied hands and I eagerly bit into it, enjoying the richness despite the dry texture. It was filled with spiced meat, a delicacy after the greens I'd had earlier.

As soon as I'd finished, Tromas took hold of my bound hands and steered me forward. "Light as you are, it would help if you could walk. I am needed to assist with our other burdens." Each step was a hazard, and I stumbled occasionally, but each time, Tromas caught me. The path seemed level. Perhaps we were nearing the town.

I was tempted to ask him to remove the blindfold, but I had given my word not to speak, and I did want them to trust me.

After a while, I heard a babble of voices, mixing into the cheerful noise of a town. Bells rang somewhere in the distance above me, giving me a sense of place as well as day. The bells rang from the castle only on Chapelday, the first of each tenday. We had come to the city that surrounded the castle. Each cautious step now fell on well-packed earthen roads, and we began to climb. A barrage of scents surrounded me: baking bread, sewage, and animals—sheep and horses, I guessed. I tripped and nearly fell, unable to recover my balance.

I was exhausted. Tromas lifted me and carried me the rest of the way.

"I bring a witch that has killed Jeiwan!" Kreig announced.

A new voice responded to his hail. "Take her to the chapel. We'll take Jeiwan's body to the king. Once Lord Nian has been summoned, we will bring her in. I will not have the king endangered." I was returned to my feet and unfamiliar hands grasped my arms.

My new guards were not as gentle as the boys had been, but I held back my power, remembering what even a hint had done to Jeiwan. I found myself pulled out of the warmth of the sun and then marched through echoing halls before being unceremoniously dumped on a cold stone floor. Behind me, a door slammed.

I pushed myself into a sitting position and noticed light glowing through my blindfold. In the silence, nothing moved. Deciding I was alone, I reached up to remove the cloth from my eyes.

"Here, let me help with that," a soft, masculine voice spoke from just in front of me, causing me to start. "Oh, I'm sorry I frightened you. Let me untie you."

I blinked in the sudden brightness and focused my attention on the small, round man who knelt before me, working with the knots that bound my hands. He was clothed in a reflect's simple white robe, plain in every way. His hair was short and brown, and when he loosed the last knot, the eyes that gazed into mine were the gentle brown of newly planted earth. A light of recognition flickered within them, and he smiled. He stood and walked into the chapel, leaving me to orient myself in peace.

The chapel's entry hall was as stunning as I remembered. The ceiling was formed from thousands of bits of glass, each reflecting the light of the sun and filling the room with playful rays of color. A ray of shimmering white in the center of the room blessed a small font of holy water. I washed my hands and splashed my face, before realizing how irreverent I was being. I opened my hands and embraced the Light in a ritual gesture of respect. Let the Shadow Lord think on that!

The open far door revealed the chapel. Beyond this I remembered only the reflect's quarters and a small storage room. The guards would have known I could not escape and trusted the Light to control my magic. Once, I would have laughed at such a thought, but now...I wasn't so sure the source of my power wasn't the Shadow Lord himself.

I entered the chapel and felt memories stir. Multicolored lights filtered through the stained glass window that formed one wall, playing across my gown and the glowing stones of my ring. Even at night, the room would be filled with a thousand candles and their reflected light. On my wedding night, the sparkles of light had caught the filaments woven into my dress and my future had seemed bright and full of hope with the Light of love surrounding me.

My gown was now ruined, a mockery of past purity.

A faint cough drew my attention to the reflect. He looked at me and smiled with surprising warmth. "Are you feeling better, Elainya?"

I stared at him. "Yes, thank you. How is it that you know my name?"

He chuckled, the jolly laugh of a friend. "I was told you were coming," he gestured at the brightness, "by my master."

"Really. Your master knew I was coming?" I couldn't remember telling anyone my name, but I must have. "You sure it wasn't a young rat?"

"My name is Reflect Rendel, child. I'm sorry to disconcert you. We don't have much time to get to know each other, but you are not to meet the king dressed like that. In my chamber, you'll find a new gown. Consider it a welcome present from my master." He bustled me toward his room before returning to lighting candles.

"Aren't you afraid I'll disappear or try to attack you?"

His eyes met mine, but his expression was unreadable. "No. Now hurry and change."

I went into the small side room, furnished as plainly as the reflect, with only a chest and a small sleeping pallet in the corner. This room had a normal stone ceiling but was still well lit by reflected light from the chapel. Tiny chinks in the walls made pools of Light throughout the room. One fell upon a gown of deep blue with gold filaments running through it, which lay across the chest. I touched the rare silken fabric in awe and watched as the Light played with the stones in my ring. This fabric could only have come from Weaver's Knot, costly as that was. When I had lived at the castle, I had preferred this fabric, an oddity among the castle women who liked the sturdy linens made locally. I'd traveled south to the Knot to bring back fabric much like this. The gown was the color of my eyes, the color of the stone in the hilt of my lost dagger, and of one of the two stones that shone from my ring. For a second, I had a mental glimpse of the artisan who had made both dagger and ring. He'd had eyes of pale blue. I put thoughts of Dren out of my mind.

I removed my girdle and the remnants of my gown. The dress slid with ease over my tattered shift. I was not surprised when it proved a perfect fit. The hem swirled about my ankles, dancing of its own accord. The sleeves trailed elegantly a few inches from my wrists. I set a gold chain belt across my hips and pulled a worn wooden comb from the small pouch that now held all my worldly goods. Removing the golden thong that had held my braid in place, I began combing out the leaves, dirt, and bits of cobweb that fouled my hair. That done, I re-braided my hair and tied it back.

When I came out of the room, even Reflect Rendel appeared surprised. "That gown was made for you," he whispered.

"How is that possible, as not even I knew I was coming?"

"The Light sees all things, my child." He gestured me back towards the anteroom, just as the guards returned.

The seneschal stopped and looked from me to Rendel in shock. "Why have you released her?"

"She is no threat to you. There has been a misunderstanding."

The guard captain frowned down at the little reflect but motioned for me to follow him into the main hall. I noticed the way he surreptitiously held his hand towards me in the same warding gesture the boys had used earlier and kept a respectful distance. I need not fear rough handling from this one; he was afraid to touch me.

The king's guards stood at attention in the hallway, hands on elaborate sword hilts. I kept my expression neutral, even as I realized how absurd the soldiers were. If I chose to use my powers against the king, what could they do to stop me? Unfortunately, I was here to win his trust, not a battle with his guardians. Trust is harder to win.

A fire burned low in the midst of the main hall. Pillars lined the sides of the room, each bearing a burning torch. With only a hint of sunlight peeking through the air vents, the room was dim after the brightness of the chapel. The walls were lined with tapestries bearing the arms of the kingdom's history. The few courtiers in the room all stood well behind the pillars.

Jeiwan's body had been laid at the foot of the dais.

As I stood waiting for the king to acknowledge me, I glanced at the wall hangings, feeling a strange sense of familiarity. A horse rampant on a field of deepest green caught my attention. I became dizzy with the sense of foreboding that came from that image.

Cydril. That was King Cydril's herald. Remembered fear, as instinctual as my fear of snakes, formed a lump in my throat. While my own personal power might be more than a match for the physical might of the king, he had held the power to destroy my life.

Cydril had known how to use that power. I remembered his face—deeply lined with age and years of anger.

The guards motioned me closer to the dais. It took all of my courage to look up into the blessed, unfamiliar face.

"Why have you killed this squire?" the king asked. He seemed angry and yet controlled. This was not a man to treat lightly. Intelligence and strength radiated from him.

I sighed. "By your leave, may I touch the boy?" My mother had spent years in service to the court. She'd made sure that I knew how to stand confidently in front of royalty, even when I was trembling inside.

A deep voice boomed from behind me. "Haven't you done enough, witch?" By his armor and sword, I judged him to be the king's war leader.

"Forgive me, sir, but I asked the king's permission, not yours."

He growled. "He was my son."

The king interrupted. "Reif, hold your tongue a moment." He looked intently into my eyes. "Why do you ask this? The boy is dead."

"I doubt it." The boy was the son of the king's war leader. I congratulated myself on my ability to thoroughly muddle an introduction.

"His companions saw you strike him down."

Exasperated, I walked over and knelt beside the squire. He looked peaceful and innocent in sleep. Someone had returned his dagger to the sheath at his side. Even without touching him, I could feel the life within him. He was in a deep healer's trance, no more.

Lightly, I touched his shoulder. As he began to stir, I stood and looked to the king for acknowledgment.

Jeiwan leaped to his feet and drew his weapon. "You don't know what you're in for," he yelled, advancing on me in fury. He was still disoriented from the trance, unaware of the change in his surroundings.

I stepped back and prepared to defend myself.

"Jeiwan!" Reif shouted.

The king watched in silence as Jeiwan froze and looked around the court. He acknowledged the altered venue with remarkable calm, and sheathed his dagger with a mutter. His gaze returned to me and his eyes grew wide.

"My lord, I came upon Jeiwan behaving in an unspeakable manner towards a young woman. When he moved to attack me, I merely quieted him until I could bring him to the light of your judgment."

"What is your name, Lady?" asked the king.

"Elainya. I am a healer, my lord." The room grew silent after a series of shocked whispers. I heard the word Draska echo through the room, and saw more than one warding gesture. Something was wrong. I'd never seen people react to a Draska in that manner.

I'd thought the boys' fear was from the belief that I'd killed their leader. Now I wondered.

"Why have you come here?" the king asked at last. He was a middle-aged man, with light brown hair and eyes the color of sand, very unlike my previous lord.

"I was returning home to Aurora when I was attacked, tied up and brought to you. I have come seeking a new life. Have you a healer in your court?"

"There has been no healer here for at least eighty years. I am told the last healer killed herself after one of my barbaric predecessors threatened to have her lover murdered. No one has dared attempt to fill her place—they fear her spirit will return to haunt them. She was also named Elainya."

"Elainya is a common name for Draska healers, my lord. It is hereditary and a recognition of skill that runs within a family. I do not doubt that the lady's spirit haunts this castle, but I have no fear for myself. I am a healer and have had some small success as a matchmaker, as well. If you would allow me to prove myself, I would serve you well." I spoke clear and loud, knowing that everyone was straining to hear my brash words. Eighty years!

So the wizard had been telling the truth.

"You are very young." The king steepled his fingers and eyed me with skepticism. "Yet you say you are returning home to Aurora. Do you think me unaware of the state of that town? Aurora was not far from here. You could not have been gone long enough to return."

His words made no sense. I decided truth was the best response. "I am far older than you imagine."

"You are a sorceress, then." His tone was not kind.

I raised my eyebrows. "Try me by whatever tests you deem necessary. You will find me an asset to your court." The shadows in the room stirred.

"You seem very sure of yourself."

"My lord, I am."

The king seemed lost in thought. Smoke floated lazily through the room, causing the light to dim further. I tensed, knowing the shadows to contain more than the absence of light. I had not done the Shadow Lord's bidding. There would be a price to pay for that disobedience, but I was still too angry to care.

Would my abilities desert me if I needed them?

There was eagerness within the shadows. They seemed to play with the hem of my gown.

"Never seem anxious." My mother's training words echoed in my mind. "Only confident and at peace. This breeds trust." I hoped I would appear half as calm as she had in her day. Always elegant, always in control, my mother had been a true asset to the court. How would she have handled King Cydril's proposition?

Smoke danced around the room and I remembered another night...a night when the torches had shone blood red. "Stand before me, Lady Elainya," King Cydril had said.

"My lord?"

"I do not approve of this match." His eyes had been shadowed, his hair unkempt, his breath reeking of strong ale.

"For what reason?"

"It is enough that I have reason. It is enough that I forbid it. Speak no more of this marriage—or you will watch Drenil die." The echo of that pronouncement lay still within these stones. In all else, I had obeyed him. In truth, I had watched Drenil die, and joined him in death.

The new king turned to his right and spoke toward a figure standing deep in shadow. "Nian, I would know more of this woman."

For a moment, I thought he might be speaking directly to the Shadow Lord, until the shadows resolved themselves into the shape of the man who had greeted me on the mountain, the man I thought would be waiting for me in Aurora.

I should not have thought it would be easy to avoid the Shadow Lord's plan.

A black, flowing cape made Nian appear to float rather than walk into the dim light of the torches. His shoulder-length gray hair was tied back with a leather thong. Slate-colored eyes were buried deep within a face lined and worn by the passage of time, partially hidden by a long, grizzled beard. He exchanged soft words with the king and then turned to study me.

His magic licked at the edge of my senses, and I steeled my mind against the probing. So, the king did allow some magic to be practiced in his court, and I could feel the darkness within this man's energy. His searching was focused, and for a moment it picked at the chinks in my mental armor, but did not penetrate. I reached back with my own abilities and found him similarly guarded.

We were not wasting any energy on trust. His mouth twitched as he rebuffed my mental approach, and he nodded slightly in acknowledgment of his own failure. Hardly a test, more like a gentle sparring match. I recognized his mind as the one I'd felt in the woods, and stifled a gasp. It hadn't been Dren, it had been this man, attempting to direct my will.

Though he spoke to the king, he did not look away from me. "My lord, she has great power balanced with a great capacity for caring. She is honest in her ways and deeds—and yet she hides her past behind walls of steel. She is trustworthy—if a bit of a mystery. Certainly her abilities as a healer will be more effective than my feeble attempts have been."

The king examined Nian before returning his thoughtful gaze to me. "I am not fond of magicians or witches," he grumbled. "Yet I cannot deny that my people are in need of a healer. You may remain as a member of my court and practice your art as you wish. As you do not fear Elainya's spirit, you may inhabit her rooms. Chamberlain, see to her needs."

Attention shifted back to Jeiwan as I left the room. Volume in the court rose as Jeiwan protested his innocence and the war leader joined in. I could feel Nian's eyes boring into my soul long after the doors closed between us.

Chapter 3

Settling In

Elainya

Being thus dismissed, I followed the portly chamberlain into the hallway, fascinated by the way the torchlight shone off his bald head. Two doors stood to my right, and I paused, trapped in the echoes of time.

Light spilled from the doorway to the chapel's anteroom, tracing patterns on the smooth stone of the hall, worn away by years of servants eager to be about their tasks. Drenil's workroom door was closed, a dark patch in the otherwise well-lit hall. Only it wasn't Drenil's anymore. Perhaps Nian used those rooms now?

Thoughts of Nian reminded me of the trap I'd managed to walk into. His power had an oppressive sense that I had never felt from a Draska before. There had to be a way out of this net. Wasn't that the way the legends always spoke of deals with demons? There was always a way out, because demons were basically stupid. The creature I'd met in the cave hadn't seemed stupid, though. Powerful, strong, intense—yes, but not stupid.

He'd tricked us easily enough.

Or had Drenil known who we were dealing with?

"Lady Elainya!" summoned the chamberlain for what I realized was not the first time. His lips pursed and his eyes narrowed. "I am to show you to your room. One of the servants can show you around the castle later."

"I'm sorry. I know you have much more important things to do. Perhaps it would be better to have a servant show me to my room, as well."

Nian stepped out of the shadows. He nodded towards the chamberlain. "You do indeed have more important things to do. The king is already missing you. If you'll allow me, I'll see to the lady's needs."

The chamberlain beamed. "Lord Nian, you come to my rescue again."

"Can you send someone to clean her rooms?"

The bald head shook. "No need, sir. The reflect had them cleaned two days ago."

The two stared at each other in silence for a moment before the chamberlain shrugged and bustled off about his business, eager to be free of me, no doubt.

As soon as he was out of earshot, Nian's cold eyes met mine. "You were to meet me in Aurora."

His was the raw power of nature, but not the power of forests and streams—I sensed the impending threat of a winter storm on the northern seashore.

"You aren't in Aurora."

He nodded, and a faint smile flickered across his face. He held up my eating dagger. Odd, I'd thought his hands gnarled this morning, but now they seemed strong, dangerous. A trick of the lighting, perhaps? He turned the dagger in his fingertips, causing the shadows to move hypnotically along its length as it shifted.

"You forgot this when we spoke earlier. A fine piece of work."

I took the knife and returned it to the sheath on my belt. "Thank you. It has sentimental value."

His nod was slight.

We stood in the hallway, unmoving. His eyes smoldered, meeting and trapping my gaze. Each of us probed deftly at the other's defenses, neither willing to make a more forceful affront.

What did he want from me? Couldn't he see that I had no intention of working with him? I could feel his gaze physically, as if he ran his hands over my body in search of clues. The familiarity and depth of his inspection infuriated me. My muscles tensed and my nostrils flared. He would not break through my mental barriers. With a surge of my abilities, I ended the intimacy of contact by shoving his mind away.

He grimaced. "You don't need me to show you to your room."

"No."

A small cough disturbed our concentration. I turned to see the reflect standing in the doorway to the chapel.

"Sorry to interrupt, but I was wondering if I could have a moment of the lady's time?"

I could have kissed him.

Nian turned to him and his eyes glinted as the knife had a moment earlier. "You may have her after you have answered one question."

"Of course!"

"How did you know she was coming?"

Rendel stood in a pool of dancing light and laughed. "A better question, old friend, is how did you not know?"

A further narrowing of his slate eyes was Nian's only response before he crossed the hall and jerked the door open to his workroom. With a slam, I was alone with the reflect and his Light.

My stomach growled ominously as I followed the reflect into the chapel's anteroom. Hopefully, dinner was not too far off.

He smiled at me. "I've a meal prepared in my chambers."

Talk of food was all it took to overcome my natural reserve around this odd stranger. He'd spread a white cloth over his storage chest and pulled a pair of stools in from the chapel. He motioned for me to sit and proceeded to surround me with platters of dried meat, fruit, cheeses, and freshly baked bread. A flask of water completed the arrangement as he poured some into a stone cup for me.

I sipped the water, expecting the sludge that passed for water in town. He laughed as my eyes widened. "Is it not true that the Draska drink only water from the river near Aurora?"

"It is our preference. Sometimes it can be hard to get." The water was sweet and cold, as if it had only just come from the spring. To me, it was the taste of life. At last, I could wash the dust from my throat!

"Drink slowly, my child, or you may become ill."

I nodded and picked up a piece of cheese, marveling at the richness of flavor. For a moment, I was too engrossed in eating to speak. Mindful of the need for caution, however, I stopped and looked at him. Unlike Nian, this man posed no threat. His air did not speak of high intelligence, but rather a pleasant disposition and love of life.

"So, you knew I was coming and you knew I would be hungry?"

His head bobbed up and down vigorously. "My master told me all about you last tenday. He said that on the first day of the month of Hope, I was to expect a visitor from the past. I was to tell no one that she was coming, but make preparations to greet her and tend to her needs. I had plenty of time to go to Aurora for the water. A Draska! How amazing!"

"Lord Nian is a Draska. You called him an old friend."

Reflect Rendel's brown eyes held only the hint of a frown. "Yes, so he is." He paused to pick a piece of dried meat off of a platter. He chewed slowly. With a large swallow, he continued. "Still, your people are rare. I wanted to greet you with honor. I'm sorry you were treated roughly."

I shrugged. "That doesn't matter. No harm done. I hear that I have you to thank for my room being clean?"

"I did speak with the chamberlain about it, yes, but he thought I was raving and ignored me. I got one of the servants to clean it for me as penance."

"Do you rave frequently?" I took a sip of the invigorating water while studying him over the rim of the cup.

His laughter reminded me of the way the light played within the crystals that surrounded the candles in the chapel. "Oh, frequently enough for him to ignore me." He picked up a spiced roll and began nibbling at a corner. "At least the cook humors my wishes."

"From the taste of these rolls, I look forward to what she has planned for dinner."

A mischievous gleam twinkled in the brown eyes. "Oh, I think you'll be pleased. She agreed to make something that should please a visiting Draska with a weak stomach. One of the servants will bring it to your room, so you can rest."

"You mean, you told the cook where I came from?"

He looked offended. "Of course not. I merely said that I expected you to be ill from traveling. My master said I was to keep quiet about your past."

"Forgive me for asking, but I need to know. Your master... who is he?"

The small man blinked at me in silence. He glanced into the chapel and down at his robes before squinting at me suspiciously. "I thought it would be obvious that I serve the One, Source of all Light...."

I shrugged. "Appearances can be deceiving. I've been fooled before, you see."

"Ah," he nodded knowingly. "Was that how you came to be sleeping in a cave for eighty years?"

A piece of the roll caught in my throat and I fought a coughing spasm. I looked at him without comment. Perhaps he wasn't as harmless as he seemed.

"You are the same Elainya who supposedly killed herself on the night of her wedding?"

"Yes."

"Eighty years, then. Tell me, did you dream? What was it like?"

"I don't remember anything. I was dancing with Drenil, and then I woke in the cave. That's all I remember."

There was more, but no need to burden the reflect with my nightmares.

"Ah, a pity. You've come closer to the other side of life than anyone I've ever met." The lighting in the room changed subtly. I could not define the change, only that it seemed as if it moved, somehow. "Well, now that's not what I meant...." Reflect Rendel laughed and then whispered, "My master reminds me that he will tell me all I need to know of such things."

"I see." I began to understand why the chamberlain had ignored his request.

With a flourish, he dropped the contents of the platters onto the cloth and bound it up in a tight bundle. "A snack for later, my dear. I know you need to rest. If you want for anything, have a servant come to me."

Shocked at the abruptness of my dismissal, I accepted the bundle and the flask of water before finding myself escorted into the hallway and abandoned outside the chapel. I heard voices coming towards me. My arms full of what could be seen as purloined goods from the kitchens, I wasn't eager to meet anyone. There were back stairs to my room, if I was brave enough to use them.

Nian's workroom door was open and appeared empty. With a glance around to make sure no one was watching, I slipped in. This room was as familiar to me as my own would be. Drenil had always kept it littered with the remnants of his latest projects, just as my father had, just as Nian did. Was it just that the room leaned to disorder or the personalities of the inhabitants? If I could get to the staircase before he returned, Nian would never know I'd been here.

A charcoal fire burned low in the fireplace. Something noxious simmered within one of the black metal pots hung over the fire on swinging rods. The rough-hewn table was strewn with various unidentifiable lumps and precious glass beakers. A thick book lay open next to a half-filled vial and a dead chicken. It was not much different than it had been the night I danced my wedding dance within these walls. "Come dance with me, Elainya," Dren had whispered as the potion entered our blood. He'd shoved the table aside, and we'd danced until oblivion overtook us. How I longed to feel his arms around me, guiding me through the dance.

I swallowed hesitantly. Whatever Nian was concocting made my stomach churn. Perhaps I had eaten too much.

This room had always felt old to me, solid, built into the walls of the castle. The beams of the ceiling were heavy and permanent. This had been a place of safety for me. I'd come here to tell Dren about the king's ultimatum. Could it really be 80 years ago?

Dren's argument had started with reason.

"He knows we're promised to each other from birth. Why would he want to interfere? He has no say over either of us when it is a matter of Draska custom."

"Dren, I think…" I'd found myself fiddling with a tapestry he used to cover the windows, and had forced myself to look at him. "I think he wants me to be his next wife."

He chewed on his lip for a moment. "The queen lies in childbed."

"The queen is dying. She won't live more than a few days—I've seen this type of failed birth complication before. He has no children. After three women have died, he wants someone who can bear his child."

"Then let him take someone else's wife." His voice was taut with contained emotion.

"I think he's looking for a miracle. He thinks perhaps his chances will be better, that perhaps a Draska woman could survive the curse and bear him a child."

Drenil picked up a bowl he'd set to cool on the hardwood table. He crushed the contents with a pestle, and I was amused to smell chicken mixed with roasted grain. He stared into the fire, not looking at his handiwork. A scratching at the door roused him. "Let the dog in, will you?"

The queen's pampered companion sauntered in, sniffing the air expectantly. I closed the door and resumed my favorite perch on Dren's stool. I'd sat here at least once every day since I'd come to the castle, watching either my father or him brew up some special potion, purify a soft metal, or experiment with treats for the dog.

Notoriously fussy, this dog had learned that Dren always had something stewing for it to sample. It rarely ate offerings from anyone else, but Drenil had found some success. "I suppose you'll be out the door as soon as the queen dies as well. Maybe you and I should run away together, eh, dog?" He patted the fluffy white beast on the head and set the dish in front of it. With a wag of its tail, the dog began to eat hungrily.

"Dren..."

"Do you want to marry him, Elainya?"

"No, of course not!" I felt my face grow hot that he should suggest such a thing.

"Then marry me now."

"He'll kill you."

"Not if we go away."

I shuddered at the memory. Why hadn't I suggested that we go home to Aurora and seek counsel from the elders? I knew the answer now as I had then: the chance to finally be married to him, to enter the bonding ceremony with the man I loved and end the constant delays had been too strong of a lure.

Nian's room was cold and dark, despite the fire. I didn't remember it being this dark. I shook my head to dispel the reverie. I didn't want to be found skulking about in Nian's study, so I moved to the door across the room which led to the secret stairs added years before my parents' time. As the magician and healer were customarily a married, bonded pair, it had seemed prudent to add a staircase between the rooms of the only two Draska at court.

Of course, the door was stuck solid from disuse. Exasperated, I put my bundle and flask on the stone floor and pulled at the handle with both hands.

"Allow me, my lady," Nian stepped from the shadows, terrifying me. I leaped backwards, nearly upsetting the flask. I grabbed it up and clutched it to my racing heart.

He laughed.

"If you're going to enter my rooms, uninvited, you shouldn't be surprised to see me." With most people, I could get a sense of their emotions, but Nian was as cold as the stone wall he stood next to.

"I'm sorry. I thought you were out. I was just..."

"Sneaking up the back stairs."

I shrugged. "Yes. Reflect Rendel gave me some food. I didn't want people thinking I'd raided the kitchen."

"No one here knows about these stairs. Even I don't use them." He waved a hand over the handle, and then pulled. The door opened with a creak and a puff of dust. I coughed and gagged while Nian stared at me. "If you intend to use them, at least offer me the courtesy of knocking, and I will do the same."

He stooped and retrieved my provisions. "As we aren't short of food here, I don't think anyone will mind your having this. Just watch out for rats."

"Thank you." I backed into the darkened stairwell, grateful for the bit of light that fell through the open doorway.

"My pleasure. I will see to it that the servants clean the stairs this evening." He nodded with mock courtesy and closed the door, leaving me in total darkness.

I felt my way along the winding staircase, mindful of the rats he'd mentioned, and shivered as a spider skittered away from my touch on the wall. After a moment with my eyes closed to calm my nerves, I continued. I was not going to wait for the servants to come and find me here. That wretched, evil old man had locked me in here on purpose without a torch.

The thought of a lock made me pause. What if the door was locked at the top of the stairs? I took a deep breath and relaxed, extending my senses until I could feel the stone around me. Calmer now, I found it easier to climb. After all, I knew this passage well. I had used it only yesterday, by my sense of time. Except I'd had light then, and there hadn't been this many spiders. The door at the top opened with only a firm shove. I stumbled into my own well-lit room.

I placed the bundle on my storage chest and set the flask on the desk. Looking down at my dress, I gasped at the spider webs and began brushing them off. A small hand mirror lay on the desk. I picked it up and confirmed that my hair was yet again fouled with dust and webbing. With a shudder, I plucked a wiggling spider from my braid and crushed it underfoot. I sat down and focused on once again untangling and combing my hair, removing any living ornaments.

The cook's servant came as I was finishing. Timidly, she laid the tray on the desk and curtsied, eager to be away.

"One moment, please."

She froze like a mouse that thought a cat had seen it but was afraid to move until it was certain. "Yes, my lady?"

"Could you have someone bring me a pot of hot water?"

"Of course, right away." She scurried off.

I examined the room's new tapestries and linens. While it was far from what it had been, at least it was clean. The bed was soft, with a thick down mattress and warm furs. Thin, pale blue drapes surrounded the bed, creating a nest of warmth. As tempting as the thought of sleep, the cook's offering of soup and bread drew my attention. A warm fire had been laid in the hearth, and I was pleased to note my iron cooking arm was still in good order. I pulled this out and sat down to sip the soup while I waited for the water. My hunger seemed endless.

I finished my meal with some of the fruit Reflect Rendel had given me, and placed the remainder of my stash into a niche hidden behind a tapestry to one side of the bed. I added the small pouch of coins and my dagger to the food.

This was still my home. Familiar.

I let the tapestry fall back into place and was jarred by the unfamiliar pattern.

Curious, I opened the chest and was relieved to find that it contained a new shift and another gown, this one a plain earthen brown, woven of the local fabric. Someone had embroidered it with tiny pink and green flowers. Beneath this was a deep green walking skirt and bodice, sturdy and yet finely made. At least I would be well clothed and fed.

There was a light knock at my door.

"Come in," I called.

The knock repeated. With a sigh, I got up and opened the door to find myself facing a squat, blond young woman holding a kitten.

"Terror!" I exclaimed, shocked at seeing the cat again.

The girl blinked and looked around in confusion. "Excuse me?" She continued petting the cat and I noticed that her eyes were the same pale gray as his fur. He pushed his little face against her nose and then jumped towards me, shoving away from her in a flurry of miniature claws and fur.

I caught the little beast as he flew through the air. "Come in! Where did you find him?"

Her long gray dress was well made, of a fine material. This was no servant, and yet she was a timid thing. "He was wandering in the hallway, mewing. He seemed intent upon this door so I helped him get it open. I didn't know whose he was."

"Cats don't belong to people. This one thinks he owns me."

Her lips twitched, but she did not smile. She held her arms crossed over her ample bosom. With a shrug, she turned away.

"Thank you," I called.

She stopped and turned back to face me. She straightened her shoulders. "You're welcome," she whispered.

"Is he..." she paused as if looking for the right word. "There are legends of cats who could speak in their masters' minds. Familiars."

"Witches' familiars?"

Her frown was deep, bordering on anger. "I'm not saying you're a witch. I just wanted to know if the cat could talk."

"He's too young to know for sure. Many of them do, actually, if you take the time to listen."

She nodded and fled down the corridor, nearly upsetting a young boy who was struggling towards my room with a steaming pot of water.

I pointed him towards the metal arm that hung over my fire. With a quick bow, he was gone before I could ask him about my visitor.

Terror was purring in the crook of my neck, his cold nose seeking the warmth of my ear. With a laugh at the tickling, I dropped him onto my bed.

I drew the bolt on the door, locking out this strange new world. With a deep sigh, I started to remove my gown before remembering the back stairs. Hurriedly, I drew that bolt as well, shivering at the thought of Nian so close at hand.

I leaned against the door for a moment.

Now safe, I stripped off the gown and the remains of my shift. I used the latter to wash myself, feeling at last free of the clinging dust and cobwebs. Placing a few more logs on my fire, I rinsed my hair in the warm water and fell asleep wrapped in the soft fur of the bed coverings, Terror purring by my head.

Nian

He laughed as he heard the girl stumbling her way up the stairs. It had been a shock to see her there, so at home in his work-room. So beautiful. Her image haunted him throughout the evening, keeping him from sleep. He paced the dark confines of his room, enjoying the feel of movement again. The master had kept his word: the pain was gone.

Well, the physical pain at least. Seeing Elainya, brushing her mind in those brief instances when she'd let her guard slip...that was a pain he doubted even the Shadow Lord could heal.

Jauer came in as the evening wore on. "Lord Nian, would you like me to bring you some dinner? I noticed you didn't eat."

Always attentive. "No, I'm not hungry this evening."

"How was your gathering trip this morning?"

"I found more than I expected to." He sighed at the under-statement. The girl would be a challenge. He'd have to break her will quickly. Jauer had never required such treatment. Life had broken the boy's will long before Nian found him.

The young man nodded and moved to the corner of the room where he slept. Nian watched as he arranged his sleeping furs with his right hand, his left hand an unwieldy lump.

"Practice the spell I taught you last week, Jauer."

With a twist of his lips, his apprentice stared at his left hand until it shimmered and changed, appearing whole and hale. He then picked up the blanket in both hands, a bead of sweat forming on his forehead. With a flick, he straightened it, and then let it fall into place. The illusion spell shimmered and then vanished as he let out a yawn.

"I'm sorry, my lord. I'm tired tonight."

"Illusion spells are not easy, lad. You'll have to practice every day until it becomes natural.

Jauer ran his right hand through the mop of reddish blond hair and grinned. "I will. It's the telekinetic part of the spell that's hard, though, making things seem to move as if I'm holding them." He waved the stump and shrugged. "This is useless."

"You are strengthening muscles you have not used before." Nian clapped the boy on his shoulder. "You will master this as you have every other spell I've taught you. I'm proud of you. Get some rest."

"Will you be going to sleep?"

"No, I think I'll go for a walk."

"Good night, sir."

Nian smiled warmly at the boy and left so at least Jauer could get some rest. It didn't matter whether he prowled the grounds or his rooms. Either way, he doubted he would sleep for several hours yet. His body might be tired, but his mind was fresh and needed time to gnaw on the problem of Elainya.

He walked out the main entrance to the castle and passed the guard on the inner gate without being seen. He found himself drawn to the small herb garden he'd tended for many years: Elainya's garden. He leaned on the sturdy rock wall and breathed deeply of the woody scents. The moonless night air was cool, fresh with the newness of spring. The lavender had begun to bud early this year and he could already smell its night scent. He'd have to trim it back from the path or soon he wouldn't be able to get the gate open.

For now, he pushed the overenthusiastic stalks back and listened to the squeak of the gate. He should bring some oil down for that.

What was blocking his entrance into Elainya's mind?

True, the Shadow Lord had enhanced her abilities, but it was her will that shut him out. Maybe he could find a way to bend that will out of the way, make her feel that she wanted to open up to him, teach her to trust him. That would be easier than trying to crush such a wild spirit.

He picked a stalk of the lavender, grateful to it for showing him the way past Elainya's defenses.

Laughter would be required. Much laughter, some music, and perhaps dancing. He smiled knowingly. Yes. Dancing. Now that his body was able to move again, he'd put it to good use.

Elainya

I woke in the early afternoon of the next day. Stretching contentedly, I laughed as my stomach growled. I sat up and recovered the small stash of food, enjoying bread and cheese along with the fresh spring water. It was not as cool as it had been in Reflect Rendel's chambers. He must have a cellar for storage, I realized. I'd never been very close to the reflect before. He'd been an older man, silently disapproving of me. He'd liked Dren, though. Everyone had liked Dren.

My fire was long dead, but the room was warm. I dressed in the new shift and brown gown. It took a long time to comb through my hair and braid it, tying it back with a bit of plain brown ribbon I'd found tucked inside a fold of the gown. Necessities dealt with, I unbolted the door and set the pot out for the servants to empty.

One wall of the room had once held a set of narrow shelves on which I'd stored my herbs. The wood had long since rotted and the pots and bottles moved on to new homes. I would need to find a potter to replace them.

A knock at the door disturbed my inventory. I opened it to see a small boy, fidgeting from one foot to the other. "Pardon me, Lady, but my mam said she wanted me to let you look at my leg."

Word was spreading. Good. "Come in, then. Show me."

He turned red and shoved up the left leg of his breeches. There, just below the knee was a nasty cut, likely infected. I frowned. "What's your name?"

"Muathmarus, son of Kreig, but Mam said we weren't to tell my pap that I'd been to see you. She said he doesn't understand that the Draska were the Light's gift to mankind. Is it true what she said? Did the Light send you to us to make the men stop dying in the war?"

I looked into his trusting eyes. "I am a healer, and a good one, but whether someone lives or dies is up to the Light, child. You know that."

"But you help. You channel the Light. How does that feel, Lady?"

Wonderful, I longed to answer. "I've never really thought of it. It simply is. Now, hold still and let me look at this closer."

I touched his knee, letting my newfound abilities seek out and remove the poison. Light healing had been an effortless experience, the Light rushing through me like warmth from the sun on a cold spring morning. This felt more like strength, like moving a huge boulder with only a small touch. I could see how this raw power could overwhelm a person's natural resistance to darkness. Still, without healing, this infection would have spread. Did the source of the power that cured him truly matter? "How's that?"

"Feels some better."

"Good. Wash it every night, try not to get dirt in it and it should heal fine."

"Thank you, Lady."

He started to leave and then turned back. "Mam said I was to look for the Light, that there'd be light coming out of your fingers..."

Bright boy.

"It isn't always that way. I wouldn't worry your mother. Just enjoy having your knee better."

He laughed. "I doubt she's ever met a real Draska anyway." He dashed out the door, leaving me glancing over at Terror, who lounged on my bed. With a shrug, the cat stood and leapt to and then out the window.

I gasped and ran to the slit in the wall but could not see any sign of the kitten. Well, perhaps it was time to pay the magician a visit. Lyricat had used this window as an exit, leaping from my ledge to Dren's.

I unbolted the back door and went in search of my wayward kitten.

True to Nian's word, the stairs had been cleaned in the night. I placed a freshly lit torch outside my door and carried another to place in its holder outside Nian's chambers. This time, I knocked and waited. The door opened smoothly. He had not bothered to throw the bolt. Why should he? He had nothing to fear from me. I frowned at the thought. With barely a nod of welcome, Nian returned to his work.

The floor in the workroom was bare—perfect for dancing to music that would float down the hall during feasts. The room seemed deep red-orange from the torchlight—darker than I remembered, even in full daylight. A fire burned in the hearth. With his face in shadow, for a moment, I almost thought the figure hunched over the table was Drenil.

"Forgive the intrusion, but did Terror come in here?"

The magician did not look up from his bubbling concoctions as I wandered around the room. His fire shared my chimney. How often I'd fallen asleep, comforted by the smells of Dren's latest project.

"No fear is allowed past the door," he said after a long pause.

"I mean the kitten."

"You've named your kitten Terror."

"He will be fearsome some day."

He glanced from me to the window. "I do not think he cares for me."

"Probably not."

"As you do not."

He waved away any response I might have made and looked at the hunk of coal he held in his hand. "I see no need for more gold in the world."

"You sound like a man who has everything he desires."

He held up the piece of coal. "Oh, you think so? I think I sound more like a man with a lump of coal that refuses to turn into gold." He threw the lump into the grate and dusted his hands on his apron—the hide of some animal. I could not guess what kind as it was heavily coated in coal dust.

I started to suggest that he try lead but decided against it. "I wanted to thank you for your help yesterday."

He gestured me towards a high wing chair, the only comfortable seat in the room. "With the king or the door?"

"With the king." I ignored his jibe about the door.

"King Romert is a very generous man." He shoved a candle to one side and hoisted himself onto the table, shifting the dead chicken out of his way.

"He does not trust me."

"Should he?"

"I will cause him no harm—and I could aid his court."

"Which is why you are here. But why should he trust a lady who appears from out of nowhere?" He began picking feathers off the sleeve of his simple dark tunic.

"Apparently, because you do."

He smiled, the expression unpleasant. "Wrong…I don't trust you. But I don't fear you, either."

"You told the king…"

"I told the king what he wanted to hear. He would not enjoy hearing that you are a vile sorceress sent from the darkest pit, come to destroy his land." His expression was unreadable.

I sat upright in the chair. "Surely that is not what you believe!"

He hopped off the table and threw the feathers into the fire. The stench was horrid.

Instinct had led me to trust the only other Draska I'd seen. His cold behavior took on an ominous cast as I thought about it now. He was in service to the Shadow Lord, however improbable that seemed for a Draska.

"Not precisely." Nian started to comment further, but instead frowned into the fire. The shadows danced within the flames, and he seemed hypnotized by them. Varied emotions flickered in the reflections of the flame on his face. "You'll be my apprentice in time. Why not just accept it? You made that vow years ago."

"Under false circumstances. If you know anything about me, you know it was a trap."

"That is irrelevant."

"Not to me. I'll fight you, and your master."

His lips turned up in a smirk. "You are no more dangerous to me than your kitten."

"Maybe I should turn you into a newt," I said.

"You couldn't." This time he did turn and face me. His stance was calm, but prepared for whatever attack I might launch.

"Only because I hate newts."

His laugh had a dry, rasping sound. Slowly, he returned to his perch on the edge of the table. "Ah, Elainya, I do trust you. Perhaps not for the reasons you wish, however."

"You were Draska-trained."

"Why would you say that?" His eyes were black holes in the dim torchlight.

"Something in your bearing. You remind me of a magician I knew long ago."

"The one who haunts this room?" He looked into a pot and stirred at the contents before setting it aside in disgust.

"Draska don't believe in ghosts."

He snorted. "Oh really? The Draska are gone, Elainya. You and I are the last. I learned what I know from Drenil, and from your new master."

I paused as his words sank in. He'd mentioned Dren before. "You knew Drenil?"

He shrugged. "Drenil took care of me as a child. He died of the Draska plague shortly after he brought me to Sun's Apex. His spirit is strong here. It seems some spirits can be trapped after death, at least in the case of unnatural bonding." His dark eyes stared into mine and he raised his eyebrows, inviting me to comment.

I shivered, despite the warmth of the nearby fire. Drenil had lived without me for a time.

Loss was sharper than the dagger I'd hoped to plunge through my heart. Surely, the real blade would have hurt less.

The magician was staring at me. This was no time to give way to the pain of Drenil's death. I walled my emotions away to be unearthed someplace safe and alone.

Nian's eyes were hard, perhaps annoyed by my lack of response. "I know who you are," he said. "More than that, I know why you are here." His lip twitched as he looked at me. He picked up a clay dish and knocked over a vial of something that began to smolder as it splattered onto the table. Swearing, he threw the vial into the fire and quickly spread white powder over the spill. The flames behind him turned an impressive shade of green.

"Why do you think you are here?" he asked when he had the disaster under control.

"I had nowhere else to go. You've denied me escape from this wretched life. I just want to forget." What I truly wanted was to wake up and find this had all been a dream.

More than anything, I wanted to lose myself in Drenil's arms. "I thought work would help."

His voice was a growl. "You're flighty and you need training before you can be of service. You were supposed to meet me in Aurora."

"And be trained in dark magic? I think not."

Nian nodded. "It was dark magic that separated you from Drenil. I can understand your resistance." He picked up the chicken and tossed it into the fire in frustration. By the way he ignored the stench, I decided his sense of smell must have died long ago. "Still, you made your choice. It is too late to change your mind now."

"We were desperate...we were in love. Cydril wanted me to marry him instead of Dren. I could not—would not! Drenil and I were bound together...it had to be. Nothing was wrong if it brought us together...." My emotions threatened to overwhelm my control and I bit down on my lip to silence the flood of words.

His eyes were sad as he pronounced, "It has separated you more surely than Cydril ever could have, and you have sold yourself in the bargain, no matter how hard you try to deny it now."

"He would have killed Drenil."

"If you truly detested the Shadow Lord's bargain, you would have let Drenil die. You accepted the agreement. It is done." He dusted the powder into a clay jar with some straw, and then dumped it into the fire where the chicken smoldered. A bit of marrow snapped in the bone. He stared at the fire, his back to me. "Drenil would have preferred an easy death to the torment he has endured."

"Will you betray me to King Romert?" I swallowed my nausea as the flames turned bright blue, and then began to die down.

His voice was a whisper I strained to hear.

"Your secret is safe, spirit."

He stirred a smoking pot for a moment. "Besides, I'm here to help you." His voice was strong again. "You think you're here against the Shadow Lord's will? You are exactly where you were intended to be."

"What do you mean?"

Nian turned and leaned across the table to stare into my eyes. "I have another, more malleable, pupil. But the master has chosen you, so I will obey him." The shadows formed by the torchlight played across his face, highlighting deep wrinkles as he frowned down at me.

"You don't like me, do you?"

"You have no place in this world, Elainya. You abandoned and destroyed your world for a romantic fantasy. You are a naive child whose willful disobedience will only bring harm. So no, I don't like you." He took a deep, rasping breath and turned away. "However, the master does not require me to approve. I will train you and I will see that you have a place here. Now what is it you have need of?"

It took me a moment to understand the question. "Charts, books, patients—everything!"

"Some things I can provide you with. What I do not have can be bought on Marketday. We will go...if you do not mind being accompanied by an old man."

"I prefer the company of old men—do you know any?"

He harrumphed. "I detest empty flattery. Answer a question for me and then I'll decide whether to lend you some of my books and charts."

"Ask."

He leaned close. He smelled of smoke and coal. "Do you enjoy making people laugh?"

The question caught me off guard. "Yes...."

His smile was lopsided, as if his face was out of practice. He gestured to the piles of books and scrolls that littered the room. "Then borrow whatever you wish. Tonight, sit with me at dinner. I will introduce you to a few patients—and we shall give our very stern king," at this he made a face like Romert had made in the throne room, "a taste of Draska humor!" I saw the glimmer he projected of what he had in mind and chuckled. So, he was not entirely cold.

"Can I ask you a question, then?"

He nodded.

"What was the chicken for?"

His laughter boomed throughout the room. "Didn't fool you, did it? I keep some form of talisman around at all times to dissuade the curious from prowling around my rooms. I find it works better than a lock on the door."

He leaned back against the table and fixed me with a stern gaze. "The court has need of laughter. You have a large responsibility as healer here. This war is not corporeal. You will not understand until you see the wounded. I haven't been much help. I serve better as a warrior than a healer."

"I've never known a Draska to be a warrior before."

"You will find that I am unique in many ways as you learn what I have to teach." His gaze was sad and distant, but not unkind.

"I haven't agreed to be your apprentice."

"Your agreement is no more necessary than my approval." His shoulders straightened, and he began to gather some basic supplies for me. All the while, he spoke of a puppet play he'd had in mind for months but needed assistance with.

I returned to my rooms with my arms and my mind overladen.

If the Shadow Lord wanted me in Sun's Apex, maybe I would go to Aurora for a time, after all. But first, I was desperately in need of dinner and more rest. The servants had returned and my room was well lit with a fire burning in the grate. Candles burned in their niches, removing the lingering musty smell from the room. The reflections of candlelight danced with the shadows around the edges of the room, leaving me a few moments of peace.

I straightened my hair and changed back into my blue gown. After a meal and a decent night's sleep, I would be better prepared to make decisions about my future.

Chapter 4

Dinner and Dancing

Nian

Dinner was the usually elaborate affair the king preferred. Elainya sat to Nian's left near the front of the carefully arranged U-shape of tables. The king and queen sat in the center with Reif and his cohort arranged to the right of the queen. Nian sat to the king's left with other courtiers arranged down the table with them. Across the room, separate tables held the younger nobility and those visiting from the king's lands.

Elainya had been at court barely a day, but Nian noted the matchmaker's watchful eyes turned upon the youth. She would be noting who made eye contact with whom, and cataloging each marriageable person in the room.

"Shall I begin with the ladies?" he asked innocently.

She looked at him, her eyes wide.

"I guessed you were eager to get to work."

When she nodded, he began. "The dark-haired woman on the right is Miatra of Westridge castle. Her father is eager to form alliance with Bright Range. There is some potential in the girl. She's plain, but her position is attractive. Shy, though. Bookish. Doesn't enjoy the company of the other women."

The girl looked uncomfortable as the bright sparkle of a girl next to her carried on a running conversation. Miatra occasionally nodded, but Nian wondered if she heard a word her companion said.

"The next one is trouble," Elainya offered.

Nian laughed. "What gave it away? The red hair or the overflowing bosom?"

Elainya looked scandalized, and Nian modulated his tone. "Lady Eavyn. The king would have her spend time with her cousin's son—Jeiwan, but she will have none of him. The squires all seem to lack the energy she requires. She has, however, flirted with every eligible male in the court, regardless of age."

"Even you?"

His eyebrows raised and he coughed deprecatingly. "Only briefly. I am not true nobility, you see."

"She fancies nobility?"

"In all honesty, it is difficult to say what Eavyn fancies, other than her freedom. She does enjoy her position as court beauty." He saw Elainya looking back and forth between the girl and Reif. Perceptive. "No. She does not look like our war-leader. Eavyn is the exact likeness of her cousin Neelysella, who was Reif's wife. Sadly, Neelysella died shortly after the birth of her second child. Fell off a cliff, or so the stories go."

Elainya pointed to a girl farther down the table, skipping over several others. "That one, the one in gray. I met her last night. She looks like a dove. Who is she?"

"Ah, the ever-silent Trillia. That is Reif's daughter, Neelysella's second."

"She is always quiet?"

"Scared of her shadow, that one. You'll not find a match for her." The rumors around the girl's birth and life were many, but he had no evidence and didn't want to fill Elainya's head with gossip. He watched as Elainya reached out with her senses, probing the girl's mind. Across the room, the girl glanced towards them and then back towards her plate.

Elainya sighed. "So much sadness."

"She was raised harshly, having no mother to guide her. At least here at court she is well treated. She has no interest in men of any sort. She'll likely need your services as a healer. She's a fragile one."

"She found my cat and brought him to me last night."

Nian snorted. "You and your cats."

"What do you mean, me and my cats? I only have the one kitten." Her eyes were points of light seeking a chink in his mental barriers.

He would have to be more on guard with her. He lowered his voice and allowed anger to filter into his tone. "I have climbed that mountain once a year for forty years, girl. I assure you, there was always at least one cat on duty outside your cave. Generations of cats watched over you. I know about you and your cats. Drenil said you used to talk to them."

"Only the interesting ones. Some are too old or set in their ways to be amusing." Her sneer would have charmed him in his youth.

He felt the barb in her words and sneered back. "Then it seems you are well suited to your current, infantile companion."

She laughed, and he barely restrained the instinct to touch her. How many times had she flirted with him like this?

With a shake of his head, he gestured towards the other girls. "Most are too young or too flighty to worry about matching yet. Their families sent them here to become courtly ladies. Still, there are only so many positions available. Then there are the squires." He pointed at one handsome youth. "Joln is the son of Cedric, Lord of Bright Range."

"We've met," she muttered. The young man in question smiled at some remark made by the blond man seated next to him.

"Tromas is heir to Dayspring Castle. Joln and Tromas are almost always together. For propriety's sake, they often keep company with Jeiwan, as association with him does well for their families. Miatra's father hoped she would fall in love with Joln. Unfortunately, Joln and Tromas spend so much time together they've managed to confuse the girl. From the looks of things, she's managed to fall in love with both of them."

"Does Jeiwan favor one of the ladies?" Elainya asked before biting delicately into a fresh loaf of bread.

Nian watched her chewing for a moment before he coughed. "He favors all of them. He's a loner mostly, unless he's leading the younger boys into trouble like you've seen. We've had several complaints against him, but he is the king's nephew."

"And the king is childless," she finished his thought.

"Yes." He glanced to his right where the king sat, talking to Reif across his pretty, bored queen.

"Perhaps I could most aid the kingdom by seeing if Queen Laurel has any need of my services," Elainya said.

"That would be a gift to the court," he grumbled.

Elainya glanced around. "I don't see any representatives from Pelage."

"That would be me." She was perceptive to note the absence of the dark-haired, heavily built northerners.

"Where are the young people?"

"Lord Kevan hasn't seen fit to send any of his brood here, mostly because of the dangers involved in the trip. Personally, I think he doesn't want his children influenced by the luxuries of the south. He'd rather have them marry hearty peasants than have them bring home a weakling who would only die the first winter."

"Not many people make the trip south now, do they?"

"No."

"But you did."

He looked at Elainya closely. "Yes."

"You're very good with magic, then."

He smiled. "I'm more than capable of taking care of myself. Even now, Elainya. You could learn a lot from me."

She broke off another piece of bread but didn't eat it.

"I'll work with you, Nian, as befits our positions. But I will not be your apprentice."

He shrugged. "We start with what we have."

Elainya

The king's fool, Jauer, was a delightful young man, bright and cheerful despite his crippled left hand. He entertained the crowd throughout dinner with so much energy that his hand was almost unnoticeable. I gestured towards him with a chicken leg I'd been savoring. "Tell me about him."

Nian pursed his lips and drew his brows together. "A very ambitious young man. He's an orphan. He came to court a few years back, right after he lost the use of the hand. I mended it the best I could, and he has been with me ever since."

I felt my eyebrows lifting. "Somehow, I hadn't imagined you as a parent."

"Don't start." His tone was gruff. "I'm too old for parenting. Jauer helps out in my workroom. Keeps things clean in exchange for a warm place to sleep."

"What happened to his hand?"

"Run over by a cart."

I watched as Jauer tumbled through the great hall, chasing dogs and servant girls with equal glee. Neither seemed to mind the torment, and several vied for his attention. I watched as a young woman smiled at him and offered him a cup of ale. He blushed furiously and ran off to roll on the floor with one of Sir Reif's hunting dogs.

The king's war leader stood as if to intervene, but the king pulled him back into his seat. Reif frowned across the room at Jauer, who wisely abandoned Reif's prized beast and took to feeding scraps to the queen's lapdogs. He randomly snatched bits of food from some of the diners' platters. Most took the theft with good spirits. Some offered morsels freely, causing Jauer to pause and entertain them with further antics.

When the dogs grew satiated, Jauer left the room, and peace reigned for a moment. "Nice-looking lad. He seems well liked. Why didn't he see a proper healer?"

Nian's dark eyes turned cold. "I'm the closest thing these people have had to a healer for years. I might not have your abilities, but at least I was here."

"You blame me for his injury?"

"No, not for that," he answered, but he did blame me for something.

My reply was cut off by Jauer's return astride a horse. He rode a midnight-colored stallion through the great U-shaped arrangement of tables and then coaxed it to bow before the king's raised dais. The horse was a terrifying beast, but the lad seemed to have it under control. A low growl came from Nian.

Queen Laurel, much younger than her husband, suppressed her laughter when the king only nodded. She hid her giggle behind a long drink of wine. The interplay surrounding the king held Nian's attention. His face was set in a frown that deepened the wrinkles around his mouth. Those wrinkles were a map of an unhappy life; no laugh lines showed amidst the remnants of anger and bitterness. If I could not avoid association with the Shadow Lord's representative, perhaps I could learn of some weakness.

I saw him gesture towards the horse, a slight, dismissive wave of his hand, and it reared back, tossing Jauer onto a table so that he landed neatly amid the remnants of a goose.

With a snort, the horse stalked over to our table and lowered its head so that it was eye to eye with Nian. He patted the black muzzle and offered it a carrot from his plate. "You haven't met my horse Singe yet."

I blinked up at the horse. "I have never been introduced to a horse over dinner before."

"And I hope you never have the unfortunate experience again."

The horse turned to meet my eye. He offered no communion, but I had the oddest sense that I had been evaluated and found lacking. He snorted in my direction and turned back to Nian. "You did well, Singe. Let Jauer take you back to the stable now."

I almost missed the furious look Nian gave the lad as he handed the lead to Jauer. He seemed to be a bit overprotective of his horse.

"Isn't it difficult riding a stallion?" I asked, trying to distract his anger from the boy.

Nian turned to me. "Singe loves magic. He can only be ridden by a mage. As such, he is an ideal horse for me. He fears nothing and has seen me through many battles. That is the best horse I've ever met. His wildness gives him strength."

"Do you ride him into battle often?" My mind spun with the concept. I'd never known a Draska to fight, but this one clearly did. In my day, the Draska had been a peace-loving people known as the Children of Light.

"As often as needed." He glared at me. "Or would you rather have me sit safely in my hut in Aurora, contemplating the sunlight on the water while the kingdom falls into the hands of barbarians?"

I shrugged. There had been no war in my day.

Jauer returned and bowed to Nian, as the serving girls cleared the remains of the meal and served more ale around the hall. Nian nodded, and I realized our turn had come.

The king's eyes followed the exchange with interest. "What have you planned now, Fool?"

"Not I, Sire! You'll have a magic show tonight."

The entire hall grew quiet as Nian stood and moved to stand near the fire. Sir Reif, seated to the king's right, whispered something to his brother-in-law. The king motioned him to silence with his hand, his eyes never leaving Nian.

"Ladies and gentle sirs, this fool has asked that I assist him in bringing cheer to the evening." Nian's voice boomed ominously in the silence of the room. His voice was rich with intent but held no hint of merriment. He drew every eye to him. I let my senses expand and roam the Great Hall. The mood was charged with anticipation.

Nian turned toward where I sat and gestured with a sweep of his hand. "Since cheer is not my strength, I have asked the assistance of Lady Elainya. We are fortunate to have a Draska healer in our midst." Murmurs of confusion filled the room and were hushed as I stood and walked to Nian's side. The gold threads in my deep blue gown reflected the warmth of the firelight. The torches cast puddles of light amidst the comfortable evening shadows, making the room seem close.

This introduction to court held little promise of improvement over my prior one.

I supposed being summoned like one of the queen's dogs was better than being seen as a murdering witch. Maybe.

Reif's eyes moved to focus on me. He raised his cup, and I wondered what he intended by the gesture. His gaze no longer held the malice I sensed when he stared at Nian. Perhaps he had decided to forgive me for the fright of seeing his son apparently dead at the king's feet.

Jauer bounded up with a box, from which Nian drew a set of three puppets. He handed me a female form, dressed as a peasant. "You can work a puppet, I assume?" he whispered, his eyebrows daring me to argue. I nodded.

The court bard began to sing and play his lyre, accompanied by musicians with lute, drum, and flute. I recognized the old song at once, a bawdy tale of a milkmaid wronged by a knight. She sought aid from the lord, who forced the knight to marry her.

The music was lively and spirited as Nian and I worked the crude puppets, using our talents. I hadn't done this since I was a young girl, but it wasn't difficult. I glanced at the king and noted his smile. He chuckled and then laughed outright as the lord puppet began to address the knight and the maid.

Nian worked both the male puppets; not a complicated performance, but it required his attention. He gestured to the lord's puppet as it spoke in a grand, deep voice. His seriousness in such a playful task made me laugh. The fool jumped up, smiling, and imitated Nian's movements, pretending to work the lord puppet. As he did, Nian's attention shifted back to his knight, and although he pretended to be controlling the lord puppet, I could feel that his attention was not on it.

I'd tried to avoid using my enhanced abilities, unwilling to risk another episode like I'd had with Reif's son. Jauer made me unbearably curious. I let my senses reach out and follow the invisible lines of power surrounding the play. The boy was working magic! I looked at Nian and raised an eyebrow. He shrugged, giving me a half-smile that was as much challenge as acknowledgment. So, this was the "more apt" pupil he had mentioned. I should be insulted, but instead I admired Jauer's achievements. Parlor tricks and fool apprentices—what would Nian do next?

The tale ended with a raucous peasant dance, fast-paced and wild. The court roared with laughter as the puppets spun and dipped. Such dances were seldom done at court, but I remembered dances like this from my childhood, as much athletic competitions as play. For a moment, I forgot the Shadow Lord and everything that had happened and allowed myself to relax.

I was startled when Nian wrapped an arm around my waist and spun me away, leaving our puppets apparently working themselves. His mind touched mine, offering only the surface-level linking required to harmonize our movements. It felt natural to relax and allow our energies to merge. He was a strong leader, clearly directing each move so that we seemed to whirl as one.

Amidst laughter and cheers, we danced around the fire in time with our puppets. The diners kept time with the drum, knife hilts pounding the table. I could feel the music consuming my heart's beat. I'd always loved music, and this was rich and rhythmic. The sorrow of the past two days retreated into a corner of my mind as I enjoyed the movement.

"Let's show them what Draska can do," he whispered in my ear. I forgot his age and the court as we spun and dipped in an outrageous display of agility and ability. I had never imagined seeing anyone dance like this outside the Draska city, yet here I was, romping like a child. Enhanced by the power that flowed with the pulse of the music, we leapt and twirled. Hot and as red as the torchlight, the blood rushed through my veins. I threw my head back and laughed, intoxicated with the freedom of movement. Dancing with Nian was an exercise in power and passion. The audience clapped and cheered us on.

As the music ended, the puppets bowed before the king and returned themselves to the box, except for my puppet, which curtsied to Jauer. He bowed to me and took it up.

King Romert was still laughing as he waved to the musicians to continue playing. "After such a display, we can not help but continue this evening a while longer. Let us all dance—at a slightly more dignified pace."

I strove to catch my breath and watched the knights shove the tables towards the walls. The couples formed up, and I focused on the pairings.

The beat still pounded in my ears as Nian turned and bowed to me, sweeping his dark cape aside. "Will you dance with me, Elainya?"

His words turned my blood to ice. We'd ended up in one of the pools of torchlight. A bright ray focused on his outstretched, ring-less hand, triggering a buried memory. I felt myself caught and drowned in the recollection.

The music had floated down the hall as my lover's friends played in celebration of our secret marriage. I'd stood in Dren's workroom, darkened to keep from attracting attention, and whispered the vows of the linking ceremony that followed our chapel wedding. From this day forward, our lives were one. We could no longer live apart. Our assistant, a traveling Draska, had mixed a potion that would help us escape the king's anger over our marriage. Fenshad, as he'd called himself then, had witnessed the rite and set two silver cups on Drenil's worktable.

Dren handed one to me, and raised the other in a toast. "Now my love, we will be free." I noticed the way the dark liquid churned within my cup. Dren drank deeply and smiled at me. As I tilted the cup back and drank, I looked up into Fenshad's eyes. In his moment of triumph, the spirit's mask slipped and revealed the Shadow Lord hidden beneath the innocent disguise.

The universe stopped in that moment. The Shadow Lord had mixed the potion. It might be poison. We would die together. Whether we would return or not was uncertain. I would have spoken, but it was too late for words.

The bitter taste of brimstone lingered on my tongue as we set the cups on the table and embraced. The wine and herb mixture flowed through my veins, bringing both fear and joy, and then Drenil took my hand. "Thus our hearts shall be entwined—my soul on fire for only thee," he whispered. Our rings glowed with our joining and our power as the spell began to work.

"My soul entwined with thine...on fire for only thee," I murmured in response. I could feel the pulse of the magic replacing my own.

"Will you dance with me, Elainya?" Dren had asked.

They were the last words he spoke to me. The last words before we held each other close and surrendered to the music and the magic. I remembered laughing with victory as the tiny room glowed red from the torchlight, or was it the power?

Slowly, darkness had replaced the light in the room and left me in nothingness. I had awakened to a world without Dren.

My love was gone, and I was alone in this world as if he had never lived. As if we had never met...or loved...or died....

Yet again, the room faded into darkness around me.

Nian

Nian grabbed Elainya as she fainted, silently cursing himself for being so careless as to trigger the memories he'd seen flickering across her face in the instant before her collapse.

Did some traitorous part of him want her to remember? No, it had been the ray of light that had drawn her attention. Cursed be the Light. The master would be most displeased. He'd formed a tentative link with her, gotten her to relax, and then lost all the ground he had gained in an instant. A shiver ran over him and he lifted the girl's body into his arms. Holding her protectively close, he whispered a prayer of repentance to the darkness and carried her from the all-too-brightly lit room.

As he carried her from the hall, she awoke with a terrified sob, and he took that moment to reach through her defenses and send her consciousness into deep oblivion.

Chapter 5

Awakening Again

Elainya

I woke wrapped in warm furs. The dizziness was gone, but I still felt weak. The sensation wasn't painful, more like being overly tired and resting in a patch of summer shade while the lazy afternoon breeze cooled my soul. I could not seem to come fully awake and didn't feel the need to. I stretched and purred like a kitten, trying to remember where I was. My purr was echoed by the tiny creature on my chest.

The room was dim, lit by a single flickering torch somewhere beyond the haze of my bed curtains. A slight indrawn breath to my left caught my attention, and I turned to see Drenil sitting on the bed beside me. He touched his finger to his lips and tilted his head towards the form of a woman, sleeping peacefully at the desk across the room. Her head lay pillowed on her folded arms, her soft hair falling in a cascade of gold-edged chocolate. Even with her face hidden, I would recognize Brenna, my dear and loyal friend.

There was something odd about Dren being here... something I should remember. I fought to clear the fog from my mind and lost. I let my eyes linger and feast on him. His face was close-shaven and his arms showed the muscles gained from his metalworking. I could not resist sinking my fingers into his wavy brown hair and drawing gentle lips down to kiss mine. He groaned and leaned towards me, not taxing my limited strength.

The important part of my thoughts struck me abruptly like a blow. Dren was alive. I could barely hear my own voice. "I dreamed you were dead. What's happened to me?"

He took my hand in his and twisted my wedding ring playfully. "We'll talk when you're better, but right now you still need to rest. Do you know that I love you?" His pale blue eyes met mine and his smile held a pain that frightened me.

"Of course." I tried to sit up and failed.

His voice was the faintest of whispers. "Good. That's all that matters." He placed my hand back on the bed and patted it gently. "Sleep." He brushed my forehead with his fingertips and I felt myself drifting into a healer's trance. I'd taught him that spell. I would have protested his using it on me, but I was already falling back into sleep, banished into oblivion with his kiss on my lips.

Nian

The Shadow Lord leaned against the wall and watched him pace.

"You did well, Nian."

"She collapsed in front of the entire court!"

The master shrugged and crushed a bug that wandered too close to his booted foot. "So she will be seen as incompetent and weak. That can only make it easier for you to gain her trust. You made great strides tonight. Oh, and you danced well."

Nian swallowed and controlled his pacing. "I have you to thank for that, my lord. Dancing has always been her weakness."

"Yes." He sighed. "I would have preferred more entertaining means of breaking her will, but I see that you are getting through her shields. You tranced her with almost no resistance."

"She was completely open. She saw me as Drenil."

"Are you sure that's wise?"

Nian looked at his master. "What can it hurt to heighten her confusion?"

"As long as it is her confusion that is heightened. Can you manage that, Nian?"

"Of course, my lord." The master excelled at sowing confusion. Nian had learned the techiques well. He'd always been a fast learner, faster when the lesson was taught in pain.

"Before long, she'll be as comfortable with the darkness as I am." Nian bowed towards the laughing shadow as it swirled and vanished.

He cleaned his work area and waited for Jauer to come to bed. The boy was late—hiding, no doubt. When he at last appeared, Nian was exhausted, beyond patience.

Jauer looked at him and paled. "I thought you would be asleep, my lord."

"I'm sure you did. I've been waiting to talk to you. What were you thinking of, riding Singe like that?"

"He was completely under control. You know Singe responds to magic. He's as tame for me as an old mare would have been."

"So you want the entire court to know you're a magician now, do you?"

"I wasn't working magic!"

"But there were many in that room who have tried to ride Singe over the years, and all of them know that it takes special abilities to ride him—abilities which they believe only I posses."

"You and the new healer."

"True."

"You think they'd figure it out just because I rode your horse? Lord Nian, don't you think it might be possible they would think that the horse has become accustomed to me? Everyone knows I'm your lackey."

"Reif is not an idiot. You think life is hard as a fool? Let him learn you are a mage before you're able to defend yourself. Don't take risks like that! And leave his dog alone."

"Sorry." The boy was sullen.

Jauer glanced toward the door to Elainya's room. "So, how long will this woman be staying? I want to continue my lessons."

"We will continue them, but for now I need to keep an eye on her. I'm hoping you learned at least one lesson today, though."

Jauer held up his vest and wiggled a finger through a hole in the back. "Goose bones are sharp?"

"The next time you act like a goose, I'll do more than toss you on a platter. You'll find yourself trussed and stuffed. Am I clear?"

"Yes, my lord."

Nian turned away before the boy could see him smile.

Elainya

When I opened my eyes again, I was alone. Still tired, I watched the curtains stir with the morning breeze. I knew Drenil was dead, and yet I'd seen him. Last night had not felt like a dream, or at least had felt less like a dream than other parts of this nightmare. I couldn't be sure. I pulled the furs closer to stop the trembling that wracked my body. I could hear women laughing in the distance, and the air was thick with honeysuckle.

The narrow shelves that lined one wall of my room were broken. One shelf still held almost true to the wall, and on this shelf sat one unbroken glass vial. I stared at it, watching the way the sun's light played with the facets. I'd always stored my herbs in jars. Where had that vial come from? Had I felt stronger, I would've gone to pick it up, but in my fragile state, I only stared at it, allowing time to pass around and through me, unregarded.

My wedding had not been a dream. My fingers played with my ring, acknowledging this bit of truth. I felt as empty as one of the broken pots that sat on either side of the vial. No matter how hard I tried, I could get no sense of Dren. Exhaustion or madness threatened to overwhelm me, and I did not care which.

Some time later, I came to my senses as gentle hands bathed my face with a cool rag. The bed curtains had been tied back on the side where I lay, and sunlight filled the room. Grateful, I looked up into Brenna's earth-brown eyes. If I had slept for many years, this young woman could not be Brenna, and yet here she was. Nothing made sense. I reached up to grasp the tan hand that held the rag, feeling the warmth of her delicate fingers. If I let go, would she disappear?

"Are you better, Lady Elainya?"

"I'm not sure." Every muscle in my body ached. I sat up and looked around the room. Several bolts of cloth were stacked on the large chest, with a small chest for jewelry next to them. Quill, ink and paper were on the desk, and new tapestries hung about the window. "Brenna, what day is it?" The light floral scents of the air spoke of spring freshness.

I had wed in winter, in the month of Darkness. In my nightmare future, it had been spring. I leaned back against the headboard of the bed and willed my mind to clear.

The girl pulled her hand from mine and twisted the rag she held, causing a drop of water to land on the fur in front of me. It glistened in the sunlight as she stammered. "I...I must call the magician, Lady. He has been most worried over your illness."

"Yes, please do." She would bring Drenil and he could kiss the nightmares from my mind.

The girl rushed from the room. I heard her whispering in the hallway but could not make out the words she spoke. I watched a small gray cat sunning on the narrow window ledge, cleaning one paw with great attention.

"Leave me with her," strong masculine tones ordered.

I sat up, "Dren, how dare you trance me..."

Abruptly, Nian pushed into my view. He frowned at the open window and thrust the tapestry across the opening, plunging the room into semi-darkness and causing the kitten to jump down with a spit and a hiss. "Elainya, I fear you overexerted yourself last night. You should be resting."

As I stared at his dark, wrinkled visage, the tears of loss began to fall. "But I saw Brenna," I sobbed. I could not catch my breath. My throat was closing in an effort to deny his existence. "I saw Drenil!"

He glanced toward the closed door. "I believe Miatra is the great-great-granddaughter of a lady that served here many years ago. I suspect she looks like her ancestor. After your collapse, the queen asked her to watch over you." He picked the hissing kitten up by the scruff of its neck and dropped it onto my stomach. "I assure you, this is not a dream, Elainya."

"My room..." I gestured towards the new accouterments before reacting to the kitten. I pulled it close to my heart and felt him fighting for freedom.

"Ah—that would be the chamberlain. He came to me yesterday bustling about this Draska woman and asking what she really needed to keep from embarrassing the king in public."

Shoving stray bits of hair back out of my eyes, I sat up straighter. I must look like a madwoman, and I had certainly been acting like one.

Nian's stare was one of calculating concern, as if I was a hungry lion and he expected me to choose him as my next meal. His laughter was feigned. I saw his eyes glance over me and then look away.

I drew my emotions under loose control. Realizing I wore nothing other than my shift, I pulled the furs up to my neck and lay back in the bed, still clutching Terror close to my heart.

Nian relaxed somewhat at this return to modesty and sat down on the far corner of the bed. "The chamberlain sent this for you. He didn't want to trust it to your maid." He placed a small leather pouch in my hand. It clinked.

"But he did trust you?"

Nian shrugged.

With a nod, I hid the pouch under my pillow. "Thank you."

"I suspect you were well liked at court," Nian said. When I said nothing, he changed the subject. "As I am the only one who knows what mysterious ailment has caused you to become ill so abruptly—in front of the entire hall, no less—I offer my services as healer to the healer."

"Not a very good way to win people's confidence, is that what you're saying?"

His crooked half-smile made me think he was out of practice. "No, but a very normal reaction to stress too soon after such a powerful trance. You really should let me take you to Aurora to rest." He was almost charming.

"No."

"Elainya..." his voice was soft, entreating.

"I am not your apprentice."

"Why are you fighting this?" His eyes were dark with a hint of future threat. He would be patient, but I suspected there would come a time when that patience would be exhausted. He had his anger under tight control, for now.

"I am a Draska. My people do not serve the Shadow Lord." I tried to distract him. "Silly for me to tire so easily. I should have been able to keep up with you!" I started to rise, and then sat back, drawing the furs up around my shoulders to cover my shift.

With an annoyed harrumph, Nian glanced away as I adjusted the covers. "You aren't making this easy for either of us."

"Nian, I am not going along with anything the demon has planned. You'll just have to accept that."

"So what? You'll stay here and become one of the queen's ladies? Will you sew and mewl, simpering praises to royalty while your race vanishes from the forests?"

"The court must think me very weak to faint after only one dance."

He glared at my change of topic, and then shrugged. "No, I explained that you were ill."

"And what did you tell them?"

"The truth."

"You what?" My voice sounded a bit too loud, and even I shivered at the shrill tone.

Nian glanced towards the doorway where the girl had appeared. He smiled reassuringly, and she disappeared. He lowered his voice to a whisper. "I explained that you had been traveling with your husband when you were attacked. He was killed, and you were left for dead. You awoke and were on your way to the castle seeking refuge when you met up with Jeiwan. You were justifiably tired and I overtaxed your abilities when I should have been sensitive to your recent loss and allowed you to rest."

"Did they question how you knew that? Or why there were no visible signs of my having been attacked?"

"They are used to my knowing the unknowable. Since we had obviously spoken, no one wondered. As for your appearance, Jeiwan's companions provided a vivid description of what you looked like when they met up with you." His lips twitched. I suspected that he was trying to control a laugh and glared at him.

"I can imagine."

"They thought you were a tree spirit at first. If you hadn't just murdered the heir apparent in front of their eyes, they probably would've started fighting for their three wishes."

"Jeiwan had already made his wishes more than plain."

Nian's frown reminded me of a thunderstorm about to burst. At me, I wondered?

"Who is the young woman I just upset so? You think she may be Brenna's descendant? Miatra, you said?" I'd heard the name before.

Last night. At dinner.

Nian shrugged. "I can not be sure that she is related to the woman you knew. Probably best not to pursue that with her, though. Miatra is one of the queen's ladies, but she has asked to look after you. The queen thought it would be appropriate for you to have a maid."

"That was kind. I'm better now, though. Just startled, mostly. Do you think she would stay and help me get settled?"

Nian leaned conspiratorially closer and I smelled smoke in his hair and ale on his breath as he whispered, "I'm certain she will. Miatra is more bookish than the other ladies with Queen Laurel. She is bored out of her mind with them. You may even find her good company." He rose to leave with a bow and raised his voice for Miatra's sake.

"You should stay in your room and rest for the next few days. There will be time enough for work later." He then lowered his voice so that only I could hear. "You will become my apprentice, you know. It is only a matter of time."

The cat spat at him and I wondered how much longer it would be before the creature learned to project its thoughts in words. Terror clearly knew his own mind already.

Nian swirled away, the black cloak floating around him as he spoke with Miatra. "She should rest. Keep the room dark so that she will sleep. Bring her simple foods and strong ale from the great hall, and try to keep her quiet. Perhaps you can help her settle in and arrange her room for patients. That should keep her mind occupied. If she shows any other signs of...illness...call me at once."

The girl nodded gravely and closed the door behind him. Illness indeed. My head had cleared. As much as I despised my circumstances, there was no way I could hide from reality forever. Drenil was dead, but I was alive and even more in the Shadow Lord's clutches than I had been in the forest.

I needed to think. For now, I was safe. The world had changed, and if I used the gifts I'd been given, I could make a place for myself.

Once I understood where the battle lines had been drawn, there would be time to fight the Shadow Lord. For now, I would settle for getting dressed. I climbed out of my bed and began searching for my gown. Miatra rushed to help me.

"Lady Elainya, the magician said you should sleep." I'd found the gown and pulled it over my head. Her fumbling fingers plucked at it, half helping with the laces and half trying to remove it.

"Probably, and I will rest, but I'd rather not meet any other callers in my shift." I laced on my sandals against the chill of the stone floor, pulled open the curtain, and turned around for Miatra's inspection.

"You look lovely, Lady Elainya." Her smile was pinched. Poor dear thought she was in a room with a madwoman, no doubt.

"Thank you. Now let's see what the chamberlain has left for me...." The cloth was more suitable for drapery than for my clothing. I preferred lightweight gowns, which would flow around me. Mother had taught me the importance of clothing to enhance my image. I would need gold thread for embroidery, and other thread for sewing. Perhaps a needle—so I would not have to borrow from the queen's ladies. Some ornaments would be nice, but I needed supplies for my trade as well.

My mental list completed, I sighed. There might be enough coins in the pouch the chamberlain had sent. We would see come Marketday. I would have to make do with what I could afford. Miatra fidgeted with the covers of my bed and then went to stand beside the window slit. I glanced at her as she tried to ease the tapestries across the opening, and she dropped them as if she'd been burned.

I sighed. "I'm not going to bite you, Miatra."

"Oh, no, my lady! I don't think you would."

I could have said the sky was green and she would have agreed with me.

"I need light and fresh air."

She nodded and stepped away from the window.

I searched the stack of fabric and found some that would serve as a divider to separate my room and provide a public area for my patients while providing me with some privacy. "Can you get me a length of hemp rope long enough to span this room?" I asked my timid companion.

"Yes, my lady," she replied and left on her search. I suspected she was eager to be away from me.

My lady? There was a difference between Miatra and her ancestor. Brenna had been far too familiar with me to call me "my lady." The child would learn to know me soon enough! She was what? Maybe 16 years old? I paused. Brenna had a great-great-granddaughter. She'd borne children, then, after I left. Had she been happy in the match I'd arranged for her? Would Miatra know? Perhaps I could ask? I shook off the thought as one leading to madness. There was no way to ask such a question without enhancing the girl's fear. Best to concentrate on things at hand.

Things like the wall in front of me. Solid. Now if it had not been altered.... I pulled the chair closer and climbed up to search for the rings my mother had ordered drilled into the stonework. A few moments of searching behind the tapestries revealed that the ancient iron rings were still in place and still strong enough to hold the weight of my divider.

Very few women of over one hundred could stand on a chair behind a tapestry inspecting the walls of a castle! I laughed to myself.

A faint knock at the door signaled Miatra's return. "Come in," I called, not turning from my inspection of the rings. "Just hand me the rope."

A masculine cough caught my attention. It was not Miatra.

I looked down at Reif's head. I hadn't noticed that bald spot among his blonde curls before. He glanced around and then looked up at me in confusion. His eyes were the color of bittersweet nightshade.

With as much grace and dignity as possible, I stepped down from the chair. He was dressed in a linen shirt, open at the throat, revealing an unkempt mass of fur. His embroidered linen vest matched the tan of his breeches. He looked both comfortable and elegant, a gentleman with land and power.

"Lady Elainya, I have come to offer you an apology for my behavior. I was concerned about my son."

"As well you should be, sir, but it is forgotten. It was nothing but a misunderstanding." My hands were covered in dust. I glanced around the room and found nothing to wipe them on.

"Thank you for your understanding." With a flourish, he pulled a spotless handkerchief out of his belt and offered it to me. I wiped my hands and returned it to him. We stood there, not looking at each other, for a long moment.

"Is there something else I can do for you?" I hoped he would take the hint and leave.

"You are very lovely." His eyes wandered over my body with as much hunger in the expression as if I had still been in my shift, or less.

"Thank you, sir." I disliked the tone of his voice. I disliked the purple glimmer in his eyes even more. He moved a bit closer to me, and I found myself up against that all-too-solid wall.

"A lady such as yourself should not have to face life without resources. I heard about your recent loss. You must feel so very alone."

"I will manage well enough, thank you." I stepped sideways, keeping as much distance between us as possible. Even this early in the day, I could smell that he had been drinking. While Nian had smelled of ale, this man smelled of something stronger...and too much of it at that.

He paused and stepped back, his hands open. "I'm sorry. I've been a widower for a long time. My manners are put to good use on the battlefield." He coughed and glanced out the window.

"Lady Elainya, I seek a match."

I pretended to think for a moment. "I am too new here. Give me time and I will find you a wife. You never remarried after Jeiwan's mother died?"

He looked out the window and took a deep breath. "My wife... was given to certain mental afflictions. When Trillia was a babe, she threw herself off a cliff into the sea. I suppose I should have remarried, but the children and the war held my attention, until I saw you last night at dinner."

"Ah." My brain ground to a halt and refused to provide me with any rejoinders.

He took a step closer to me, and I shifted so I could rest my hands on the chair. "I want you, Elainya. You have enchanted my heart. Last night when you danced, my blood boiled. Your eyes are beams of radiance that strike through me. Your hair," he reached out and touched my hair. "So soft."

"Sir, the incident with your son has strained you. I think tomorrow you will feel differently." I stepped around him to place the desk between us—but then I was trapped in the corner. He did not move to press the advantage, merely smiling at the way I'd cornered myself.

"I will love you more tomorrow than today."

"I am but recently widowed...."

"I offer you wealth, devotion, a castle of your own. You would be step-mother to the next king."

"Lady Elainya!" Miatra exclaimed from the doorway.

The knight backed away from me and I shivered. "Sir Reif, I thank you for your offer, but I'll thank you more to refrain from such rambling. Draska marry for life. I was married and now I am a widow. I have no desire for love. I have drunk my fill and now I am free of it. Good day, sir." I took the rope from Miatra's trembling hands and stepped back onto the chair to tie my end of the rope to the ring above me.

Ignored, Reif left, closing the door with a resounding slam.

The kitten crawled out from under the bed and pawed at the loose end of the rope.

"Thank you, Miatra," I whispered, climbing down. I was annoyed to find my own hands shaking. I glared at the cat. "You were no help at all."

"Are you unharmed?" the girl asked, glancing from me to the kitten. It occurred to me that talking to cats might not be a normal thing in her life.

"I'm fine, merely surprised. He was a perfect gentleman." I smiled to reassure her as much as myself. "Now, I want to hang this cloth over the rope to make a private chamber."

"But...Sir Reif..."

"Is gone. This doesn't require sewing, so why don't you help me?" Her eyes flicked from the door to the rings in the wall and then to the cloth in my hands. Her fear was obvious.

I sighed and put the cloth back on the chest. "Sit down, child."

She sat on my bed and glanced from me to the door. I pulled my chair over to her and held her hands in my lap. Her brown eyes showed white as they met mine. "Sir Reif frightens you?"

She looked down. "You are very powerful."

"Miatra, we are going to be friends. I'm not anyone you should be nervous around. Understand?"

"Of course, my lady."

"Queen Laurel is your lady. I am merely Elainya, someone who'd like to be your friend. Do you understand?"

Miatra nodded in awe. "Yes...."

"Now, are you frightened of Sir Reif?"

"Everyone is—and his son is worse!"

"I've met the young problem." She nodded and a faint smile lit her face like the first flush of dawn. Word of my encounter with Jeiwan had spread quickly. "Why does everyone fear Sir Reif?"

"He has the king's ear."

"So does the chamberlain, so does the magician, for that matter."

"The chamberlain does his job. Besides, he's old."

"Ah, and that would include Nian as well?"

"Lord Nian is...well...no one fears him. I know he's very powerful, but he keeps to himself most of the time." She chewed on her lip.

I smiled. "He does seem good with magic."

"But Lord Nian...well, he's funny sometimes. It is hard to be afraid of him."

I wasn't sure I agreed with her on that point, but I ignored it. "So everyone fears Sir Reif and his son?"

"Yes. The king listens to him more than he listens to any other. They are fast friends, as well as relatives." She fidgeted and her hands clasped mine.

"Relatives?"

"You didn't know! Queen Laurel is Sir Reif's sister." A sob escaped her lips. "I should have stayed with you. I'm sorry, my lady."

I had managed to offend the most influential man in the kingdom within a day of coming to court. The second most influential man in the kingdom had already admitted to hating me. Some days my brilliant wit astounded me.

"So what troubles you about what you just saw?"

"I would not see you hurt—and I don't think he could hurt you—if what they say about you is true...but...."

"You're afraid I've gotten myself in trouble?"

"Yes. You denied him. He will not accept denial of his desires for long."

"Well, it is nothing new for trouble to seek me out. I promise to be careful. Does that help?" I squeezed her hands to soothe her. "Really, though, he was very polite, in an intense, forward sort of way."

She nodded and her smile brightened a bit. Terror climbed onto my desk and looked her over intently. Miatra laughed at his scrutiny.

"Now, will you help me hang this curtain?"

"Of course, my...." She stopped and looked me in the eye for the first time, holding my gaze. "Of course, Elainya. It will be my pleasure."

Nian

Nian stood in the shadows as he watched Reif leave Elainya's room. His teeth were clenched, and he longed to draw the spirit-sword he carried and cut the predatory leer from the man's head. He'd sensed her fear but allowed her to deal with the man. Perhaps Reif would be helpful. Maybe he would drive Elainya to seek assistance.

The man was a bully, pushing his son to imitate his excesses and his daughter to hide behind walls of stone. It was no wonder Neelysella had killed herself. What woman wouldn't to escape him? Elainya.

Elainya would know how to handle him. Wouldn't she?

She hadn't known how to handle King Cydril's advances all those years ago. But then maybe she'd learned something in the meantime.

He stopped and thought. A deep frown lined his face. What was that time to her? Two days?

She would learn the depth of her mistakes, though. She was bright. She'd learn quickly. If not, he'd have to teach her.

Reif would bear watching. But then, he always had.

Chapter 6

Swirling Shadows

Elainya

Miatra made me laugh with her mothering ways. She brought me a plate of fresh fruit from the great hall around time for the noon meal. I craved much more but didn't want to hurt her feelings.

I sat in my chair by the window and tried to ignore my grumbling stomach. I hated just sitting around pretending to read the books Nian had loaned me. Ancient writings weren't enough to interest me today. When the tall, redheaded girl came in carrying her basket of sewing, I was thrilled by the distraction. Terror glanced up from where he was napping and then sat up to take notice.

"Miatra, dear, you haven't eaten yet. Take a break and I'll keep Lady Elainya company for you," she smiled, her green eyes twinkling at me. She saw the cat and squealed. "Oh, what an adorable creature!" She reached out to stroke him and he purred against her hand. "You are the most darling little thing!" Putting her sewing basket down on the chest, she lifted the kitten and cuddled him to her heart. I was surprised he would allow such familiarity.

Miatra looked skeptical but went quickly. I had not noticed that the girl hadn't taken time to eat. I had been self-centered and missed her discomfort.

Once we were alone, the lady flopped down onto my bed, her deep green gown flaring out around her and my cat by her side. "My name is Eavyn. I thought you might need a break from Lady Dull and her book work." Her hand rested on the cat, and I noticed that each nail was a perfectly shaped half moon.

Even if I was glad of the diversion, I didn't like the implied insult to Miatra. I pointedly closed the book on my lap and set it on my desk. "I like books."

Lady Eavyn laughed. "Well, YOU would. Not me. I'm just here to get married—and for that I hear you are now the most important person for me to get to know. So, I brought you a present." She whipped back her sewing to reveal a cloth-wrapped package, which she deposited in my lap.

Amused, I opened the package to find a roll of bread and some chunks of dried beef. "You are buying my favor with food?" I eagerly bit into the finely spiced meat.

"No...just your friendship. No one could survive on the fruit Miatra brought you earlier—I checked. I liked the way you put Jeiwan in his place. I figure, you're a good friend to have. If it helps me get the best husband, well that's a bonus. Everyone knows I'm to have the best man anyway."

"And why is that?" I looked into her dancing green eyes and wondered if it was because she was the most beautiful woman at court—that would be believable. She was certainly more vibrant than anyone I could remember.

"I'm the heir to a large piece of land in Dayspring. My brother inherits the title and the castle, but since I'm older, father offered me a worthy dowry." She blinked in the overly honest way she had, and I liked her despite my desire to see her brought down a notch.

"Such honesty!" I laughed. "Would you like to share some bread?" I broke the small loaf in half and held out part.

"Oooh, no! I've no magic to help me keep this figure," she giggled.

I looked at her with a healer's eye. "Well, you do look fit!" In truth, she looked more than fit. She was thin, but in a tight, muscular fashion, and she had curves in all the right places. Her facial features were delicate with only a hint of freckles to give her cheeks a playful character. I couldn't see that there would be much challenge in finding this one a husband.

She pulled the beginnings of a bodice from her basket and resumed attaching lace to the neckline. Terror became fascinated by her thread. She dangled a scrap for him and laughed as he stood on hind paws to bat it from her hand. "I want a man to want me for more than my father's land," she sighed.

"I'll add that to the list of qualities to look for in a husband for you, but I suspect they will find you as attractive as your dowry. Do you have any favorites?"

"Not really. Most of the boys around here are so childish. I like a couple of the army captains...."

I sensed dishonesty for the first time from her. "No, I think you have a favorite."

She laughed. "Remind me not to lie to you about anything important. Captain Bertrand is quite handsome, but the reflect says his family is not worthy. Something about insanity."

"Ahhh." I swallowed a piece of meat and wrapped the remainder of the food up, thinking to save it in case dinner was as meager as lunch.

Miatra entered at that moment, rescuing me from continued conversation. I turned and put the food in the niche. If Miatra noticed, at least she didn't comment.

Eavyn gathered her sewing with a toss of her red curls. "I dare say, Miatra, you eat too fast! You'll be down with a stomach ache and then who will assist Lady Elainya?"

I stifled a giggle as she sauntered out.

Miatra sighed. "She can be such a boor. All she talks about is men."

"If I'm to be matchmaker to this court, best I learn the gossip as soon as possible."

The girl twiddled her fingers at the cat, who ignored her. With a sigh, she sat down on the chest at the foot of my bed. "I suppose so. I'm more interested in helping you take care of people, though."

"The Draska do not see the world the same as your people, I suspect. To us, love is as much a part of the body's well-being as the beating of the heart. Love gives a young couple the energy to succeed in life. It heals many physical ailments just by its existence."

"My mother used to talk about the Draska. She learned about them from her mother. I thought your people were all dead."

"Dead?"

"From the Draska plague." Her expression said she was worried about me.

"Oh, yes," I said, before she could call for Nian. "The plague. Some of us survived."

"Did your mother tell you stories about it?"

"Actually, she never spoke of it." Terror was feigning sleep on the window ledge. He looked up at me with one eye and then sighed back to sleep. He could not speak yet, but I could already sense his amusement. Some pieces that had puzzled me fell into place. Draska were more unusual than I'd imagined. No wonder I'd been treated as if I were half witch, half ghost.

Miatra's eyes held a dreamy look as she remembered tales she'd been told as a child. "The stories were sad, so romantic, but tragic. Whole families found huddled together. My grandmother used to say that it seemed the Light had gone from the world when the Draska died. The women in my family have served at court, as I do, for many generations." Her eyes met mine. "You called me Brenna this morning. Brenna was my ancestor's name."

"I was not fully awake."

"That's what Lord Nian told me."

Bright girl. Brighter than I'd realized. How close was she to guessing, I wondered? I ran a hand along my temple. She was so much like Brenna.

"How did she die, that ancestor? Do you know?"

"Peacefully in her sleep with her children around her." She smiled.

A tear slipped from my cheek before I realized I was crying. "Thank you for telling me about your family, Miatra."

"Something told me you might want to know." She seemed lost in thought for a moment. At last, she asked, "Will you stay here or go to Aurora?"

"I haven't decided yet." I took a deep breath to quell the ache in my heart. "I need a walk."

She paled. "Lord Nian said...."

I sighed. "I don't really care what Nian said. I need sunlight."

The corners of the room were deep in afternoon shadows. The Shadow Lord or one of his minions could be hiding in any one of them.

I pulled the tapestry further back from the window slit and looked out over the castle grounds. So much was the same, so much different. How could I carve a place for myself here where no one had ever seen a Draska healer? I shivered and picked up my cloak.

If I didn't do something soon, I would give in to the madness that lurked along with the shadows in the corner of this room. "Don't worry. I won't be gone long," I said.

The kitten scampered after me as I went out to explore my new home.

Outside, I let my feet wander where they would, following familiar paths that no longer existed. I came upon a small clearing and stood staring at impossibility: my garden lay before me, untouched, just as I had left it two days and 80 years ago. The garden gate swung in on leather hinges, and the river rock of the path crunched beneath the soft-soled shoes I wore. The hem of my gown brushed an early growth of mint and came away wet with dew that had not dried on this gentle spring day.

I had planted bulbs in the far bed before my wedding, a ritual of calming, reaffirming that there would be a tomorrow. I'd left the trowel in the iron garden box Dren had crafted for me. The box still stood beside the dormant rose bushes.

This was a dream, of course, but I couldn't break the spell. I lifted the lid, noticing the gleam of the recently polished surface. Inside were my hand tools, worn and aged, but the ornately carved handles were the same. I took the trowel in hand and knelt in the soft earth, heedless of the dirt now staining my borrowed gown. The soil gave easily and I came up with a bulb, roots fully developed, and a pale shoot emerging from the tip. The bulb had been in the ground for months, from cooling to warming. Not the same bulb, then, but perhaps a descendant. I sat back on my heels and glanced around the garden. There were subtle differences, a bush here or there out of place, yet it was my garden.

A shadow passed over me, leaving me chilled. "I knew I had a mole in the garden. I hadn't pictured one quite so large, however."

I looked up into Nian's sparkling gray eyes. "I'm sorry.... I...." Words failed me as I fought to explain what I was doing digging up his garden.

He laughed. "It's not a problem, child."

I stood up and put the bulb in his hand. I looked at the trowel and dropped it back in the box. The lid clanged shut, echoing in the silence as I fought for words. "You see, this place...well, it brought back memories. I thought I was dreaming."

Nian nodded. "It is a healer's garden." His eyes were on the well-tended roses just coming out of dormancy along the fence. "When I came, it was in disarray. I could tell what it was supposed to be. I saved what I could and guessed at the original design."

"You did well."

He nodded. "Such a garden is useless for alchemy. It has been a distraction that I cannot afford any longer. The war demands what time and energy I have. Since you are to be my apprentice, I give it to you to tend."

"I haven't agreed to be your apprentice."

His lips pursed, and he seemed to be thinking. "You know this place. It calls to you."

"Yes."

"Well, then, one step at a time. Perhaps after you find your place in the dirt, you will find your place in life." He put the bulb in my hand and curled my fingers around it. I could feel the strength in him, held under tight control. "You never know what may grow from such a small start."

The gate swung shut behind him, and I was alone with the growing things. I put the bulb back in its hole and patted the dirt over it. I had made perfume with flowers just like this one in my years at the castle, delighting the queen and her ladies. Perhaps I would again.

Images of the past lay lightly over the world I saw, no matter where I was. Here, all was as I expected it to be, nothing was foreign or harsh. It was restful not having to think about then and now, just to exist.

A supply of fresh compost lay ready for the roses, and newly hewn stakes were ready for the climbers. I gave myself to the garden, clearing away the damage from the cold season, and encouraging the newly emerging plants. Peace washed over me as I gathered the early herbs and tamed the wandering weeds.

At sunset, I filled my skirt with cuttings and carried them to my room for drying.

Reality awaited me. My drying racks were long gone, storage shelves rotted, bottles and jars long escaped to new owners. I dropped the bits of herbs on the hearth and sat on the chest at the foot of my bed to think.

Only the one shelf remained, that one bottle reflected the torchlight with a ruby red light, seeming almost the color of blood. I stood and picked it up, turning it over. I would have remembered a vessel of workmanship this fine. Each facet reflected dancing torchlight in the swirling depths. It seemed about half-full of some black liquid. I tilted it from side to side, watching the way the liquid flowed and sparkled. Magic, and not my own.

Carefully, I slipped the cork loose and took a tiny sniff. There was no odor. The absence of smell told me more than I would expect. Was it water? No, not the way the liquid pearled as I gently shook it. So, perhaps some fine oil, pressed from the newest olives? Perhaps a well-boiled alcohol mixed in to dilute the potion? I put the cork back in and returned it to its resting place on the shelf. I'd need to ask Nian what it was.

My eyes wandered upward to where I had once hung herbs to dry near the fire. The hooks were still there, bits of rusted metal embedded in the stone. I fished among the contents of the chest for bits of thread.

Dinner was past by the time I tied the last bundle and hung it to dry.

I had thought there was no life for me without Dren, but I now realized I had been a healer from birth. There was a place for me here, a life with purpose. A weight lifted from me and I dusted the dirt from my skirt.

Miatra brought me a meal, complete with a treat for Terror.

Tomorrow I would inventory my supplies and see what could be done to prepare for the future. War was at hand. I feared my skills would be needed. It was time I reconnected with my people and learned what had passed in the time I'd been gone. The trick would be to get there without Nian.

Nian

Nian turned away from the window in his workroom and smiled softly to himself. It was good to see Elainya in the garden. Her protest had been half-hearted. Already her resistance was weakened. Gently, given time, he could lead her wherever he wanted and she would follow. Time was the issue. Would the master give him the time he needed? She could be spared the painful lessons he'd learned. She could keep her heart mostly in one piece if he was careful. Perhaps it was better that she hadn't gone to Aurora. This way he could prepare her for what she would find.

Elainya

Sleep came easily, but my dreams were troubled, full of memories of Drenil and the emptiness of his loss. Just before dawn, I dressed by feel and the feeble moonlight that came through the window.

I'd found a simple walking dress in the chest; warm and sturdy, it would serve my needs. I hid the small pouch of coins in my bodice and tied the knife to my belt. A scrap of cloth served to bundle up my small food reserves. I would need more, but I was certain to find food in Aurora. I petted the kitten and urged him to stay in the castle where he would be safe. Images of Trillia, Miatra, and Eavyn flickered through his mind. He knew where food could be caught or charmed, and he preferred that to another trek through the woods with me.

I willed the guards not to see me and slipped from the castle. The road was not well traveled, but it was not overgrown, either. Someone still passed to and from Aurora regularly, despite what Miatra had said about there having been a plague. Maybe the girl was wrong.

The walk felt good at first, but I soon began to tire. Exhaustion overtook me and I was moving slowly by mid-morning. The world spun. Perhaps Nian had been right when he said I needed rest.

At that thought, I heard hooves approaching from behind and stepped to the side of the road. The huge black beast came to a halt, and Nian swirled into view. I was having trouble focusing on him as he seized my arm.

"What are you thinking of going off alone this soon after your waking? You aren't strong enough to travel."

"Let go of me!"

He released me just as another wave of dizziness hit and knocked me to the ground.

"And what good does letting you fall serve?" he asked with more than a hint of mirth.

I sat on the ground and tried to control the urge to cry. "Just leave me alone, Nian."

"You could die out here."

"I should be so lucky," I grumbled. "You think your master would allow it?"

"Let me take you to Aurora. You can ride Singe. You'll be there in just a couple of hours. We can argue whether or not I should leave you then."

"I hate you," I mumbled, and he laughed.

"You'll hate me worse once we begin your training, but for now, I'll accept this level of hatred as a good sign." I didn't have the strength to resist as he lifted me and placed me on his horse before jumping up behind me.

He was strong for his age.

The next hour trotted by in silence, and I was grateful. When the small band of men blocked our path, it took a moment for me to focus on their intent.

"Brigands," Nian whispered and slipped off the horse. From behind his back, he drew a broadsword. I had not noticed that he was armed and it took me a few moments to understand. I'd heard of magicians who could form their power into a weapon, but I had never seen a spirit sword before. It was a beautiful weapon, if such a thing could be called beautiful. Nian's glowed with an eerie dark light, slicing through the air in a warning arc as he took up a defensive posture.

The brigands paused, sorting out a plan of attack.

I wanted to help, but I was so wracked with dizziness that not falling off the horse was the best I could manage.

One of the men lunged forward. Without hesitation, Nian swung the sword, slicing the man from shoulder to the opposite hip. I watched in horror as the two bloody halves of the body fell to the ground.

The remaining bandits stepped back in shock. "Leave now," Nian commanded.

The brigands were only too eager to comply. The sword vanished and Nian swung up behind me without a glance towards his gory handiwork.

Amidst the wave of dizziness and nausea, I focused on what had happened. "You really are a killer."

"Maybe I should have given you to them for sport and ridden off peacefully. It would have required less effort." He felt distant, his touch cold where his arms brushed mine as he held the reins.

"I can defend myself."

"Not right now you can't."

I tried to summon my power to prove him wrong and was frustrated to find him right. "In time."

His sigh echoed. "No. Your power won't work on me. Learn that, girl, and we'll get along much better."

My head ached with exhaustion.

"Just go to sleep. I'll wake you as we get close to Aurora. There are things we need to speak of, but for now you need rest."

I didn't argue. I hated him for being right, even as I fell asleep.

Nian

He held her as she slept. Her loathing hurt more than he wanted to admit. With a swallow, he kicked Singe into a lope. Well, she would hate him more soon enough. He looked down at the top of her hair. Innocent. Stupid. She dared call him a murderer. He shook his head. True, he'd killed. He'd killed many men in battle, but she had killed an entire race.

Chapter 7

Aurora

Elainya

Nian woke me when we reached the Draska forest. I took in my surroundings. "Almost home," I smiled.

"You understand, Elainya, that Aurora is not as you left it."

"I didn't expect it to be." The trees were as varied and tall as I remembered, the air fresh with moisture and new growth. In the distance, I could hear water cascading over the rapids as the river flowed down towards the stream that would feed the pond I loved so much.

"Miatra mentioned that there'd been a plague."

"Yes." His voice was almost gentle as he continued. "I meant it when I said there are no more Draska, Elainya. Aurora is abandoned."

"What do you mean?" I'd heard his words, but they made no sense. Aurora was a thriving town, the home of my people.

"Do you know the ancient saying that there is a healer for every disease?"

"Yes." Grandmother Nala had taught me philosophy as well as medicine. I knew many such wise sayings.

"There was no healer for the disease that killed the Draska."

I tried to follow what he was saying. "But you survived."

"I was in Solitude at the time. I survived by not being here, just as you did. I returned to find Aurora a place of death. I burned the bodies in case the disease should live on and spread to other areas." His voice was thick with an emotion I found hard to name. He coughed as if clearing his throat.

"How can you be so sure it was a disease?" He had to be wrong. Truth tugged at my stomach and I felt a warning twinge of nausea. The Draska couldn't be gone.

"There were no marks on the bodies. Most of them lay in their beds as they died. A few children survived. I found homes for them in the surrounding towns, but I made sure their new families did not know where they'd come from."

"Jauer was one of the children?"

"Not exactly. He is one of the children's children. Your home has been vacant for a long time."

A question from days earlier led me from one bread crumb of information to the next. "Is that why the king had trouble accepting that I am a Draska healer?"

Nian let slip a bitter laugh. "As the last of the Draska died some forty years ago, you can see why it was implausible."

Wherever I looked, flowers were blooming with the newness of spring. Honeysuckle twined into the branches of the trees that grew along the outskirts of the forest, filling the air with perfume I remembered from my childhood.

The River Gleam was easy to cross in the hills, but as it narrowed, it became a rushing torrent from the rains. The forest was full of dappled light—here shadow, there patches that were so bright my eyes ached. Wherever the light fell, tiny flowers bloomed. As we neared the Glint, the stream that led into Aurora, I felt an ache swell in my heart. Here was the land I'd loved in childhood. I'd played in the meadow to our right. All was silent, empty, as if even the birds feared to break their vigil.

I motioned for Nian to stop and slipped to the ground. He made no attempt to follow me. "I can't believe they're all gone," I said.

The sun was warm and a breeze played with the length of my gown as I wandered into the middle of the meadow. The stream passed through here and I sought out the pool where Dren and I had shared many a lesson. I found the spot and sat down upon the sun-baked rocks, dipping my hand into the ice-cold water.

"Oh, Drenil," I whispered into the emptiness.

My mind drifted back to another time I'd sat here. "Are you ready for the testing?" he'd asked.

I could almost see him sitting across the way and I surrendered to the memory. "I suppose I'm ready. What if we aren't placed together?"

"We're a team. They'd never separate us. We're too good together. Besides, I'd never survive without my own personal healer!" He'd laughed.

"You, sir, are clumsy." I'd splashed him.

"Am I really?" He jumped to his feet. "I bet I'm faster than you, though. Race you to the city!" He'd challenged and we'd been off.

We'd run through the woods, both of us tripping over roots hidden in the rotting leaves that blanketed the forest floor. Through light and dark, we'd run until we emerged into the clearing that surrounded the city. There had been children and dogs playing everywhere, chickens underfoot, cows wandering untended, generally a scene of bustling laughter and activity.

Drenil stopped and turned to me. His face was gentle as he grabbed my hands in his and held them tight. "We will never be separated, Elainya. Do you understand?"

In the echoing silence, I stared deeply into his misty eyes. "Don't make promises you can't keep."

"I'm here, Elainya. All you have to do is accept that. You'll see me again. I swear it."

My hands tightened on nothingness as the memory trance vanished.

I found myself alone in the vacant city, dizzily trying to sort now from then. Empty. Some buildings had been damaged by age, while others looked almost normal. I wandered from house to house, finding only abandoned ruins and rotting wood. Dirt had blown into buildings. Decades of disuse had taken their toll on my home. I stood in the city center and turned in slow circles, trying to understand what I was seeing.

Nian

He watched her turn. She still hadn't fully grasped what had happened. The past intruded into her reality, making it easy to bind her to him. He could sense the master waiting in the shadows. Now was the time to destroy the last of her reserves. If he'd had a few more days to gain her confidence, perhaps he could have done it in a gentler fashion. As he watched her spin in place, though, he knew it to be a vain hope. She would never be ready for what he had to say.

Elainya

I walked back to the clearing, unable to think of anything except the silence and the dust shifting across my sandals. Nian had tethered the horse at the edge of the forest where there was some sweet grass it could eat. The wizard sat on a fallen log, watching me.

"You drifted into memory."

"Drenil was here."

He nodded. "That doesn't surprise me. His spirit is tied to yours." He paused for a long moment. "I wonder if you are ready for the life you've returned to?"

I shrugged and sat down next to him on the log. "I don't know." I gestured to the emptiness. "I trained here."

"Then it is fitting that you should begin your new training here, as well," he said.

"There is something different about me. I noticed it when Jeiwan threatened me. I felt it again when I spoke with his father."

"Your power is greater than it has ever been."

"Why?"

Nian glanced towards the shadowy forest behind us before continuing. "You used the powers of Darkness when you and Drenil cast that spell. You bound your souls together for eternity, but in so doing, you sold yourselves to the spirit who aided you."

"How can you be so sure of that? You weren't even there." I was angry, but I knew his words were true.

"I've seen your handiwork. Only my master's faithful servant could have created destruction at that level."

"What are you talking about?"

"There is a healer for every disease."

"Yes." I could not understand what he was saying. "And this was a plague...."

"Elainya. For some diseases, there is only one healer with the gift and understanding to cure it. Sometimes it is merely a matter of bringing the right healer to the right place. But if the healer is gone, or somewhere beyond time due to selfishness...."

"You're blaming me for the plague?"

"You killed those people by your failure to act."

"I didn't even know there would be a disease!" I realized I was screaming and decided I didn't care. There was no one left to hear. "You don't know what passed between us and Fenshad. It wasn't like that. We were only supposed to be asleep for a few days."

"The only ones who knew of that pact were yourself, Drenil, and..." he gestured towards one shadow in particular, "our master."

I gasped, recognizing the form and substance of the Shadow Lord. Standing to my feet, I moved away from the spirit. "He is not my master."

The forest echoed with laughter as Nian stood and put a calming hand on my shoulder. "Elainya, the pact was made and sealed with your own blood. You can not escape any more than I can be free of my own agreements with him."

"What was your bargain?" I questioned, trying to think of some way to divert the conversation. More than anything I wanted to flee from the Darkness, but I'd already tried to run from Nian twice. I knew he would be there waiting for me, wherever I went.

"I asked for things that I felt were important at the time."

"And now?" I needed time to think. My head had begun to spin again as the dizziness echoed.

"The master is not demanding. He asks only small favors, and he repays service well. You have to admit, he has given us both significant power."

"What if I don't want it?"

The master seemed to grow darker in his manifestation. He stepped forward as a cloud hid the sun. "The time for wanting and wishing is over, Elainya. Don't worry, I will not ask you to do anything that is beyond your nature. The power I offer can be used to heal the sick if that is your wish. You can search the future and find the best possible life mate for those in your care. I can give you other gifts. You may retain this fair form for the rest of your life, aging very little. I can even arrange for you to spend more time with Drenil's spirit."

The last was tempting, but my heart ached for more than spiritual contact with my lover. "You've already cheated me. I do not think our bargain holds."

"Elainya, Drenil is with you now and always will be. I have kept my part of the pact. You will keep yours. You have no choice."

"These gifts that you offer...what do you gain from them? Why would you wish me to use your power to heal?"

"That is not your concern. Do good, Elainya. No explanation is required. Perhaps it is merely that I wish my servants to be happy. I am watching you. Nian can teach you all you need. Obey him as you must obey me."

The forest glade seemed to grow warmer as the Darkness left.

Nian stepped away from me. He pulled food from his saddlebags, placed a blanket on the ground, and prepared a simple meal, all without looking at me. "Come and sit. You should eat something." His voice sounded hoarse.

"You serve that being willingly," I said.

"Here, have some ale." He handed me a flask.

"Why?"

"Because you must be thirsty."

"Not the ale. Why do you serve him?"

He turned an infuriated gaze on me. "We all have a price, Elainya. He offered me my heart's desire and I took it. It is enough that he has kept his word and that he has allowed me to do some good with his gifts. What do you truly know of life, anyway? You're just a child. Eat your food."

Silenced, I munched on the fresh bread and rich cheese. The ale had a strong bite I didn't like. "The Draska drink only water from the spring in the heart of Aurora."

"We are the Draska now. You will find that little inhibits shadow magic, so you may drink whatever you wish."

I handed the flask back to Nian and walked to the stream to drink of the fresh, clear water. Sitting down on the warm stone, I let the afternoon sun bathe me as I tried to make sense of this new life.

Nian did not interrupt my thoughts.

Did it matter whether I used this new power or not? My heart knew itself to be condemned. If what Nian said was true, I had killed an entire race.

I had killed my own people.

If I could do some good, bring some healing out of this darkness, maybe then I would not feel so wretched. The power was in me already. I had felt it coursing through my blood decades ago, and I could still feel the warmth. Controlling Jeiwan had been effortless. Indeed, I'd not even known what I was doing. He had not been harmed, so the power was not totally evil. Perhaps the source did not matter?

Nian draped a cloak over my shoulders. "I brought this for you." I had not even noticed the chill as evening fell around me. "It will be night soon. You should come and rest."

He led me into the village and to a hut that was in good repair. My mind could not recall whom it had belonged to. "I've started a fire within that should keep us warm through the night."

I nodded and followed him into the dwelling. He'd made mattresses out of leaves covered by blankets on either side of the fire. As I lay down upon the surprisingly comfortable bed, I smelled the sweet herbs he'd mixed with the leaves. Despite my intentions to think throughout the night, I fell into a deep sleep. In the darkness, I dreamed.

Nian

The master had allowed him one more day to reach her. She was close to surrendering. Gentle handling would bring her around. He sighed, the fear he'd hidden slowly drifting away on the night breeze. By tomorrow night, she would be safely in the master's care, the need to use force past.

Elainya

I woke in the middle of the night to find Drenil kneeling beside my pallet. "Hello, my love," he whispered.

Sitting up, I glanced across the fire to where Nian lay sleeping. Drenil's eyes reflected the firelight, sparkling with life. I brushed a stray lock of brown hair out of his eyes. "Have you come to torment me some more?" I asked.

He sat and put his arm around me. "No. You need someone to talk to, so I am here. Also, I brought you a gift." He placed a shining silver brooch in my hand. Elaborately twisted silver surrounded a glowing blue sapphire. "For your cloak," he explained.

"How lovely." I wondered if it would still be as solid when I woke. "I do need to speak to you." I sighed. "Drenil, this master...must I serve him?"

He touched my chin to direct my gaze into his eyes so I could see the truth of his words. "Elainya, if you do as he wishes, you can bring good to the world. If you do not, he will kill you, and this time death will be real. I fear that if he kills you in anger we will be separated. Live, my darling. Besides, is it service if you may bend his power to serve your own ends?"

"If this is the price he asks of me, what did he ask of you?"

Dren glanced away and then kissed me. "Do not trouble yourself. I am with you, even if only as a spirit. It is enough for me." He held my hand tenderly. "Will you at least try to do as he asks?"

"For you I would do anything."

He ran his hand over my hair, tugging my braid. His touch felt real. "Sleep now. You have a long day ahead."

I awakened the next morning to a sharp pain in my right hand. Opening my fingers, I gazed at the workmanship I knew all too well. Only one hand could have made such a delicate creation. I drew the cloak tightly about me and pinned it together at the throat with the brooch. I unbraided my hair and combed through the thick brown waves. On a whim, I let my hair hang loose to my waist.

Nian greeted me with fresh berries and a flask of cold water from the spring that tasted of melted snow. "How are you feeling this morning?" he asked.

"I am adjusting."

"Good. That's a lovely brooch. I don't think I've ever seen anything like it."

"Drenil brought it to me in a dream last night. How is it possible that a spirit can give me something this solid?"

Nian stirred the embers of the fire, scattering them. "He is a spirit, but he is also in service to the master. Perhaps the Shadow Lord allowed this contact to give you courage."

I sat and munched on the berries. After a while, Nian handed me bread. He seemed to know my eating habits well. Finished, I drained the flask and handed it back to him. "What is it I need to learn from you?"

"You have a good beginning. You know who you are and what you are to do. You have questions: ask and I will answer them."

"What really became of the Draska?"

"Weakness, men's hatred, battles on the spiritual plain which they were not prepared for, time...many different things worked together to destroy them. Stories say that when the invasions began, the Draska were the first line of defense. When their powers failed to overcome the enemy, some turned to shadow magic for added strength."

"You are saying that the Draska served the Shadow Lord?"

"No. They tried to draw upon his power without commitment. That is when the plague began. Understand, Elainya, the Shadow Lord is not the servant of our kind. The Draska's abuse of his gifts created a poisonous environment that eventually became a disease. Your absence destroyed them."

In that moment, I saw the truth. The pollution could have been drawn out. I could begin to see the combination of ritual and herbs that would have saved them.

He was right.

I could have saved them.

"What do you think the master will do if I choose not to use his power?"

Nian seemed to stare at a pattern of clouds as he leaned back against a tree trunk. "If you do not use his gifts, he will not have any use for you. He can be very persuasive, though." He plucked a bit of leaf from his beard and threw it into the remains of the fire. "You have already lived beyond your lifetime. I doubt he would allow you to continue. Can't you find some good to put your abilities to?"

"If he will allow me to do good."

Nian nodded approvingly.

"Why are some of the buildings untouched?" I gestured towards the hut we had stayed in last night, and remembered who had lived there.

"I've repaired some of them."

"That was Drenil's parents' house."

Nian nodded. "I come here whenever I need to recuperate from overextending myself. It is peaceful. I keep some supplies here and have used it as a place of rest. You may come here whenever you need to. I know Drenil would have wanted you to use it."

"Why are you overextending yourself?"

"Up until now, there hasn't been a healer in the kingdom, certainly not one who knew how to treat a Draskan mage." He shrugged. "I've fought with our troops and tried to heal the wounded, but these creatures who attack us seem immune to magic. All I've succeeded in doing is making them mad."

"Miatra credits you with keeping them out of the kingdom for as long as you have."

Nian laughed. "Miatra is an innocent child. All I've done is raise an army...something that should have been done immediately. Gerald was not ready for such a challenge. Romert has been a much better king."

"Who holds your loyalty...the king or the Shadow Lord?"

He glanced towards the forest. "Kings come and go, but Shadow, like Light, has remained since the beginning of time. He will be as he is now until the end. He demands total allegiance, Elainya."

I could think of nothing else I wanted to ask. He'd given me too much to think about already. I felt dirty. "I would like to wash in the reflection pond as I did in my childhood."

Nian nodded and went back to Drenil's house to set things to rights, giving me privacy.

The reflection pool lay in a sun-brightened clearing, a short distance into the woods. How many times I had bathed here! I laid my clothes on a sunny rock so they'd be warm when I emerged, and dove into the ice-cold water. It washed over me, tingling every inch of my skin and fanning my hair. Still, the feeling of filth remained. I dove again and again, brushing the soft sand over my skin until it shone pink and new. At last, I lay on the sun-warmed stones and allowed the rays to dry me as I wrung the water from my hair.

Gently, I ran a comb through my hair until all the tangles were gone. Thus cleansed on the outside, I snuggled into the warm shift and let the folds of my gown flow around me. I looked at my reflection in the pond and heard Jeiwan's voice inside my head, calling me witch. Perhaps the boy was right.

I ran my fingers through my hair to set it flying about my shoulders and returned to the city.

As I approached, I heard Nian's voice raised in anger and hid among the trees.

Nian

"She is little more than a child."

The Shadow Lord's human guise stood over Nian just outside the hut. "She is old enough."

"Her loss is too recent. She's still weak. Jauer is nearly ready. Let him lead the way and release me."

"No."

"Master, please, another day is all I ask. I am too old to deal with her stubbornness. I can't do this."

"You can and you will. She would never learn from Jauer. Of course, I could just kill her. If you truly feel she is so unworthy, perhaps we are both wasting our time."

"No," Nian answered quickly. "Wait. Just give me time to prepare her. She must recover first. When the time is right, she will serve you. Let Drenil speak with her some more. That will help."

"I am not patient, Nian. I want this done." The Shadow Lord vanished and Nian sank stiffly to sit upon a nearby log.

He picked up a rock and threw it hard across the clearing. "I hate this," he muttered. He'd been close. He'd sensed it, and then as she'd bathed, he'd felt her pulling away. Which way would she go when he demanded her answer?

Elainya

I stepped out of hiding. "I seem to have complicated your life."

Nian chuckled. "You hide well. I'm surprised I didn't sense you. I thought you were still bathing."

"What am I not ready for?"

He looked at me. "You must swear allegiance to him."

"I will not." I was more surprised by the strength of my answer than he was.

Nian's voice echoed in my head, but his lips did not move. He stared intently into my eyes. "Hush. He is good to his servants and harsh to his enemies. Do not give voice to your thoughts."

Aloud, he said, "We will speak no more of this today. Rest. Be silent—that is the next lesson you must learn. Think on your situation. All I demand of you today is silence."

He rose and stalked off into the woods, leaving me confused. So, the Shadow Lord could not hear thought-speech. That was indeed a valuable lesson.

I walked through the village. Silence came easy in this place of death. I wandered the forest, gathering a few herbs. As I had as a child, I roamed the area, eating roots or berries as I became hungry, drinking water from the stream. I felt young again, and my strength began to revive. At dark, I returned to the hut and fell asleep next to the fire Nian had built, just as my grandfather had so many years ago.

In my dreams, I slept in Drenil's arms, safe and at peace.

Nian

He watched her sleep, knowing he'd stretched the master's patience to the breaking point. He could feel the flames of anger drawing nearer with each breath. Today. This was the day it would begin. He did not sleep, but sat tending the fire and seeking strength, locking away any hint of emotion. Caring for the girl was not allowed, and yet....

How could he not?

Elainya

I awoke to find Nian sitting outside the hut, with a warm breakfast prepared. "How are you?" he asked.

"I'm feeling stronger."

"Good. Yesterday you returned to your childhood. This is a good place for your lessons to begin. You obeyed me without question. This is also good."

"I have more questions."

"The time for questions has passed. The time for thinking has passed. Today is a day of testing."

I remembered testing days. My teachers would ask questions about the lessons we had learned from the forest. Based upon our answers, we would be given greater responsibilities, or a wider range for our explorations. I nodded and sat up straighter. Somehow, I had become his apprentice without meaning to.

"How have you come here?"

I thought carefully. What answer would he be looking for? "By choice." That sounded better than by horse.

"Whose choice?"

"My own."

"The power of choice is immense. You have a decision to make now, but it is necessary that you understand."

I listened, sensing an urgency in his tone—a warning?

"There is more at stake than life or death. You must agree to serve the Shadow Lord. In his service you will be with Drenil's spirit, you will have unparalleled power, and you will have freedom."

"If I do not serve him, I will die," I added.

He frowned at the interruption. *Be quiet,* echoed through my head. "No. You will live. But you will be alone, and you will beg for death."

"Being with Drenil only in my dreams is not enough."

I felt a chill and knew the master had joined us. "She doesn't understand, does she, Nian?"

He stood and faced the being behind me, an urgency on his face that I did not understand. "Not yet. She's not ready yet. She's not strong enough."

You must swear allegiance to him if he asks. There was fear in his mental voice.

"I say that she is strong enough. I have already waited far too long. Girl, will you serve me, or must I explain the alternative?"

I stood and faced the creature. "I will not serve you."

The Shadow Lord seemed to grow and Nian stepped forward. "She's not ready! She's still a child."

"BE SILENT." The command echoed through the clearing, and I felt the Shadow's attention focus on me.

Nian stepped back and placed his hands on my shoulders. *Now, Elainya, please.*

"I am old enough to choose for myself and I reject you," I spat.

The response was instant and violent. The world dissolved around me and I was surrounded by pain. Burned as if by fire, I screamed. The pain swirled and I could not find a purchase against it. I tried to force my body to run, but was held by Nian. His grasp was inescapable, the agony rippling from his hands, echoing through every inch of my body.

I could not breathe. I was dying and the pain would never end. Incredibly, the agony intensified, and then it was gone.

I was lying in the dirt, trying desperately to bring air into my lungs.

"Now she understands," the Shadow Lord growled, and was gone.

Young idiot, echoed through my mind as Nian lifted me and carried me into the hut. His tone was bitter and angry.

Nian

The first time Nian set foot in Aurora, he'd been assaulted by the stench of unburied bodies, overwhelmed by the taste of death. The buildings were in various states of disrepair, but there was no sign of fire or assault.

He'd stood at the edge of the village in shock. A few animals roamed the spaces between the huts; if this was the result of attack, the raiders had been less than thorough. "Is anyone here?" he'd called and listened as the silence echoed. An emaciated cow flicked an ear in his direction as it stepped over the rotting corpse of some form of fowl.

The huts were arranged in a loose circle around a central meeting area where communal cooking fires were often lit. The path here was less overgrown than the one he had just traveled, but even it screamed of abandonment. He walked toward the center and then searched the ring for the home he remembered as belonging to his grandparents.

The rough wooden door hung ajar. It fell off the hinges as he pushed it aside. The air was thick with death and decay. The two of them lay together on the floor in front of the hearth. Signs of disarray tugged at his mind, but the sight tore his soul. He stepped outside and vomited into his grandmother's flower bushes.

Enraged, he drew power about him and called a burst of fire from the long-dead hearth, intending to destroy the carrion, the hut, village, everything until the ache in his heart could be quenched. Instead only a wave of choking black smoke emerged and enveloped him in darkness. With a swirl of dust, the master took form. "No, you will not destroy the evidence of what you have done."

"What do you mean, I have done? This is your doing! Evil on this scale...."

"Required an invitation before it could be created." The master laughed. "I must say, the illness was more effective than even I dreamed it would be. With no healer to decipher the code of how it spread, it moved quickly."

"The best healers in the land lived in Aurora!"

"Ah, but only one healer had the clues that would have allowed her to understand this disease. Regrettably, she was not available."

Understanding swept over him. "Elainya."

"Elainya." The Shadow Lord waved him inside to where the bodies lay. "See how his head is in her lap? He collapsed suddenly, trying to help her build the fire. They were freezing anyway. She drew his body close and died crying for the loss of all she'd known, never realizing her grandson was still alive." He shook his head in mock despair and then turned his dark gaze on Nian. "I could not have done better myself."

Nian, blind with fury, moved towards him and was thrown through the door and into the dirt.

"Your penance is to clean up this mess. By the time you have it to my liking, I think you will have learned to serve me."

Elainya

I remained senseless for a time. When I did come around, I fought against my fear of the shadows in the hut. Nian was firm that I must stay inside during the daytime, thus surrounding me with a darkness filled with mocking spirits. Ripples of remembered pain echoed through my body causing me to gasp and cry out in the few moments when I slept.

Drenil's visits were brief. He would appear, urge that I choose the easy path, and then leave.

At last, I began to adjust to the darkness and the trembling passed. My thinking cleared. Nian approved and allowed me to walk in the clearing at night. Gradually, my strength returned.

We sat across the fire from each other and stared into the flames. "You failed that test," he said.

I laughed for the first time in days. "I gathered that."

"I would have spared you had you listened."

"You helped."

He was silent for a long moment. "Yes. And if you choose to die, it will be my hand that kills you."

"You'll enjoy that."

He glared at me. "No."

"I feel old," I sighed.

His response was a snort of laughter. "At your age, you should."

"So I have a choice, but not a good one, is that the lesson?"

Nian did not answer.

I sighed. "Call the master." I knew I couldn't bear that torture and would only grow weaker if I fought. Nian had been right, and for that I hated him.

Nian glanced towards the shadows and I watched the master take form. "What is your decision?"

"You will give me the power to heal the sick?"

"Yes." The Shadow Lord stepped closer to me, tipping my head up to look into the depths of his black eyes. Enchanting eyes. Eyes that devoured my soul.

"You will allow me time with Drenil?" I asked.

"Of course."

"Then I will serve you."

I heard Nian sigh with relief.

"Then kneel before me," the master commanded.

I knelt, fighting down the bile that rose in my throat. "I despise you," I whispered, "but I will serve you and do your bidding without question."

The Shadow Lord's laughter was joyful. "Rise, my good servant!" He pulled me to my feet and kissed me, his tongue forcing my lips apart. I fought down a choking gag. "I delight in your hatred. You and I will have an honest relationship. We will work wonders together." I felt the weight of oppression lift from my shoulders. I was committed, and in that there was a strange sort of freedom, just as Nian had said.

As the master disappeared, I turned and left the circle. I did not look at Nian. I did not speak to him that night. I slept by the pool, wrapped in the assurance that I would not die of the cold and nothing in the darkness would harm me. Now it was only the light that I had to fear.

Nian

Nian waited outside the hut for Elainya's return throughout the night. He'd spent many sleepless nights here, so one more didn't matter. In truth, he was relieved that she had surrendered as easily as she had. His own battle with the master had lasted for months, but then he'd still had someone he thought he was fighting for, and there had been the children.

He'd been dragging the carcass of a dead cow into the funeral pyre when he'd seen the blond head peak around the edge of a collapsed hut. He'd run after the fleeing child, only to be brought up short by an arrow-wielding teen. The older children had witnessed one of his battles with the Shadow Lord and had kept the younger ones hidden as long as possible.

It took every bit of negotiating skill he had to convince them to allow him to find homes for them. He'd known even then that the master would not suffer anyone to remain in Aurora. Whatever his plan was, he intended the village to remain livable, but empty.

The night passed in a cold fog that cleared to crystal stars and faded to the washed-out gray of dawn. In that faint light, Elainya returned. She didn't speak, but entered the hut and gathered her things. A blind fool could tell she was angry. She would not understand what he'd risked to try and delay the testing. Even now he shivered at the thought of the variety of torments the master could have employed. It was best this way. Having her angry and alive was acceptable.

She left as silently as she'd come. With a sigh, he gathered his own belongings and saddled Singe. Best to let her walk off her anger. He deliberately took a deer track through the forest to avoid passing her on the road. At the castle, he turned the stallion over to the stable hands with directions to pamper the beast, and went to stand outside the gate and wait for Elainya to climb the hill.

Chapter 8

Matchmaking

Elainya

Iwalked toward the castle through swirling mists that dragged at the hem of my heavy brown gown. The road was quiet as I let my thoughts wander: to Dren, the Shadow Lord, my past, and my future. The morning sun seemed unable to break through this sodden haze, only occasionally basting me with warmth as a patch curled away.

Sound echoes in such a mist. I heard the horse long before it appeared. Could anyone harm me? Unlikely, so I continued on, choosing not to vanish into the forest. I felt the darkness in my blood, writhing like the fog, changing me in unknown ways.

The rider pulled a large brown gelding to a stop next to me. "Lady Elainya? What are you doing out here...alone?"

I stopped and looked up at Reif as he sat on the shifting, restless horse. "I was visiting Aurora and now I'm returning to the castle."

He frowned. "I thought Nian was with you. Will you allow me to give you a ride back? This area is dangerous. You should not be here alone. The walk is long and these mists hide much evil."

"I know." I smiled and allowed him to help me up in front of him.

He clicked to the horse and it settled into a steady walk, not hurried or uncontrolled. I felt more at ease on this well-trained animal than I had on Nian's beast, and I enjoyed the sense of controlled strength responding to the warlord's commands.

Reif was dressed in practical clothing: leather breeches and vest covering a linen shirt, open at the neck, with the sleeves removed. His sword hung from the saddle within easy reach. He looked at ease, confident. He was at home on a horse as he was not in the castle. His dogs explored the forest floor as we traveled, shadows playing in the woods. He smelled of the woods and wild places. "Were you hunting?"

"No, running errands for the king. I have been riding a sweep of the eastern shore to check for invaders. There was an attack on a farm there sometime within the last few days."

"Are there any wounded?" I'd heard enough to know that caring for the casualties was expected to fall to me.

Reif was silent as he guided the horse over a rocky patch in the path. Once we were steady again, he answered. "No. There were no survivors. There rarely are in the raids."

"I'm sorry. That sounds like a grim errand."

"It was, but seeing you helps." His arms around me tightened only a little as he looked down at me. "I'm sorry if I was too forward the other day." He shrugged. "I'm comfortable on a battlefield. At court I feel awkward. It is all my brother-in-law can do to keep me from making a fool of myself most days."

I tried to think of an answer that would be kind and yet clear. "You were flattering. It is just that I believe in the traditions of my people. I hope you can understand."

He fixed his gaze on the road ahead of us, and his expression remained neutral, impossible to read. "I do respect your feelings. I'm just curious about something. I've studied Draska traditions. Your people were a vital part of this world. It is my understanding that the Draska bonding ceremony made it impossible for one spouse to outlive the other."

"Yes." At that moment, I realized that in this world, the Draska ways were a mere historical curiosity. There was only the smallest hint of doubt in his voice as he continued. Was it real, or was I only imagining his skepticism?

"And yet you are here—the last Draska woman, widowed. Certainly that should change the rules. If you do not marry and have children, then there will be no more Draska."

He adjusted the horse's direction with a slight tug on the rein. "It seems to me that Draska tradition at this point would encourage you to marry."

I hadn't thought that far yet. I'd been focused on my confrontation with the Shadow Lord. Had that been his plan all along? Eliminate the Draska? What would happen to the kingdom if we were gone? A horrible realization sank into the pit of my stomach. All those years ago, he'd said he wanted help with a land deal. Nian had mentioned that the Shadow Lord demanded Aurora be kept habitable. My people's land was empty now, vacant. It belonged to...whom? Nian? I'd missed the clues. Lord and lady were not generally titles given to Draska...they were reserved for landowners. What was the Shadow Lord up to? That land had been given to my people by the Light centuries ago. The water that ran through the town was said to contain special powers that gave the Draska their abilities. Could that land be given to another people? What would they become if they lived there, drank the water?

My long silence must have troubled Reif. "Forgive me, Lady Elainya. I didn't mean to upset you."

"Elainya. Please. Call me Elainya."

His eyes brightened. "I would be delighted to do so. And will you do me the honor of calling me Reif?"

I smiled up at him, but felt the way my lips twitched in denial of the expression. "Of course. I do appreciate you giving me a ride back to the castle. I'm suddenly feeling unwell."

He nodded and urged the horse into a gallop. He did not speak again but focused on getting me home. Odd to think of the castle that way, but Aurora would never be home to me again.

Nian

Elainya arrived in a flurry of hooves only a few moments after he'd stationed himself to watch for her. He stepped into the shadows, pulling a few about him to aid in concealment, as Reif helped her down from his horse.

Nian felt his hands clench as he watched the man set her gently on her feet and touch her shoulder to make sure she was steadied. She looked up at him with simple gratitude, but no affection, thank the darkness. He relaxed. How had she come to be with that boor? The warlord certainly seemed to turn up at inconvenient times. There was an intensity in her stance that bothered him. She was focused on, what? Flirting? That didn't seem like Elainya.

He listened as they exchanged pleasantries.

"You should not make that journey on foot, Elainya. Among my more pleasant duties, I help my brother-in-law manage his stables. I've actually bred a good number of his horses myself. If you would allow me to, I'd be pleased to have a horse placed at your disposal. There is one in particular I have in mind...."

"Oh, I've never been good with horses. I don't think that would end well."

"You've met Singe?"

Elainya paled prettily. "Yes. He terrifies me."

Her cat dropped from above to land at Nian's feet. He startled and growled at the creature who bounded into Elainya's arms. She petted the kitten before settling it back on the ground.

Reif laughed. "Singe does have that effect on people, and for good reason. But he has some unusual characteristics that are also evident in a young mare he fathered. She is as gentle as he is wild, but she seems to respond to certain talents the way her father does, the way that cat does."

"And how would you know that?"

"I watch. Singe was impossible to control until Nian claimed him. Even now, I could not ride that horse, and yet even Nian's servant has some luck. Ember—the mare—has always seemed drawn to Nian whenever he comes to the stables. Anyone can ride her, but I've often regretted the lack of a Draska woman to develop the abilities I think she possesses. I'd like you to take a look at her once you are recovered. She's a good horse. She'll keep you safe."

The blush that crept up Elainya's throat made Nian sick. The man could charm a snake. He could not hear Elainya's soft-spoken response, but Reif smiled and tenderly touched her shoulder before taking his beast to the stable.

Elainya picked up her bundle of belongings and turned to the castle just as the sun burst through the mist and burned away the shadows surrounding Nian. She met his eyes and nodded in acceptance of his scrutiny. Her expression was grim, her lips tight. Anger was a palatable cloak around her. He stepped away from the wall.

"My apologies. I did not intend to intrude."

Her expression changed to one of confusion for a moment before it cleared. "Oh. Reif. No, no intrusion." She stopped and looked up at him, seeming suddenly small in his shadow. "I have a question. Aurora—who owns it?"

"I do. Or rather, we do."

"Has the Shadow Lord asked you for it?"

He blinked. She wanted to discuss land titles? Perhaps her absorption had not been directed at Reif. "No. Why would he?" His hands relaxed and he reached out to take her bundle.

"I don't know, but I think perhaps he will."

Nian laughed. "Elainya, the master is a spirit. He doesn't need land. He rules wherever he pleases. As he rules us, he already has control over Aurora."

She paled. "Does he?"

"Of course, but it doesn't matter."

"What happens to my land if I marry?"

Now it was Nian's turn to feel the blood drain from his face. "Why then, I suppose I would give it to your husband as your dowry." He coughed to clear his throat. "Are you considering a marriage?"

The mist swallowed the sun and he shivered. What was the girl playing at?

"No. I was just curious." She glanced at the castle. "You know I can't remarry."

He shrugged. "You're still young. Stranger things have happened."

She twisted her wedding ring around her finger. "I think Dren might object." Her voice was soft, sad.

He longed to reach out and touch her, erase the loneliness he heard in her voice, but held his feelings behind a stone wall. His tone came out harsh and he regretted it immediately. "I'm sure he would." Nian took a deep breath and softened his voice. "Still, Drenil is dead. He would want you to be happy. If you found someone you could care for...."

Her eyes spat fire as she glared at him. "No." With a soggy swirl of plain brown fabric, she grabbed the bundle from him and stalked away. Terror glared at him in a feline imitation of Elainya's expression as the kitten followed his mistress.

He glanced after her with a faint smile. She needed some better clothes. She'd always enjoyed nice things. He'd send one of the squires to Weaver's Knot to ensure her favorite weavers were represented on Marketday. Maybe that would improve her mood.

Elainya

Why was everyone so worried about my love life? I was supposed to be the matchmaker, not these men. Reif? His children were almost my age. Well, the age I appeared to be, at least.

I stormed through the entrance to the castle and turned toward the stairs. Terror bounded ahead. Distracted, I collided with Reflect Rendel.

He gasped at the abrupt contact and stepped backward, his eyes looking me over with an intensity I would've expected from Nian, but not from him. "Lady Elainya! I was hoping to run into you!"

There was no controlling the frown his pun brought to my face. Mother used to warn me about the wrinkles on my forehead when I made that face. With a sigh, I twisted my facial muscles into a more socially acceptable greeting. "Reflect! I'm sorry. I didn't see you!"

"I would've been crushed had you done it on purpose," he jibed. "Did you enjoy your trip to Aurora?" Despite the banter, his eyes held a slight frown of concentration.

How could I answer that? Looking at the little man, I found I could not lie to him. "No. No, I did not."

His expression warmed. "I'm sorry. It is a sad sight to see the Light's chosen ripped from the land. But now that you are here, who knows what recovery might be possible." His smile was not a leer and yet his meaning was clear. He saw me as the mother of my renewed race.

"Not you, too!"

He laughed. "Have you found yourself the focus of some attention? Well, you are a beautiful young woman. You've got to understand, Nian has lived alone for a long time."

The wheels in my mind ground into silence. "Nian?"

Rendel blinked and coughed. "Oh, dear. Ignore me. Everyone else does. I'd best get back to tending my flames." He turned and left faster than I would have thought possible.

Nian? He must be, what? Sixty years old? He could have grandchildren my age. Besides, I had just spent enough time alone with Nian to know how he saw me—as a tool for his master. I trembled, remembering the torment I'd experienced at his hands. The reflect was insane.

I followed Terror up the stairs, lost in thought. When I entered my room, the time confusion overwhelmed me. Where my shelves had hung in ruins, fresh tapestries now hung. I dropped my bundle on the floor and pulled one side of the heavy fabric back to reveal the neatly restored shelves, empty save that vial I'd yet again forgotten to ask Nian about.

Miatra walked into the room behind me. "You're back! Did we get them right? I had Joln and Tromas help me. Tromas picked the fabric. He said it would protect the herbs from sunlight." Her face glowed with pride.

"Yes, you've done a fantastic job. This room is...." I changed my wording at the last moment. "This room is exactly what I would have wanted. Now all I have to do is gather more herbs and buy more pots."

"It's three days until Marketday." She placed the books she'd been carrying on my desk. "I borrowed those from the reflect. I hope you don't mind, I've moved into the room next door. That's the room my great-grandmother used when she assisted," she paused, "your predecessor."

Our eyes met. Yes, this girl was bright, and she would keep my secrets. I could not have hoped for a better assistant. Brenna would have been so proud.

"I want to change out of this dress and into my blue one. Close the door, will you?"

Miatra rushed around while I unpacked my bundle. She held up the blue gown and fingered the fabric. "Elainya, where was this fabric made? I haven't seen any like it before."

I smiled. "The Draska favored fabrics from Karakul. They spin the fibers strong and thin and then weave them into this fabric. Each weaver favors a different pattern. In Weaver's Knot, there is a family that makes this cloth. It has always been my favorite."

"It is like silk! Won't you be cold?"

"My people wore this fabric before you were born, child. I'll need a good woolen cloak for winter, but I'll be fine the rest of the year."

She held up the dress and spun around, watching how it flared and moved. "I could almost enjoy sewing with fabric like this."

"We'll make you a gown next."

"Oh, I could never afford it."

"I'll trade you for the fabric."

She looked at me and laughed. "What could I have that you'd want?"

"Consider it my thanks for the shelves." I thought for a moment. "I would like something else from you, though. Information. I need to know more about Lord Nian."

Miatra helped me change and nibbled on her lip. She shivered. "Well, he isn't a real lord, or he wasn't born one, at least. He came to serve at the castle during the reign of King Gerald,

Romert's father. We'd been without a healer or a magician since right before King Cydril died."

I tightened my belt and did not look at her.

"King Cydril died the day after Drenil and Elainya were buried. It is said the lovers put a curse on him so that his heart stopped."

I frowned. "No they didn't."

"Why not? He was an evil man."

"Well they were Draska…I mean, Draska don't generally go around killing people…with curses or anything else. They are…were…a peaceful people."

Her eyes rolled. "Nian isn't peaceful."

"True."

"Lord Nian helped Gerald raise an army. He found a war leader and began to fight the invaders. If we hadn't had a good army, I doubt we could have held them off this long."

"These attacks have been going on for over forty years?" I asked in amazement. "Why hasn't someone taken the battle to the enemy's lands? For that matter, who are they?"

"That's just it, they come only at night. We don't know where they're from. In the morning, they're gone, leaving nothing other than destruction."

"You're from Westridge…have there ever been any attacks in the west?"

"A few, but our coasts are rocky. In West Ridge, we don't build our towns right on the water. We prefer to be near the good pasture land.

"Did you know Nian came from Solitude?" she asked.

I laughed at that. "I'd heard, but no one comes from Solitude. In all my life, I've never heard of anyone leaving there. The way is very dangerous. The only safe way is to cross Beast's Retreat and come down the coast road and then over. That's why they named it Solitude. Once anyone went there, they never returned."

"Lord Nian did. He came across the Northern Way, too."

I raised my eyebrows. So he said. Maybe he flew.

She nodded. "Anyway, King Gerald was too desperate to refuse his help. He's been the only Draska here for years. King Gerald made him lord of the Draska lands in gratitude."

"Does anyone know why he left Solitude?"

"No, but I've heard it had something to do with a tragic love affair." She sighed dramatically. "Supposedly he left to escape the memory of his lost love."

"Really." Despite these revelations, I could not imagine Nian as a love-lost soul.

Nian

Elainya came to dinner dressed in the blue gown the reflect had found for her. Nian's breath caught in his throat at the way the shadows made the light flicker on the embroidery. She was cold and distant, yet she joined him as they entered, taking the arm he offered. Silence reigned as all heads turned to stare. As an entrance, it was magnificent.

King Romert's lips formed a thin line. "You have returned from your excursions. I see rest has restored the Lady Elainya to health." He motioned for them to be seated and then turned his attention to Queen Laurel.

Nian glanced at Elainya and was struck by the change in her appearance. She was glowing with health and energy. She caught Nian's stare and raised an eyebrow in challenge.

"You have been pale since you came to us. Tonight, you are radiant. If all the master's servants looked as you do, I suspect he would have more of them."

She frowned and looked around the table. Nian watched as Reflect Rendel made the sign of Light in her direction—a blessing or a warding gesture? However it was intended, Elainya seemed disturbed.

"Don't let the reflect worry you. He is a crazy old man."

She turned to glare at him and did not reply, but her eyes spoke volumes of accusation. Clearly, she had come to distrust old men.

He coughed and pretended to focus on the chicken he was gnawing from the bone. Across the table, Reif raised his goblet to Elainya and smiled.

From the corner of his eye, Nian saw her return the smile. Curse the man, he was going to have to do something about that attraction. He'd thought Elainya bright enough to see through Reif's barely civilized exterior, but who knew what the girl was thinking these days. He'd been pushing her hard. Had he pushed her into Reif's clutches?

"Queen Laurel is a beautiful woman," Elainya offered.

Had she been looking at the queen instead of her brother? "Yes, she is."

"And she has never borne a child?"

Ever the healer. He chuckled. "I've never even heard a rumor that she might be with child." *It is generally assumed that the king is no longer capable of fathering a child.* Nian sent her the words silently, cautious of the king sitting beside him.

She nodded and glanced toward the king with that same healer's eye. *Not too old. The queen looks lonely.*

He smiled and bit into a carrot. She was willing to communicate with him through thought speech. That was an improvement. One step at a time.

Miatra seemed somewhat more animated than normal. Perhaps Elainya was having a positive effect on the girl. Joln and Tromas were vying for her attention, having placed her between them. He allowed himself to be entertained by their banter and the dinner passed in peaceful companionship. He could almost forget that he'd earned Elainya's hatred.

Elainya

Early the next morning, before the sun could rise, Lady Eavyn bustled into my room. I kept the door open during my waking hours to encourage such familiarity, but such an early visit was unexpected.

The first thing I noticed about her was the new gown. Giggling, she whirled around, showing off the flowing green fabric. Her eyes sparkled—a perfect match for the pale green ribbon she had braided into her long red hair.

"My, aren't you up early!" I said as I finished tying a blue ribbon into my unruly hair.

Her face fell. "Don't you like it?"

I laughed and hugged her. "Of course I do, dear! You look lovely."

She smiled again. "You looked so beautiful when you came to court, I thought maybe I'd see what I'd look like if I dressed like you."

"You are lovely on your own, but the style does suit you. We'll have to go down to the pond later so you can see yourself. You need a lighter weight fabric, though, to get the full effect."

"Oh!" she cried and ran to look out of the window slit. "Good...I was afraid the sun was up!"

"It will be soon."

"Come on, Elainya. We're going gathering!"

I'd often joined the queen's ladies for dew gathering in the time before I'd slept. She handed me a silver pot. "I thought you might need this. I had an extra." Legend had it that if a woman washed her skin in dew water gathered before sunup in a silver pot, she would stay young forever. Some said it would remove freckles. Still others whispered that a woman thus washed could enchant the man of her dreams.

I accepted the pot. "I can't imagine you needing anything to keep you young or beautiful."

She beamed at the compliment. "It's for my freckles." She grasped my hand. With Eavyn laughing and pulling me down the stairs, we merged with the giggling girls. The air was crisp and brisk as the ladies of the castle met in the courtyard. As the first light of dawn colored the morning mist, we streamed forth, adding our own bright colors to the new day.

This was my favorite courtly excursion. We romped through the gardens, skipping and laughing as we knocked the bright drops into our pots.

The queen joined in with glee—the king not being present. She was young to be burdened by our over-serious king. I took every opportunity to make her laugh.

Glancing up at the dawn clouds, I gestured for her to look. "My lady, see, there is a hound chasing a cat."

"Where?"

"See—the cat is about to turn over the milk jug."

"Where??"

"Oh, no! It spilled the milk!" I exclaimed, spritzing her face with some of the water I'd collected.

She laughed brightly and we romped through the grasses, letting the morning fragrances make us giddy.

"Oh, Elainya, I'm so glad you came to us!"

"Thank you, my lady."

She knocked a drop of dew from a pale pink rose into her gathering pot. We were alone in a corner of the garden and she looked to me for news. "Have you any matches floating in that mischievous mind of yours?"

"A few, my lady."

Her eyes widened. "Well...tell!"

Quickly, I thought up a few bits of gossip that would please her. "I've a lady for Jeiwan..."

"Oooh! Poor girl—which one?"

I nodded to where Lady Eavyn stood knocking drops of water into her jug. "Eavyn can handle him once he gains control of his passions."

The queen looked surprised for a moment and then smiled wistfully. "You know, she would make an admirable queen."

Grasping the private moment, I broached a tender subject. "Jeiwan is the heir to your husband's throne."

Laurel's lips tightened in a delicate frown. "Yes. My brother is very proud of him."

"Forgive my boldness, but I have noticed that there are those in the kingdom who would rather see the throne pass to a child of your issue."

She looked into my eyes and I read a deep sorrow in her soul. "As would I, but it is not possible." She gestured towards the grounds in general as she whispered, "My position has a price, you know. Romert is kind, and I know he desires a son, but he is not as young as he once was."

"He is not too old to father a child."

Laurel did not speak for a long moment. She continued knocking drops of dew into her pot. Had I not been standing next to her, I would not have noticed the tears which mingled with the dew. At last she spoke, her voice so soft I had to strain to hear her. "Elainya, our marriage has barely been consummated. Believe me, it is not possible. Romert knows. He waited too long to marry, so when he did, he chose a young bride, believing that would be enough. It has not been so."

"My lady, I am a healer."

"Age is not an illness, Elainya."

"If you ask it, I can remedy this. The king is not so old. If you are brave enough to assist me, you will have the child you desire."

The eyes that met mine were cautiously hopeful. "It is said that you practice a dark magic, Lady Elainya."

"Where is the evil in seeing that the kingdom does not fall into Jeiwan's hands?" I countered.

"What would I need to do?"

"Tonight I will send you a small pouch of powdered herbs. Each night at dinner, sprinkle a pinch of the herbs in the king's ale. They will dissolve instantly and he will not notice the taste. His energy will be restored. Beyond that, you will need only see that he sleeps in your bed chamber."

The queen smiled. "If your potion works well, I will know how to get him to bed...and what to do next," she giggled.

"Miatra will bring you the pouch before dinner." I allowed my gathering to lead me in another direction as Queen Laurel began to hum a cheerful tune I recognized from our puppet play.

Our group laughed into a bright, sparkling glade. Among the flowers and the birds, the ladies looked completely at home.

In the shadows, I noticed a soft movement. Without seeming to stare, my eyes picked out a girl hiding behind the undergrowth. Her hair hung in long, black curls around her soft face. Expressive deep blue eyes watched every move of the ladies with catlike fascination. Her curiosity was almost comical. I had seen her before...somewhere.

Suddenly, she was gone. The ensuing rustling in the bushes made my heart stop. The other ladies were so intent upon their gathering that they had not noticed. Casually, I moved towards the trees, listening carefully, remembering where I'd seen that face in the bushes before.

"One sound and I slit your throat. Do you understand?" a familiar voice said.

I hung my pot like a basket over my arm and feigned pleasant innocence.

"Jeiwan? Did I hear young Jeiwan here?" I moved through the thicket into his sight. I ignored the terrified look on the girl's face, and the knife Jeiwan quickly sheathed.

"Good day, Lady Elainya," he said politely.

"Good day, Jeiwan. Good day, my dear," I smiled at the young woman as if seeing her for the first time. "Perhaps it is fortunate that I happened along...to be found this way, again, Jeiwan, is not seemly. Still, if you desire a match with this lovely young woman, I can make arrangements."

He looked from me to the girl and then back at me before releasing her arm in shock. "No!"

"Tsk, tsk, Jeiwan! To lead her on so! I'm sorry, my dear, but run along home, now."

She curtsied and ran away.

After she was gone, I turned to Jeiwan and dropped my pretenses.

"You have no thought for manners, much less chivalry or seemliness, am I right?"

"I don't know what you mean."

"Every time I see you, you are behaving more like a brigand than one who would be king."

"My father says the weak exist only for the pleasure of the strong."

"If your father said that, then he is a brute, but no matter. If, by chance, I were stronger than you, then I could do with you as I pleased?"

He laughed.

"Jeiwan, the strong can fight each other if they wish. I have no care for that. But the weak are those to whom chivalry should be directed. If you could learn this now, you might yet become a fine young man."

"When I am king, I will tolerate no magic in my kingdom, so save your lectures, witch."

I smiled. "You meant Lady Elainya."

"You're not so powerful. All you've done is to put me to sleep and heal a few scrapes and cuts."

I sighed. Normally, I would not indulge myself, but...this was a special occasion.

Relaxing into the master's power, I waved my hand in Jeiwan's direction, and his knife floated into my hand. "This is a lovely dagger," I said, feeling the awkward weight.

"More tricks!" he blurted.

"Doesn't it make you a little nervous?" I gently slipped the knife into a more usable grip.

"Why should you make me nervous?"

"Oh, no reason, I suppose." I turned and walked away, casually throwing the dagger over my shoulder as I left the tiny clearing.

I heard him gasp as the dagger embedded itself in the tree beside his left ear.

I turned and smiled my most charming smile. "By the way, I won't mention your little escapade to anyone of importance, provided it doesn't happen again."

I left him still staring at the dagger. Magic did have its uses.

Turning back to where the ladies continued their play, I found myself the focus of a dove-gray gaze. Jeiwan's sister stood on the edge of the clearing, her gathering pot held loosely in her hands, her eyes wide and her lips smiling in an expression of delight.

I smiled and nodded toward her, amused by the curtsy she offered in return.

My enjoyment of the morning had been dampened. I returned to my room and traded the pot for my gathering basket. I paused at the kitchen to beg some fruit for breakfast and then walked to my garden. My garden. It was a blessing that it had survived. The herbs I needed were all at hand. Carefully, I used my dagger to dig the man's root. The knife was as sharp as the day Drenil had given it to me. The stone embedded in the hilt flashed in the sunlight. Balanced and elegant, it felt like an extension of my hand, not cumbersome like the weapon Jeiwan used.

"It is not a weapon," Drenil had explained years ago.

I had held the unsheathed blade up so the light glinted off the sharp point. "How can this not be a weapon?"

"It is like magic, neither good nor evil, simply a tool. It can aid you in your gathering, you can use it during surgery, for eating, many good and noble things can be accomplished with such a knife."

"It could also kill."

Drenil had laughed, tilting his head back slightly. "You could never kill, Elainya, just as you could never practice the dark arts." The sun had glinted off his brown hair, and the sky reflected in his eyes.

"Oh, but I can," I whispered to the shadows of the past, and gathered the rest of my needed herbs.

Returning to my chamber, I set a fire in the grate and began slicing the root thin so it would dry quickly on the stones around the hearth. I set another batch to boiling in a pot over the flames, and sat down at my desk to look out over the castle grounds.

The ladies were not in sight, having retreated from the midday sun. All was silent in my chamber. It would not be enough for Laurel to conceive a child. She must conceive a boy, a strong boy with enough resemblance to the king that there could be no doubt as to his parentage. In the past, I had left such matters to chance. And the kingdom had passed on to Gerald, I remembered ruefully. Gerald, Cydril's incompetent cousin, a child of ten when the king died. Of course, there was no guarantee that a child of Cydril's would have been competent.

But Romert seemed bright and intelligent, not having suffered by his parentage. Perhaps Nian knew another way to ensure that the child would be male.

A rumbling purr drew my attention to the kitten sitting on my desk. He stood and rubbed his face against my arm. I scratched behind his ears before standing. "I'll be back, little one. I've a short errand to run."

He turned in place and lay down upon the book open on my desk.

Checking that my fire was well set for the time required, I made the short walk down the narrow back stairs to Nian's workroom.

I rapped on the door, amused to find that the light knock was enough to open it. It had not been barred or even latched. Apparently, I had been expected.

Come in, Nian thought to me. Interesting. He seemed to prefer thought speech. The master could not read our minds. I wondered what the master would think of Nian's preference.

"Good morning."

Nian smiled, the wrinkles of his face growing deeper with the motion. "What do you need?"

I closed the stairway door and made sure the door to the main hall was closed. Nian did not comment, but his eyebrows raised at the precaution.

"I have promised to assist Queen Laurel in providing an heir for the kingdom."

With a nod, he grasped the problem. "And you can only do so much with herbs." He gestured for me to be seated. "The solution will not come by your potions, my apprentice."

"Don't you know some way, other than...?" Still, I could not bring myself to say the words.

He frowned. "Elainya, ensuring an heir for the kingdom is one of the best, most pure things you could do. Ask the master, I'm sure he can arrange to tamper with your potion. You remember how to summon him?"

I nodded.

"Then go on, I've work to do." He laughed when I did not move. "You'll have to reach out to him on your own, girl." He shooed me towards my stairs.

Help, I had expected from him, not derision. Although, why had I expected anything else? Frustrated at being treated as a child, I retreated to my chamber and threw the bars across both doors. I sat down and gazed into the focal point of my wedding ring until I was calmed. It was a step I was committed to, had been committed to for years. I'd sworn fealty, and yet I hesitated. Annoyed at my childishness, I took a deep breath and stood up.

I smoothed my hair back, straightened my gown, and forced the words of summoning from my throat. The room grew chilled, and the light refused to enter through the window. Firelight flickered from my cooking area and made the room shimmer. The Shadow Lord appeared, laughing.

"Was that so very hard to do?" he asked.

My mouth tasted like coal and my voice failed me. The sight of him after our last meeting sent a tremor through my spine.

"We have spoken before, Elainya. This is no different. What is it that you need help with?"

"The king and queen are childless. He is growing older. The heir to the throne is a tyrant who abuses the weak."

The Shadow Lord waited patiently for me to state my problem.

Confused, I realized my omission. "Such an heir is not acceptable!" I said in exasperation.

"Ah, of course not. You would want someone who is…kind." The last word he said with the same tone as I had invoked him, as if the word itself was poison. He glanced at the herbs in process and sighed. "You want my help. That is not a problem."

I stood stiffly, waiting for his directions.

He paused and observed me. He stepped closer and looked into my eyes. I closed them and turned away, lifting my chin, holding my head firm, refusing to allow the trembling in my soul to show.

"You are a proud and arrogant woman, Elainya, part of what I find pleasing in you. I would not have you this uncomfortable with our relationship. Is it the ritual calling that bothers you? That silly old teaching about words never to be spoken?"

I took a deep breath, turned back, and returned his searching, dark gaze.

"Very well, then I shall make it easier for you. Call me and I shall come, no invocation required. Pray to me, and I will do as you wish. Embrace my will, and my power will work as your own." His shadow hand brushed my chin gently. Though revolted, I could not pull away from his icy touch. "Serve me and your price for power will always be small. Treat my power as if it is your own. You may dispense with the formalities," he laughed.

He reached over to the shelf and picked up the beautiful vial that I had often wondered about. "You haven't used my gift," he said.

I looked at the jeweled container. "That was from you?"

He smiled. "No invocation needed. If you need extra power to achieve your will, a drop of this will give you all that you need." He added a drop to the pot and returned the vial to its place of honor.

With a flourish, he scraped the distillation from the pot and placed it in my mortar. Crumbling the root, he ground the substances together. I could not see all that he did, but in a moment he had wrapped the powder in a bit of fabric he plucked from my desk.

The kitten hissed and the Shadow Lord laughed.

"This should accomplish what you wish." He took my hands in his own and wrapped them around the small bundle. "You have little to fear from me, Elainya. I am as generous with my servants as I am harsh with my enemies." He ran a hand along the side of my face and down my arm. I held still and allowed his vile touch to linger on my hip. With a laugh, he swirled and vanished.

The room remained dim, however. The sun had passed over the roof of the castle, leaving my chamber in cool afternoon shade.

Shivering, I wrapped my cloak about me and sat down to regain my strength. In my heart, I could feel the master's power. As I touched the herbs, I felt them change subtly. I knew without a word that Laurel's child would be a boy, strong and true.

Unbarring the door, I went in search of Miatra. She took the herbs to the queen without question. Perhaps she'd guessed the contents.

I went outside to sit in the garden and watch the sun set.

⁂

Dinner that night was a festive affair. A passing bard entertained with tales of the kingdom and strummed on his lyre. The food was too rich for my unsettled stomach. I ate sparingly of the fresh vegetables. Nian beamed at me with pride in his eyes. "You've done well, today, Elainya."

He nodded towards the queen, who sat cheerfully at the table, striking in a deep purple velvet gown, cut to flatter her figure admirably. Her blonde hair was braided loosely and hung over her shoulder and down to her waist, accented with a fine strand of purple ribbon. Her crown set lightly upon her head. Jewels gleamed around her dainty neck, and the king seemed unable to keep his eyes from following that jeweled strand toward the cunningly designed bodice. Yes, Laurel had completed her portion of the arrangement. I noted when she brushed her fingers idly on the king's cup and smiled as he toasted her beauty and drank deeply of the wine.

Their early departure from the meal did not surprise me in the least.

Nian chuckled and raised his goblet to me. I touched mine to his, and some of the dreariness of the day lifted. Whatever the means, the outcome was certain to be fruitful.

Looking around the room, I found my gaze captured by young Trillia. Again, she smiled at me, and again I found the expression almost unpleasant. Had she guessed what I was about? The way she lightly tipped her goblet towards me and then nodded towards the queen's empty seat left me unsettled. Those gray eyes didn't miss much.

Tired, I made my way out of the hall, and found myself walking beside the smiling reflect. "Lady Elainya, do you have a moment?"

Unable to think of a quick excuse, I nodded and returned his smile. He motioned for me to join him in the chapel. "In many ways, we will be working together," he said thoughtfully. "You make the matches and I will ensure they are properly blessed, eh?"

"Yes."

"Did you notice that Sir Reif was absent from the table tonight?" he asked idly.

"No." Why was I answering the reflect in monosyllables? He seemed not to notice my discomfort and motioned for me to sit beside him on an elaborately carved pew. The moonlight filtered through the stained-glass window added to the abundant candlelight. The room seemed cheerful.

"He was called to the front late this evening. Attackers were seen on the shore. Word was sent by bird, but he will not reach the coast in time. This is an evil hour for our land, Lady Elainya."

"Why is now so evil? You have been at war for forty years."

"I suspect the attacks will come more frequently."

For a moment he seemed sad, but then he set his mood aside and changed the subject. "The queen looked lovely tonight."

"Yes."

"Do you suppose I will ever have the opportunity to bring the king's child into the Light?"

"Perhaps soon, the way the king was looking at her tonight."

"Yes, he did seem younger, more alive. Good. We will need his strength. Well, I've detained you long enough, dear lady. Will you humor an old man and speak with me often in the evening? I find pleasant company difficult to come by—everyone else sees me only as a reflect. You seem not to need my services in that area, and I would value you as a friend."

Surprised, I nodded. "Yes, that would be delightful."

"Good. I'll have some tea laid by and the next time you join me, I'll serve you a dessert in payment for the sweetness of your company."

He stood up and saw me to the door, leaving me baffled by his offer of friendship.

He was a kind man, but the shadow's weight on my soul left me uneasy around the reflect. Would he still be my friend if he realized who I was?

I returned to my room to find a small wooden box in the center of my desk. It contained a pink stone in a gold cage, suspended from a leather thong. The accompanying bit of parchment contained a note from Sir Reif professing his hope that I would enjoy it, and his sorrow at this sudden parting. Miatra entered a few moments behind me.

"Oh, Elainya!" she smiled as she looked at the bauble.

Terror sniffed at it and batted it with his paw before leaping to the floor and stalking off to find a more comfortable spot on my bed.

I sighed and put the necklace back in the box. It was a simple trinket, but the gift reminded me that I would have to deal with Reif's advances.

I had no desire to encourage any suitors.

Miatra was oblivious to my mood.

"I gave the queen the herbs you sent. She seemed so happy. I stayed on to help her get ready. Wasn't she lovely?"

Exhausted, I tried to focus on the girl's words and failed. "Miatra, we'll talk in the morning. Dress for berry picking and you can help me." Yes, berry picking would soothe the dark ache inside me.

"Of course."

I handed the box to her. "Can you see that this is returned to Lord Reif as soon as possible?"

She took the gift as if I'd handed her a scorpion. "Yes." She swallowed and then nodded at me. "Of course. I'll make sure it is done."

"Thank you."

I knew that I'd dismissed her more as a servant than as a friend, but for just tonight, I was too tired to protect her feelings.

Chapter 9

Berry Picking

Nian

In the darkest part of the night, Nian slipped from his workroom and out into the countryside beyond the echoing castle walls. There, in the open air of a moonless night, he summoned the Shadow Lord.

The master swirled to take form, appearing behind Nian. "Lovely night for a walk."

Nian whirled around and then regained his composure. The night was still, quiet. Above him, the stars shone like icicles. He hated the cold. "I would like to speak to you, my lord."

Fenshad chuckled. "I had guessed that. Come now, Nian. What is it you want?"

"I've done as you asked. The girl is yours."

"Elainya. It is a lovely name, don't you think? A lovely name for a beautiful young woman. I would think you'd take every opportunity to use it."

Nian ignored the barb that pierced his heart. He ground his teeth together and forced his tone to be level. "Elainya, then. You have her. She will do your bidding. You don't need me any longer. Please, release me."

The Shadow Lord stepped closer so that Nian could see the frown on his face. "No. I'm not done with you yet. What's wrong? Your aches are gone, you've got a pleasant companion, position, power. What else do you want, Nian?"

"She hates me."

"Of course she does. She'll get over it." The scent of night-blooming honeysuckle wafted over them and the master breathed deeply. "You smell that? Let her hatred be a thing of beauty to you. Inhale it and let it give you joy in life."

His lack of response made the shadows laugh.

"No? You don't like that idea?" The Shadow Lord leaned even closer, his breath the foul stench of ash. "Then charm her if you will. I won't stop you." The sudden crushing grip on Nian's arm made him gasp. "But I'm not ready to let you die just yet. You still have work to do."

Nian knew better than to struggle against the master's grip. He choked back any acknowledgment of pain that might encourage the demon's passion for torture. "What would you have me do, my lord?"

Fenshad released him. "I'll tell you when I'm ready. For now, keep Elainya nearby. Watch her. See that she adapts to her power. If that doesn't entertain you, go kill something." With a swirl of laughter, the master was gone.

Nian sank to the ground and rubbed the blood back into his arm. For a long moment he just sat, not thinking, not feeling.

The lone keen of a nearby wolf roused him. He looked into the forest, sensing the creature more by the tiniest sound of movement than sight. They locked eyes—two lonely hunters—and the wolf stepped from the forest. The light gray of its pelt was mottled with age. It sniffed in Nian's direction and then snorted with disgust before turning back to easier hunting.

With a frown, he got to his feet and returned to the castle. After Marketday, he'd see about killing something. That would give him an outlet for his frustrations.

Elainya

The next morning I awoke to Terror kneading my arm as he curled up with his head on my shoulder. "There you are," I mumbled as I struggled to consciousness. "You went out in the night. What did you get up to?"

He sat up, looking every bit the elegant miniature statue of a cat, and licked his lips. With his eyes closed to slits, he projected *mmmoussssse.*

I scratched him behind the playful ears and under the silky chin. "Oh aren't you getting clever?"

With a deep rumble of purr, he curled up on the end of the bed as I got up to dress.

It was best to wear a simple, close-fitting gown for berry picking. Of course, I knew berries would not be ripe this early in the season. The vines would be riddled with thorns. I donned the brown walking dress and collected my gathering basket. If all went well, I'd be needing wild raspberry tea for the queen in a few days. The leaves should be ready even if the berries were not.

Miatra was easy company. She filled uncomfortable silences with stories of the court youth, while paying close attention to each of my directions. We wandered deeper into the forest in search of a sunny glade with early-sprawling bushes.

The air was fresh and heavy with the scent of sunshine and earth.

"It is too early for berries," Miatra finally pointed out.

"True, but I want the leaves. Look for some that are a rich, dark green, as fully developed as possible. I also need fresh spearmint and peppermint," I said as we began our search. We crossed the meadow and walked down a path that led to a small stream hidden in the woods. Here the berry bushes grew thick and we walked carefully, picking only the freshest leaves for drying.

"What is this used for, Elainya?"

"It has many uses. We can make tonics or facial waters for the ladies. Placing the mint leaves in the morning dew will clear their complexions and is good for headache. A tea of these leaves is good for digestive upsets," I said, being deliberately evasive.

Miatra was a step ahead of me, however. "For the queen? When she is with child?" she asked brashly.

I feigned innocence, having not told her the contents of Laurel's pouch. "What makes you think the queen is with child?"

"She isn't yet, but she will be. It was obvious last night. She was so beautiful and the king looked at her as if he were seeing her for the first time. I know you had a hand in it, although I'd never tell anyone."

"And why would you say that?"

"You kept to yourself yesterday, and you made a very special preparation for Queen Laurel, which she took from my hand with more eagerness than I have ever seen in her eyes. You were so tired."

I decided to be truthful with my young friend. "Well, I see I will have to be more circumspect in my dealings if I'm to keep my doings secret! You're very perceptive, Miatra, and will be a good assistant. Do watch your words, though. I don't want people speculating about the child's birth." I thought of the reflect. "For all I know, the reflect would reject the child as heir if he thought I was responsible."

"Oh, he wouldn't do that. The reflect hates Jeiwan as much as you do."

How could I answer that? "The reflect doesn't seem the type to hate anyone."

"He gets angry. You haven't seen him angry? It is an amazing sight to behold! It is as if the very Light itself bursts from him.

He's always right, when he is angry, though." A very pretty tremble went through her arms and she wrapped the arm not holding the basket around herself for warmth. "I hope he never gets upset at me. He caught one of the girls stealing candles from the chapel one time and the hall echoed with his tirade for hours."

I tried to keep the skepticism out of my voice. "I can't imagine anyone getting mad at you, so I don't think you have anything to worry about."

"I can keep a secret," she smiled.

"Good." Considering what she knew or suspected about me, that was a good thing.

"Elainya, I wanted to ask you...." She was suddenly shy, hesitant.

"What?"

"Do you think I could learn to use magic the way you do? To heal?"

"No!" The word came out more harshly than I'd wanted.

I took a deep breath and started over.

"I'm sorry, but no, Miatra. You don't have the gift. You're bright and could work miracles with herbs and a little training, but I wouldn't want you trying to practice magic. There are consequences that you don't need to understand."

She yanked a leaf from its vine and stuffed it roughly into her basket. "Fine. At least I'm bright enough to help you with menial tasks."

I watched her wander off, longing to call her back, but not wanting to talk about the Shadow Lord on this sunny day.

In a moment, she'd rushed ahead and stood smelling a conical cluster of white blooms atop a tall, bluish stem. The sunlight was playing in that corner of the grove, highlighting her beauty and making the white of the flowers seem to dance. For a moment, I leaned back against a tree and enjoyed the sight of her freshness and innocence, surprised to find myself jealous.

"I love this plant. I've never known what it is, do you know? It smells just like honey!"

A shiver went up my spine as I looked more closely at the tall feathery blossoms she was stroking. I had gathered them before. It was beautiful and could be used for treatment of fevers and stomach upsets. But now, I feared it. "That's witches' bane."

"Witches' bane? What an ugly name! I think it should be called light's spire." She breathed deeply of the heady scent. "Or maybe sweet beam."

"Legend has it that it was given to mankind by a messenger of Light to counteract pestilence. It is very potent." Supposedly, it would kill a witch or at least drain her power if she even touched it. Of course, what made one a witch?

The thought nagged at me. What was a witch? My definition had always been someone who relied on demonic sources for power. A breeze stirred the branches of the nearby trees, and I could almost hear laughter from the deep shadows. I was being ridiculous to fear a plant, but I could not bring myself to touch it. "Leave it. I have other plants that fill the same purpose."

I could feel the echo of the Shadow Lord's torment running through my veins. What would happen if I touched the plant? Would it kill me? Would it set me free?

Would I die?

"I'd love a bouquet of the flowers," the girl continued, oblivious to my tension.

"Leave it, Miatra," I snapped, my voice suddenly hoarse. She obeyed, but looked hurt by my reprimand.

The incident shadowed the morning. We ate some rolls I'd filched from the kitchen for our midday meal and then headed back.

"Elainya, have I upset you?" Miatra asked quietly.

"No, child. I'm just still tired from yesterday. Will you hang these herbs to dry over my fireplace while I go to the garden to rest? You know how to hang them?"

She nodded. "I'll take care of it. Just rest. You'll feel better this evening."

We parted company, and I went to my garden to pull weeds, trim the existing plants, and train the wanderers to my design. For the first time, I kept to the afternoon shadows as I worked, feeling the sun warming my skin uncomfortably when it touched me. The activity was soothing and I was calm by dinner time.

Nian

He'd followed her movements throughout the day, sticking to the shadows. She was afraid of the bane. Needless superstition. After the two women left, he stood over the bush and picked one of the flowers. The scent was rich and sweet. Unless he found himself sneezing to death, he sensed no danger from it. It was, after all, just a plant, its only power in the superstitions of those around it and in the healing substances it could be turned into.

A bee buzzed around the flower in his hand and he shooed it away, dashing the blossom to the ground in the process.

If only he could chase away her superstition as easily.

His eyes focused on the flowers. They were pretty if someone liked flowers. Elainya did. He picked a bouquet and carried them back to the castle. Along the way, he added wild roses and a late-blooming tuber to the mix.

He placed them in a vase in his workroom and watched for her to finish her gardening.

Elainya

I returned to my room to find Nian sitting at my desk, staring at a vase of flowers. The floral scent filled the room, giving me a momentary smile before I realized what he held. "How dare you," I sputtered.

He stood. "I dare because I am your teacher and you are behaving like a foolish child. Come here."

There was no denying the command in his voice. I looked up into his eyes and took the two steps to his side. "Why?"

He plucked a single stem of bane from the vase and grasped my hand. His touch was not harsh, but I could not escape as he wrapped my hand around the fluffy petals and closed my fingers, crushing the blossoms into my skin.

"That is why," he muttered and left through the back staircase.

I held the harmless flower, letting the perfume waft over me, clearing the trace of fear from my blood. He was right. I had been childish. The petals lay strewn across my desk, where I left them to freshen the room.

Changing with relief into my traditional blue gown, I braided my hair and went down to the great hall in time to respectfully take my place beside Nian for dinner.

Again, Queen Laurel was striking in her beauty. The evening meal was simple, consisting of mixed fowl and fresh vegetables from the castle gardens. I watched the young people chatting pleasantly. Joln and Tromas had seated Miatra between them again and they talked across her in eager voices. She seemed at ease.

Nian's searching eyes stayed on me like leeches. What did he want from me? I turned and met his stare face to face. With a cough, he returned his attention to the roast turkey leg he was holding. Whatever it was, he didn't want to talk about it here.

I looked around the room again and noticed the empty chairs of the king's men who had gone to deal with the raids along the coast. Only the older men and a few of the squires remained at the table. Several of the ladies looked tired, with red-rimmed eyes. Sniffles occasionally echoed through the room as one or another resorted to hiding behind a handkerchief.

The heavy atmosphere of the room was shattered by a lady's scream as one of the older men collapsed in a heap on the floor across the room from me, his bench turning over as he flailed against an unseen attacker. I was on my feet and running before I heard Miatra call my name. The well-dressed knight lay on the floor, his eyes open and his mouth gasping for breath as tiny moans escaped his lips. His body was convulsing as he clung to life. I shoved the others away without being gentle. "Let me touch him," I ordered. Nian was only a moment behind. I felt the knight's heart beating rapidly, much too rapidly. My power responded instantly, searching for the cause of his attack.

"His name is Viron," Nian offered.

"I need mistletoe," I ordered, and felt my power responding to his need without conscious direction. His heart had lost its rhythm and beat in random patterns like a child with a stick. As Nian left, I turned my attention to the patient. "Sir Viron, there is pain in your arm and your chest?"

His recessed jaw quivered in his round face. His hair had escaped its lacing during the attack, and I brushed the thinning brown locks away from his fear-clouded dark brown eyes. I watched his head jerk out a nod in response and smiled encouragingly at him.

I closed my eyes and ran a hand along his side, easing the pain, reaching out to slow down the frantic beating of his heart. Fear would only hasten his death. I needed to tune his body's system to work at the same pace as mine until I could get the medicine into him and teach his body to take over again. "You are going to be well again, Viron. Do you understand?"

He nodded again, some of the tension relaxing from his jaw. I pushed at the rest of the fear with my abilities and felt his body relax. "Tromas and Joln, I'll need you to carry him to my room,"

I directed, keeping a gentle mental touch on his heart. The master was right about this use of power, it was good.

I'd never been this strong before, nor had I felt the power flow with such ease. Behind me a torch guttered and went out, sending up a cloud of smoke that caused those surrounding us to cough. The lady who had screamed stood by my shoulder, twisting her kerchief and sobbing.

"He will recover," I assured her.

"Someone, take her to her room. Give her strong ale and make her sleep. Her fear is not helping."

Miatra and the reflect were quick and efficient, bundling the crying woman off despite her heated protests. I noticed that the tension around my patient's eyes relaxed as the crying receded. "Don't worry. They'll make sure she's cared for."

Viron managed a weak smile, despite the strain of breathing.

Nian returned. I took a goblet of ale from the table, and he poured a few drops of the precious medicine into it. Nodding to Miatra's smitten pair, I followed Viron to the extra pallet I had added to my chamber so that I could care for the very sick.

I added a drop from the precious vial to the mix, then gently helped Viron swallow the enriched ale. For a moment, his heart fought to speed up as the medicine took effect. Then, ever so slowly, his heart began to relax. Bit by bit, I removed my mental touch from his body and allowed his system to return to normal. As he passed into an uneasy sleep, I put hawthorn in water over the fire to steep.

As his condition eased, the boys and the others who had followed us up the stairs left. I spared them little concentration, merely relaxing myself as each distraction ended. He would live. For a moment, the knowledge of his recovery filled my mind.

All of the talk of witchcraft was nothing more than fairy tales.

Nian

Nian stood in the doorway watching her, pride evident in the smile on her face. She sensed his gaze and looked up in confusion. "You've adapted well. I told the master you would not need much of a teacher."

A frown replaced the satisfied smile she'd had only moments before. With a sigh, she stirred honey into the tea she'd been brewing. The color changed to a deep brown. Tenderly, drop by drop, she eased the tea between Viron's blue-tinged lips. Within a few moments, his sleep deepened and his color improved.

"The power comes so easily to me," she whispered.

"You have been too concerned about the ethics of your position. Relax and all will be well." He knew she wanted to object, but the evidence of Viron's soft snores was undeniable.

She stood up and walked to where he was standing in the doorway. "You're right. Now, if you'll forgive me, I'm going to close this door so he can rest."

"Tomorrow is Marketday," he spoke as he stepped backward, allowing the door space to close.

"I will see you then," she whispered and closed the door.

He stood with his hand pressed against the thick wood, feeling her throw the bar across the inside. Tomorrow would be a day to distract her from these heavy thoughts and remind her that laughter could still reign.

A deep weariness settled in his bones, an echo of the age pains the master had so helpfully removed. The Shadow Lord's gifts were fickle. She would need his help at the market, so perhaps there would be some way to restore the fragile accord he had managed to forge during their days in Aurora before the master had intervened.

Chapter 10

Marketday

Elainya

"I can not believe I slept this long! You should have woken me." I dressed quickly in my green walking skirt and bodice. I'd been up most of the night watching Viron, dosing him with medicines, and keeping my senses tuned constantly to the beating of his heart. I had gone to sleep only a few hours earlier, leaving Miatra to watch over my patient once he seemed stable.

"Let me help!" Miatra protested. "You were so tired, I thought you'd want to rest."

"I didn't want to sleep all morning," I grumbled.

"Lord Nian seemed encouraged that you were sleeping."

"Nian was here?"

"He still is. He took a chair into the hall and said that he was going to take you to the market when you awoke."

"He's been sitting out there for how long?"

"Since early morning, but it isn't unusual for Lord Nian to just sit...."

That gave me pause while Miatra tightened the bodice of the gown and straightened my braids. I looked at her and she elaborated. "It is said he's communing with a demon," she whispered into my ear as she twisted up the last braid.

"Probably true," I muttered.

She secured the braids in a bun atop my head with an ornate wooden comb and shooed me out to meet my erstwhile companion. Regardless of how I felt about him, I would need his help today.

Viron lay resting peacefully in my outer chamber. Miatra assured me that she could watch over him while I was gone. Even more reassuring was the sleeping kitten at his feet. Terror was guarding my patient but seemed to have no immediate concern for the man's well-being. I'd feel better when Viron was complaining about his forced rest, but for now he was accepting the situation.

Nian sat outside the door as Miatra had said. He was dressed in hooded black robes, carefully embroidered with mystic symbols. He wore his years badly. "Good afternoon!" He bowed stiffly after he had struggled to his feet.

"I am sorry to have kept you waiting."

"I was concerned that perhaps you had decided not to accompany me."

"Did you think I had slipped out the other door?"

His smile held mischief. "No."

"And why not?"

"I barred the door to my workroom."

His smile made the comment a joke and so I laughed along with him. "Well, then, we'd best get going before the merchants go home."

He offered me his arm. "Very well, then."

Beyond the castle walls, the valley spread out before its king, green and full of life. Sheep and cattle grazed while the farmers planted their crops on the manageable hillsides. The path into town was not long or overly steep and made for a pleasant walk.

The village was alive with people and animals meandering to and fro. What caught my attention, however, were the brightly colored booths of the marketplace just outside the village.

Marketday at Sun's Apex had drawn merchants from all over the land together—everywhere colors flashed, people bantered, and animals shuffled, managing to get in the way. I noted silver from Pelage, cheese from West Ridge, salt fish from Summerstown, and my favorite cloths from Bright Range. The noise was almost deafening. Here was singing, there musicians were playing, and all conversation was yelled over the din. It was delightful.

The smell of roasting food and bubbling sweets was intoxicating. My stomach growled in anticipation.

"Now, what shall we buy first?" Nian asked.

"I need a few rare herbs, some baskets, and small jars," I began.

"The herbs I may have in stores in the castle. You will find my collection extensive. I will provide you with all you need. As for baskets—here is a weaver."

The stall was small and cramped with baskets in all sizes, shapes and colors. Stacks lined the edges of the space, while even more were hung over my head on poles. The proprietor waved his arthritic hands in grand gestures as he explained the value inherent in the various fibers he had chosen for each basket. It took me some time to choose the perfect ones for my study, but at last I chose several small and one larger gathering basket. I negotiated a fair price out of the old man, mindful of my limited funds. Nian took my purchases and placed them in a sack he carried. With a bow, he pointed the way to the potter. On the way, he pulled me to a stop near a booth where roasts were being turned lazily over a spit by a bored young man. An older man, perhaps his father, was hawking the richness of each and comparing the flavors to those of great nations no one had ever heard of. He looked at Nian. "Now you, sir, you seem to appreciate the culture of the ancient Draska. They liked their food spicy, or so the stories tell. This roast here," he pointed at one near the middle that sported a black and red crust, "is rubbed with hot spice in the traditional method."

Nian glared at the man in annoyance. I could not resist intervening.

"Actually, the Draska prefer simple foods with strong flavor but not overwhelmed by spices." I pointed at one on the end that looked not overdone. "Like that. Give us slices from there. Oh, and if you want to encourage business, I'd rather you didn't refer to me as ancient."

He looked at me in confusion. "You are little more than a child. You should let your grandfather do the bartering. He surely knows how to speak with a civil tongue."

Nian growled and I laughed.

"You are about to lose a customer," I said.

With a flustered apology, he carved off two generous slices of the roast I'd indicated and Nian dropped a small coin into his hand. We wandered towards the potter's stand, munching on the meat.

Nian's brow was furrowed in concentration as he tore chunks from the meat as if he were killing the beast with each bite.

I ignored his mood and turned my attention to the potter.

Nian

The pottery merchant was a heavy, middle-aged man with a large desire for money. His wares were of fine quality but beyond Elainya's price for the quantity she would need. Nian was prepared to offer her additional coins from his own purse when he caught the gleam of mischief in her eyes.

Seeing that sparkle, he paused to listen to her bartering.

"Sir, are you a visitor here, or do you live in the village?" she asked, examining a jar closely.

"This village is my home," he offered. "Anyone can vouch for the quality of my work. My name is Eryn."

"Is there a healer in the village?"

"Only a midwife." He seemed nervous. Nian was examining a particularly delicate vase and noted that the man's eyes did not waver from him. Did he fear magicians or broken wares? He put the vase down gently and turned to glance around the nearby stalls. It would be better if the man paid attention to Elainya.

"It must be bothersome to have no one to aid you when you are sick. Do you have children?"

Eryn rolled his eyes towards heaven. "Aye—too many—five too many. But my Taya, she loves children. Never seems to have enough."

Elainya laughed. Such fragile wares to have around children! "What do you do if your children become ill?" she asked.

"My wife cares for them. We have only lost two. We do better than most."

She sighed and put down the jar she had been examining. "You have lovely wares, and I have great need for them. I am new to Sun's Apex. I did not carry my potions with me on the journey here. Unfortunately, I cannot afford your lovely jars. A healer is useless without medicines."

Now she had his full attention. "You are a healer?"

"I would be."

"Lady, perhaps an arrangement could be reached between us—an exchange of services...." It did not take long for Eryn to take her order. He even agreed to make the special containers she needed and to have his oldest daughter, Cyndace, deliver them to the castle within the tenday. As she completed her negotiations, Nian noticed a woman standing to one side trying to attract his attention.

With a glance to make sure Elainya was engaged, he stepped to where the woman hid behind the fabric of a nearby tent. "I heard you wanted special fabrics." The old woman's hands were expressive, thin. Her arms showed the strength of a weaver.

"Yes. Did you bring them?"

She smiled, revealing a shockingly small number of teeth. "Of course. We don't have many requests for such lovelies, but we still make them. Teaches the children what fine work can be done."

He drew a small pouch from inside his robes and placed it in her hand. "Make sure the lady I am with sees them and can purchase what she wants. If she cannot afford her choices, send someone to me later and I will make up the lack, but make sure she does not know of my assistance. Can you do that?"

"Such a sweet man. I'll make sure your granddaughter has whatever she wishes. She's lucky to have you." The old woman laughed and patted his arm before vanishing into the tent.

Nian returned to Elainya's side before he could be missed. Granddaughter? Ancient? He could feel the anger struggling to escape and wreck havoc. Best to remember his place in life.

***

Elainya

The jewelers fought over who could best serve me. Nian stood back and laughed at our bartering. Despite his amusement, there was a darkness about him today that was out of place for our errand.

"Lady, here are ornaments for your lovely hair...."

"Hush there—she loves my rings for her dainty fingers!"

"Fie on you both—her small wrists will sparkle with my bracelets."

I chose my purchases for their delicate patterns, some for their style, others for their sound. At last, I finished and returned to Nian's side.

"You are a furious bargainer. Perhaps one of your ancestors was a merchant." Nian's smile was strained, but he seemed to be enjoying the exchange.

I didn't comment but simply added my items to his sack.

Something in the crowd distracted him. He touched my arm lightly and pointed to where a traveling magician was performing playful tricks for a group of children. "Elainya, can you see him?" His expression was proud.

"Mere illusions." The tricks were nothing more than any Draska child could learn to do.

"Yes, but do you see him?"

His words caused me to look closer at the gray-haired old wanderer—no, perhaps not so old. Perhaps not so gray, either. "He is not what he seems." My senses revealed the edges of an illusion spell...a good one.

"Look closer. You know him."

I looked again and saw Jauer through the cloud of his illusion. His left hand drew a gold coin from a child's ear and deposited it in an outstretched hand.

Clapping along with the crowd, I turned to Nian. "He has been well trained."

"He did not believe it possible when he was younger, but he loved magic so much, and there is power in him."

"Can anyone else see him as he really is?"

"Only those like ourselves. He will be safe. This is his first time in public with the illusion of being whole. Someday, he will be a court magician."

I stared at Nian. "But he is crippled."

"The boy is whole. His magic is whole. Sometimes I feel he is more whole than I!" Anger cloaked his face in darkness and I remembered the pain I'd felt at his hands in Aurora.

"I have nothing against the boy...I simply meant that he might have problems...." I needed to be careful not to make Nian angry. I realized I'd taken a step away from him in fear.

He controlled his anger with an effort of will that I could feel as he mentally restrained his emotions. His eyes took in the sudden distance between us and he sighed. "Forgive me, but at court—he is not well treated."

"I did not know." My voice cracked and I coughed.

"No, of course not." Nian glanced away. "What else do you need?"

"Sewing supplies and fabric."

Nian gestured towards the table of a weaver from Karakul. As I handled the precious thin fabrics, I turned back to Nian. "Jauer's magic...there is darkness to it."

"Yes."

"Is he old enough to wield that sort of power?"

"You were not much older when you chose your path."

"I had the benefit of a Draska education...and I still chose wrong."

Nian stared at me and I felt a gentle probing. "No, Elainya, you chose the only option you had. You may find that you are comfortable with shadow magic. While you slept, even the Draska came to see that it had merit."

I shook my head but did not reply. Here in the noonday sun, it was hard to think of Darkness. The sun glinted off a fine gold filament woven into a bolt of delicate sapphire cloth.

The weaver noticed my attentions and flashed a toothless smile at me. "Oh, such a pretty girl. You like my pretty fabrics?"

I tried to smile, afraid to ask how much she'd want for such finery. "They're lovely. Do you weave them yourself?"

"Did when I was young, my dear. Now I teach my grandchildren. Those are their practice pieces. I shouldn't really sell them, but I promised them I'd try."

"These are practice pieces?"

"Oh yes. Pretty playthings. Do you like them?"

I stared at her in shock. "Yes, very much." I fingered a bolt of turquoise-colored fabric and remembered my promise to Miatra. It would look lovely with her hair and skin. I chose a sapphire blue and a peach for me as well, reveling in the feel of the fabric and amazed by the prices the weaver offered.

Nian watched me pick, occasionally offering a comment about one bolt or another, until I'd found myself with several extra bolts thrown in.

I arranged for the fabric to be sent to the castle—Nian being overburdened—and we paused for a moment to enjoy the entertainment.

Nian acquired baked apples and ale for us while I negotiated with the blacksmith for my final purchases. As I ordered the infusers I would need, I noticed Jauer, now in his usual fool's garb, amusing the crowd to earn extra coins. Were it not for the crippled hand, he would be quite the catch, I thought. His hair was reddish blonde in the light and his green eyes glinted with life and mirth. I noticed my young friend from the woods among those watching him eagerly. It was good to know the girl was safe.

I turned my attention back to the muscular blacksmith and watched as he leaned his shaven face over the fire to fashion the delicate metal work for my infuser. This would take a while, but I enjoyed watching him work. Drenil used to work with metal in just such a fashion, an economy of movement with each motion creating a flourish or twist. Dren also did not have a beard. He'd always been afraid it would catch fire. I chuckled at the memory. Drenil's metal work was the daintiest in the land, but fire had never been his ally. More than once I had tended his burned fingers.

Nian leaned the bag he'd been carrying against the booth and rested a light hand on my shoulder. "I'll be back in a moment," he said and slipped silently into the crowd. I felt myself relax as he left. It felt good to be alone for a moment.

The blacksmith worked deftly as he wove the hot metal with his tongs. The tiny ball began to take shape in his large, skilled hands.

An explosion erupted in the midst of a crowd behind me, and people jumped away from the source.

I whirled to see Nian standing alone, his gray eyes blazing, with Jauer lying in a heap behind him. I pointed at the bag and spoke to the blacksmith. "Bring this to the castle tonight and you will be well paid."

In a moment, I was beside the fallen lad. He had many bruises, but most were old. What worried me was a ragged, bleeding cut on his forehead, and his lack of movement.

"How bad is he?" Nian asked, his eyes focused on the group of squires which he held at bay with his gaze and an upraised hand.

"I don't know. We'll need to get him back to the castle."

Jeiwan stepped forward. "Stay out of this, witch. This is between us and the fool, and now this wizard who has interfered."

After the last few days, I was in no mood to put up with Jeiwan's insults. I stood up and faced him. "I am no witch, boy, and I am getting tired of you calling me one."

"Ha! As this is no wizard. Magic is evil. Neither of you should be allowed near the castle." He drew a dagger from his belt and advanced on us, followed by his companions. I noticed Joln hung back from the mob. Jeiwan held up a charm which he wore around his neck. It was a tiny ball, not unlike the one the blacksmith had been making for me. Inside, it held...flowers? White flowers? "This will protect me from your witchcraft!"

Witches' bane. I almost laughed. I looked at Nian and then back at Jeiwan.

Everything seemed to be happening slowly. The clouds moved overhead, creating a dappled light on the boys' faces.

Nian looked confused, unwilling to injure the boys. Perhaps this was the time for me to explain the difference between a witch and a healer. "Jeiwan, you have a lot to learn."

I barely tapped into my abilities as I sent the lightest of sleep trances descending on him. He looked at me, annoyance frozen on his face, as he fell to the ground, asleep.

Nian smiled as the other boys gasped and jumped back.

"Let's take Jauer to my room," I said. "I'm sure these others can bring Jeiwan home." I glared at Joln. "He is just asleep, you understand me? I'll wake him up later."

Joln nodded. "I'm sorry, Lady. I did try to stop him."

I waved off Joln's apology and turned back to my newest patient.

The boy cradled in Nian's arms did not move. Nian's voice caught as he stood up and held the young man's limp form close. "We'll take him to my rooms. You have Viron in yours. I have everything you'll need." He moved up the hill with more speed than I would have thought possible for a man of his age carrying a heavy burden. I rushed to follow.

In his laboratory, Nian carefully laid Jauer on some furs in a corner. He gathered the herbs I would need without direction while I examined Jauer's head. He was frighteningly pale and had not woken during the trip.

Finding a thick, warm fur, I pulled it over him. With a small rag, I wiped the blood from his forehead. The cut did not seem deep. I could sew it closed with a needle and thread, but I could feel the shock from the injury working its damage on his mind.

He had lost a lot of blood and there was swelling beneath the skin.

Nian had surrounded me with small jars of dried herbs. Carefully, I picked some from each and began grinding them in a mortar. "Why did they do this?" I asked as the rich scent of the herbs filled the air.

"Because he is a fool."

"So they beat him up?"

"Yes."

"Why?"

"Because he will not fight back. They need to feel they are strong."

"Do they always hurt him this badly?"

"Not usually." His tone held such deep concern for the lad that for a moment I almost forgot what had passed between us in Aurora.

"So you are teaching him magic—so he can defend himself?"

"No, so he can go elsewhere."

"And what if he does not find what he wants there?" I asked very quietly.

"Then he can move on."

"Running won't solve his problem."

"Perhaps not." He looked at the boy sadly. "But it is a chance."

The torches flickered strangely as I cleaned and stitched the cut. I packed it with the poultice and wrapped a thin piece of cloth around the remaining herbs, setting them to steep in hot ale Nian prepared. When the color had changed to a deep green, I wrung some of the ale into Jauer's mouth and helped him swallow. He stirred slightly and then sighed and did not move. I eased his mind into a healer's trance and felt the first stirrings of his strength returning.

"He will sleep for a while."

"Will he be all right?" Nian's face showed his fear.

"I think so. He is strong."

"I am glad you were here, Elainya. My talents do not run to medicine."

"You chose the right herbs. You would have done fine."

I eyed the boy's sleeping form critically. We discussed his treatment, finishing just as the chamberlain bustled into the room. "Forgive the intrusion. Lady Elainya, the king wishes an audience with you."

I stood up to go with him. When Nian moved to follow, I waved him back. "Stay with Jauer." He seemed relieved as he sank to the boy's side.

The chamberlain seemed nervous as we walked.

"I misjudged you, Elainya," he said.

"Oh?"

"You have disgraced my king."

"Have I indeed?"

"Apparently you performed your evil magic in the market place."

"No, I defended myself after Jeiwan and his ruffians beat Jauer senseless."

"He is a fool."

"Which?" I asked innocently. Still, it was disturbing to think that those in power condoned Jeiwan's behavior.

The chamberlain glared as he bowed me into the throne room. Jeiwan was lying in state before the king.

"Again, Lady Elainya?" the king asked. I noticed a glimmer of humor in his eyes.

"Your fool lies unconscious in Nian's chambers, my lord. Injured by this ruffian."

The king sighed and glanced towards Reif's empty chair. "I would ask Reif to control his son, but it appears you are doing an admirable job of it."

I smiled in acknowledgment and bent to revive the lad. Having learned my lesson before, I removed Jeiwan's knife from its sheath and handed it hilt first to one of the king's guards. I knelt beside Jeiwan and brushed his forehead with my hand, waking him slowly.

He stood and glared around at the court but wisely said nothing.

The king barely hid a chuckle. "Jeiwan, brawling in the marketplace is inappropriate, and attacking Lady Elainya appears not to be in your best interest."

The boy's face burned crimson, but he managed to force "Yes, my lord" past his gritted teeth.

The king waved at him in dismissal and he left quickly.

"How fares the fool?" the king asked.

"He is injured. He will not play for you this evening. Maybe not for a number of evenings."

"Will he recover?" The king seemed genuinely concerned. Perhaps there was hope for the kingdom yet. His fingers fiddled with the hem of his shirt, pleating it as he waited for my answer.

"Yes."

"You seem very powerful."

When I did not comment, he frowned. "Lady Elainya, the townsfolk say I have welcomed an evil sorceress into the castle who has taken it upon herself to destroy my heir."

"Is this what you believe, my lord?"

"No. But use caution, Elainya. I can not long contain such talk." He blushed, an expression I'd not yet seen crossing his face briefly. "My wife is very fond of you." He seemed to think for a moment and then he sighed. I wondered what he wanted to say, but chose not to. "You may go, Lady Elainya."

I returned to Nian's laboratory to check on Jauer once more before going to check on Viron. "What did the king wish to know?" Nian asked.

"My character, I believe."

"And you passed this test as well."

"I will be more careful next time," I said and knelt to touch the boy. "We could move him to his own room, now, if you'd like. He seems to be resting quietly."

"This is his room. He sleeps here. He says it makes him feel close to the magic."

I smiled. "There is magic within him. He will always be close to it."

Nian nodded. "I felt that when we first met."

"Is he of Draska blood, do you think?"

Nian shrugged. "If he were, his life would be more dangerous than it already is. I prefer to think of him merely as any other orphan."

"He's not, though," I said, rising to leave.

Nian stopped me with a light touch on my arm. He seemed uncomfortable and glanced towards the shadows before he spoke. "For what it is worth, I did not wish you pain." I noticed that he spoke the words out loud. A challenge to the Shadow Lord, perhaps?

It was an offer of peace, and I accepted it tentatively. "I know. I'm trying not to think about the past."

"That works well...," he looked towards Jauer's sleeping form and I could not see his face. "For a while."

Chapter 11

Apprentice

Nian

Jauer woke during the night, took some of the ale Elainya had left for him, and then fell into a more natural sleep. Nian sat on the floor next to the boy's pallet and watched for any sign that the blow had harmed his mind. Elainya said he would recover.

She would know.

It had taken every ounce of his will not to kill Jeiwan when he'd seen Jauer fall from the blow. Elainya had handled the situation with her typical calm, efficient manner, every bit the traditional Draska.

And what was he?

What had he become?

The first of the new Draska? Some strange malformed throwback to an extinct race?

He shook his head and stroked his beard. Elainya was right—best to forget the past.

Leaning his head back against the stone wall, he fell asleep, one hand on Jauer's shoulder in mute comfort.

Elainya

Viron was progressing nicely when I returned to my rooms to find Eavyn watching him.

"I sent Miatra to eat," she whispered, unwilling to disturb my napping patient.

"Have you seen Terror?"

"He went out a few minutes ago."

"Good." My examination of Viron was cursory. I renewed his healer's trance and set more hawthorn on to brew. Another day like this and he could return to his own room. The cat clearly felt he was out of immediate danger, and I trusted that diagnosis. Lyricat had been the same way.

"Eavyn, could I trouble you to take some food to Lord Nian? I doubt he'll leave Jauer's side."

She looked up in confusion. "The fool is injured?"

I suppose it should not have surprised me that Jauer's condition was not common knowledge.

"Yes." I told her what had happened and she frowned. "That boy Jeiwan is out of control. I can't believe the king allows him such freedom. It will be a disaster for this kingdom if he gains the throne." She stood and gathered her things. "If the army was here, he would not have been so bold. His father would not tolerate him brawling in the marketplace." She glanced toward the window, and pushed a lock of hair behind her ear. "Well, they'll be back soon."

She slipped her cheery demeanor back into place with a tiny shift of her shoulders. "Don't worry about Lord Nian. I'll make sure he eats."

As she marched out to feed the mage, I almost felt sorry for Nian. Almost.

The blacksmith delivered my purchases at nightfall, and I unpacked the treasures to much ooing and ahing from Miatra. When she saw the fabric I'd picked for her gown, she squealed and then covered her mouth and glanced toward the portion of the chamber where Viron lay sleeping.

"You won't wake him," I smiled. "He's tranced until tomorrow. That gives his body time to heal."

She frowned. "Will you do the same for the injured when they come back from the front?"

"Probably."

"So they will go to sleep and not wake up." Her eyes clouded over. "That will be better. I hate to hear them scream."

I puzzled through her comment. "Some of them will wake up, you know. I'm not bad at what I do."

"Oh, I have faith in you. It's just that I've never seen anyone recover from those wounds."

I thought about Reif's comments about there having been no survivors from the raid. Poison, perhaps? Otherwise, how could the enemy be that thorough in the heat of battle? "Miatra, who are we fighting?"

"No one knows." She sighed. "They come from across the water. I've heard they use beasts as attackers. Some say they are spirits, others say they are just dressed in some form of blackened armor."

"Spirits?"

"Shadow spirits. When daylight comes, they vanish." She shrugged. "I'm not sure I believe that, though. The ones who get close enough to describe them are usually near death."

I wondered at that.

I ate a simple meal in my room and fell into an uneasy sleep with Terror, satiated, at my feet.

Nian

When Elainya came to check on Jauer, she seemed pleased to find the boy sitting up and nibbling at a piece of toast. She looked into his eyes and touched his forehead gently. "You're healing well!"

He smiled up at her. "You're very talented, my lady."

"And so are you. That was a fine illusion you performed yesterday."

The boy beamed with pride and gestured toward Nian. "I have a good teacher."

Nian noticed the way she didn't meet his eyes at the comment.

He coughed. "Will you join the castle at prayers this morning? Reflect Rendel came here from Summerstown. His liturgy is pleasant and he is fond of Draska. He even allows the likes of me in his chapel."

She smiled. "Well, in that case, I'll be there."

"Must keep up appearances," he said and followed her to the door to her staircase.

On the small landing, he whispered, "Jauer's magic seems hampered by the injury."

He watched Elainya as she sent a tendril of power to evaluate Jauer's condition again. A wrinkle appeared above her brows.

"It's from the injury. Something is stopping him from connecting to it. Let's give him some time and see how he does."

"You don't think it is permanent, then?"

She rested her hand lightly on his forearm, a surprisingly gentle gesture. "He'll be fine. Just be patient."

Elainya

I wondered at Nian's invitation to prayers. I'd always gone to prayers before, but then Nian couldn't know that. I had wondered if I would be welcome in the chapel—as if the reflect might somehow see into the past, and know me too well. Missing prayers, however, would immediately label me a witch, as everyone else would be there. Besides, part of me would miss the closeness to the Light I'd always felt during prayers. I contemplated my state and decided it could not hurt to try. Especially considering the king's warning.

I wore the gown of healer-blue cloth the reflect had given me, that particularly vibrant shade of sapphire which made my eyes seem to glow. The fine gold filament woven into the fabric made the gown sparkle with power. The bodice laced in the front and the neckline was modest enough for any occasion. I braided a gold cord into my hair, slipped on my belt, and carefully sheathed my small dagger. Thus simply adorned, I went to the chapel.

Reflect Rendel stood near the altar and turned as I entered. "Good morning, Lady Elainya. I hoped you would come early."

"May I sit in the back during the service?"

"Of course. The house of Light is open to all...especially to you."

"Why especially me to me?"

"Those who walk in darkness are more in need of the Light than those who walk in haze. If you do not mind, I would like to speak freely to you."

"Please."

"My master bids me tell you that you are never so far from the Light that it can not shine into your life. Do not forget this. Whatever else happens to you, the Light is always there." The reflect blessed me then and went on about setting up for the service.

I sat on the back pew, knowing that the good reflect could not know me or anything about me and say such a thing.

I was no longer just walking in darkness. I had become an instrument of the Shadow Lord. Perhaps even one who would harm the kingdom. I had certainly contemplated killing the king's heir.

Nian came and sat beside me just as the service began. I did not listen to the priest's words, but watched as the Light streamed through the stained glass that made up one wall of the chapel. I looked about the room, filled with all who lived within the castle walls. Jauer, looking pale but recovering, sat beside Nian. I saw many heads bowed in prayer, but being in the back, I could only see Nian's expression. I glanced at him from time to time, and his reactions varied from boredom, to patient toler-ance, to near sleep.

Nian smiled warmly at me as the service ended. "You see, our Reflect Rendel is a mild-mannered sort. A bit of a bumbler, and a terrible speaker, but harmless." He placed my hand care-fully on his arm and directed me to the dining hall for breakfast.

Proprietorially he piled my plate high with fruit and cheese. "You did not eat well last night. I suspect you have no appetite this morn-ing, but you will eat or you will not be able to keep up your strength."

I tasted the fruit. "Nian, do you think the Light shines on such as us?"

He snorted. "Elainya. The Light shines even on the Shadow Lord himself. No one could draw power from Darkness without knowing that Light exists. Stop this silliness. You have been giv-en great power and a supreme mission in life. Take the power, take control of your life. This self-inspection will not serve you." His tone was a sneer and in disgust, he was gone, leaving his half-finished meal for a servant to clear.

I finished what he had chosen for me and returned to my room. Miatra helped me unpack the rest of my packages.

Those tasks completed, I allowed myself to rest. Miatra brought me remnants of the evening meal and I ate them in the peace of my room.

After dinner, I found myself hungry for a bit of something sweet and some easy companionship. The reflect was probably tired from his day of service, but I decided to see if he was awake.

I slipped quietly into the chapel, warmed as always by the candlelight. The candle scent didn't quite mask the aroma of chocolate emanating from the reflect's open door.

He met me at the doorway and bowed me into his humble chambers where he'd laid out tea for two and a plate of small chocolate cakes.

"Dessert, as promised," he laughed.

"And how did you know I was coming?"

"You were not at dinner."

"I could have been sleeping."

He smiled. "But you are not."

We sat and he poured the tea. I smelled gentle, soothing herbs, exactly what I would have chosen to settle my wandering, stress-laden thoughts.

"I will be asleep after that tea," I joked.

"Then I will have soothed your spirit in exchange for the lightness of your company. A good bargain."

"You find my company light?"

He shrugged and picked up a cake. "In the same way as these cakes are light. Perhaps not good for me, but delicious."

I tasted one of the cakes and had to admit they were amazing.

He grinned. "Want to know my secret?"

I nodded, my mouth full of chocolate.

"The cook is my sister. She knows I have an incurable sweet tooth."

I laughed. "So you didn't do this just for me."

"Whenever you want dessert, I am sure to have something."

This explained the roundness of the man and probably his pleasant disposition as well.

"How is Jauer doing?" he asked.

"Mending well. I need something to lift his spirits, I think. It is hard being so poorly treated by the other young men."

The reflect nodded and was silent for a long time. "Perhaps what he needs is also pleasant company."

"I'm not sure I would be of much use to him."

"No. I was thinking of someone carefree. A young maiden, perhaps?"

I choked on my tea.

"Well, you are the matchmaker."

I found myself shaking my head in wonder. "Here I was focused on treating him as a healer. You're right. A young woman would be good medicine for his spirit."

He shrugged. "You see? We work well together."

Early in the morning, the potter's daughter delivered my special pots. I was thrilled to recognize her as my timid friend from the woods.

The girl seemed eager to leave, but I motioned for her to stay.

"Miatra, could you please bring some tea and bread for us all from the kitchen?" I asked.

As soon as we were alone, I hugged the girl. "I'm so glad to see you are all right."

"When I heard there was a Draska healer still alive, I knew it must be you who had rescued me that day. I'm so glad to have a chance to thank you!"

"You're welcome. Besides, you helped me find a home here, so I should thank you."

The girl looked confused but shrugged.

"What is your name?" I asked at last.

"Cyndace, my lady."

"Call me Elainya."

She shivered as if the suggestion frightened her. Her eyes were wide as she looked around my room. She seemed eager to explore. "My father made sure your pots are of the highest quality. Can I help you unpack them?"

"And stay and enjoy tea. You can tell me about life in the village."

So it was that the three of us spent a pleasant morning setting up my herb shelves and chatting about romance among the peasants and the nobility.

"You love the idea of a courtly life, don't you, Cyndace?" I asked curiously.

"Oh, yes. All the ladies dress so beautifully. Everyone seems so happy."

"Appearances can be deceiving, never forget that."

She nodded. "Do you enjoy making matches?"

"It is one of the more pleasant aspects of my life. What do you wish for in a husband, Cyndace?"

She laughed. "I won't have a choice...but if I could...I'd want a kind man...a gentle man...someone who will take me away from here."

"You want a knight to ride in and rescue you?"

"No, just someone I can travel with. I want to have adventures!" She twirled around in the exuberance of youth.

I laughed, and then a young man's image came into my mind. "And what would you like this young man to look like?"

"Oh, I don't care what he looks like—as long as he's wonderfully nice."

"I'll have to keep my eyes out for him," I offered.

When we had finished unpacking my jars and placed them carefully on the new shelves along the wall behind my desk, Cyndace left.

Miatra was amused by the thoughtful expression she caught on my face as I watched the girl leave from my window. "You've got a match in mind for that young woman, don't you?"

"Who, me?" I asked with a mysterious grin. The master had said I could use his abilities to see pairings, so I let my mind wander. Yes, the two would have a bright future. Idly, I reached up to the shelf and picked up one of the older jars I had borrowed from Nian. "You know, Miatra, I've just realized that this must be replaced." I went to my niche and pulled out a coin. "Excuse me while I find someone to take it to the potter."

She laughed as I dashed down my back stairs to the magician's chambers. Jauer was resting in the corner. "It is time for you to get some fresh air, young man," I said.

He leapt up eagerly as I continued. "The potter's daughter, Cyndace, just left here and I forgot to give her this pot to take to her father for replacement. Here is some money to pay for it. Could you take a horse and catch up to her for me? Why don't you give her a ride home while you're at it?"

"Of course, Lady Elainya, I'll be glad to help." Cheerful boy that he was, he was quickly off. With a brief sigh of satisfaction, I walked out of the magician's chambers, straight into Nian.

He glared down at me. "Getting rid of the competition?"

I blinked in confusion.

"My other apprentice...?"

"Oh, no! I just met his future bride and I thought it couldn't hurt for them to get to know one another."

"Hmmm, well, as long as you're sure he's well enough to ride."

"As long as he is careful. Lying around won't help him right now. She's a good match for him. Might help him get better faster."

"As long as you are sure," he repeated.

Then I caught the hint of a smile. "Of course I am." I laughed, and dashed back up my staircase.

Having the thin shelves against the wall made it possible to drape the tapestries over them—both hiding and protecting my herbs from the light.

I stood back and admired the finished project. Miatra nodded her approval. "Tromas and Joln do good work, don't they?"

"Do you fancy them as much as you fancy their work?"

She blushed. "They're very nice...."

"Do you have a favorite?" I watched her eyes.

"Well, not really. I like them both."

If she did have a favorite, she wouldn't tell me. More likely, she really did like them both. Good! I wanted her company for a while longer. She was so like her great-grandmother.

"Miatra, can you draw?"

She looked at me out of the corner of her eyes, cocking her head like a small bird. "I used to draw with a stick in the dirt when I was a little girl."

"Did you like it?"

"Yes."

There was more to it. "And since then?"

She looked down.

"What is it?"

"You'll think me foolish."

I raised an eyebrow. "You could never be foolish."

"Sometimes, I mix ashes from the fire with water—it makes a kind of ink—and I draw on leaves with a stick...but don't tell!"

I smiled. "Art is not childish, Miatra."

"Oh, but my mother was so angry when she found out! She said I should come to be with the queen and learn to sew and be a lady."

Without comment, I picked up a sheaf of parchment from my desk. On it, I had written the names of every herb I needed. The list was for Nian—but first.... "Could you copy these marks?"

Miatra held the paper reverently in her hand and looked at it. "I think so."

"Good. Then while I sew, you can make the labels for my jars."

Her eyes opened wide—I had already come to love that sparkle. No, I would not match this girl with any ordinary squire.

I gave her pen and ink—and showed her how to hold and use each.

Gleefully, she sat at my old desk and worked with the precious materials. The glimmer in her eye promised that she would waste none.

Viron moved from quiet acceptance to a healthier state of annoyance. When he passed into unbearable irritability, I sent him back to rest in his rooms under the overabundant care of his wife, confident that he would make a full recovery.

My wardrobe progressed rapidly in the next days. Flowing gowns began to fill my chest and I felt happy—or at least at peace. A series of minor complaints brought the residents of the castle and the surrounding area to my door. Most I helped with herbs, only occasionally resorting to my enhanced abilities. Within a tenday, news of the castle's healer had spread, and I had enough patients to fill my time. Many were uneasy in my presence, but all were grateful for my healing powers.

Jauer healed well, with the easy recovery of youth. He spoke often of Cyndace, leading Nian to complain that I had distracted him from more than his boredom.

His magic still seemed hampered by the blow he'd taken, though. To those who knew him only as a fool, he was healed, but Nian and I continued to worry. I thought he would heal in time. Nian wanted promises, but I had none to offer.

With Miatra's help, I worked my way through Nian's books, seeking any treatment beyond what I already knew, and finding none.

Spring blossomed into summer and Jauer began helping me in my garden. I could see the strength in the boy and admired his patience with the lengthy healing.

Terror grew a bit more each day, to a point where he could form simple words. He delighted in any errand I sent him on and became fond of Jauer.

Jauer's condition did not improve. At last, I sent Miatra, Jauer, and the cat to harvest mint so that Nian and I could discuss the boy's condition with the Shadow Lord.

We closed the curtains in my room, barred the door, and Nian summoned the demon.

"Well!" the demon laughed as he manifested in his usual handsome form, "what a delight to see you two working together."

Nian turned to me, letting me direct the encounter.

I took a deep breath. "My lord, you have said that you will assist me with healing."

"Yes." His eyes focused on me and I felt almost a hunger from him.

I glanced at Nian and then back to the master. "Jauer is not healing as I would expect. His body is whole, but his magic seems damaged, weakened."

The demon shrugged. "What is your concern?"

"I want him to be healed."

"You have already said that he is well."

"But, my lord," surely some deference would help, "he needs his magic."

The Shadow Lord made a little shaking motion of his head and ran his tongue over his teeth. He turned to Nian. "That boy is not sworn to me, yet."

I watched Nian's throat convulse. "Not yet," he said.

The demon looked back at me. "I'm tempted to insist that he asks me himself. But since it is you who asks, Elainya, I will grant your request." He walked over to my shelves and glanced over the various jars, selecting a few including the mysteriously beautiful one he had given me.

He carried them to my desk and mixed a cup of ale with the extracts and herbs before waving his hand over it. A tiny puff of smoke erupted from the cup and dissipated. With a sniff at the resulting potion, he nodded. "That will restore your apprentice, Nian."

Then he turned to me. "It is time you took an apprentice as well."

"I've been working with Miatra."

He shook his head. "You may continue, but I have another in mind. I will send her to you."

With that, he vanished.

When the gathering party returned with early mint, I added some to the brew and had Jauer drink.

Miatra watched with curiosity, not fully aware of Jauer's abilities to begin with. As he swallowed the last drop, a wind rushed into the room, causing doors to rattle and the curtains to flap as if being ripped from their cords. With a sound like thunder, the wind exploded into silence and we all glanced at each other while Jauer fought to catch his breath.

Terror jumped up on the desk and sniffed at him.

Nian was the first to speak. "Jauer? Try something simple."

Jauer looked at Nian and swallowed. He raised the trembling stump of his left hand and we all watched as it shimmered into the illusion of perfection. Miatra gasped.

Startled, he looked at her and let the illusion fade. "Please, Miatra, you mustn't tell anyone," he explained.

I turned to her. "Because of the way magic is viewed here, we have kept Jauer's abilities a secret." I tousled his hair fondly. "He gets into enough trouble without that being known."

"Of course," she whispered. "I thought...I thought the Draska were gone." She looked at me. "I thought you were the last."

"Not quite," I said, remembering the Shadow Lord's direction that I was to have a new apprentice. "Not quite."

The next day, the queen sent Eavyn to bring me to her chambers. I wore my new peach gown, delighting in the warmth of early summer.

Queen Laurel smiled at me as I entered and shooed the other ladies out.

"Thank you for the tea, Elainya." She blushed.

"You look beautiful." I took in her bright eyes, supple skin, glowing hair, and wondered if the tea might not have already fulfilled its purpose. "Did you want me to confirm that you are with child?"

She looked shocked. "No, I think I'll know that for myself soon enough. I need your help with another matter." A deep breath passed her lips and I watched her eyes flicker to the door. She lowered her voice. "It is my niece that I'm worried about."

I had to think for a moment whom she might be talking about. I knew she was related to Eavyn by marriage. "Eavyn?"

She blinked at me and a frown creased the perfect brow. "Eavyn? No. She's not my niece... More of a distant cousin, really. No, I meant Trillia."

Now it was my turn to be confused. "Surely Trillia isn't with child...."

She laughed. "Oh, no!" She gasped for breath. "I could wish for her to be married and with child! No, Trillia has other problems. I'd like you to accept her as your apprentice."

"Trillia. Sir Reif's daughter?" Surely I had to be mistaken. I suspected the girl would faint at the thought of blood. Imagining her as a healer was beyond my abilities, much less training her to be one.

"Don't judge her too quickly, Elainya." I heard the tone of affronted royalty and carefully schooled my responses.

"Of course not, my lady. I don't mean any disrespect for your niece, but she doesn't seem to have an interest in..." I stopped. Actually, I couldn't see Trillia having an interest in anything.

"Trillia has many inabilities. She rarely speaks. She doesn't flirt. She doesn't sew or read, even though I know she is able to do it all. I need your help getting her past her inhibitions."

"Have you considered just getting her drunk?" I wasn't serious and was a little shocked to find that I had been taken seriously.

"Yes. Sadly, we found her a day later asleep under a litter of hounds. She didn't remember anything after the first ale, and has refused to drink anything other than milk and water ever since."

While this explained the health of the girl's complexion, it left me with more questions. Her aunt had already resorted to what I would have considered extreme measures. Now, she was asking me to find a place in the world for the girl.

"Her father does not seem to approve of Draska methods. Wouldn't he object to her being my apprentice?"

"I will handle my brother," she smiled.

"It might be easier to simply find her a match."

Laurel frowned. "It would. With her connections, there are several young men who would have her, even with her flaws, but she does not want them."

Interesting that among the ladies in waiting, the queen would single out Trillia for special favors.

"My lady, I am already training one assistant. Miatra has been a great help to me, but I rarely have enough patients to keep both of us busy."

She waved her hand in dismissal. "You will have after the next battle."

"You expect Trillia to help with battle wounded?"

The queen's patience was being tried by my ongoing concerns. "Elainya, I am asking you to meet with her and test her... however you Draska do such things. Do not judge her until you have met with her."

"Of course, my Queen," I replied, as any other response would have been inappropriate.

Her smile returned. "Good. I'll go out and send her in to you. You can meet with her immediately." In a whirlwind of flapping sky-blue skirts, the queen was gone, and I found myself momentarily alone in her chamber. I turned around to survey the room, just as a small cough heralded the entrance of the girl I thought of as "the dove."

This was the first opportunity I'd had to see Trillia at close range since she'd brought Terror to me. Her clothes were of high quality, but wrinkled. Her hair had once been carefully coiffed, but now stray wisps of blonde fell forward to cover her face. One gray eye peered intently in my direction while its twin hid behind the unkempt veil.

"Why, hello," I smiled.

A timid smile was her only response.

"Your aunt tells me that you are interested in becoming a healer."

The smile became broader and she nodded.

The girl was trembling. I stared at the thin, twisting hands as I tried to decide how to continue the interview.

"Let's sit down." I motioned towards a fainting couch near the door.

She sat and tucked her daintily crossed ankles under the seat. Her hands lay in her lap, quivering and yet controlled.

"You don't need to be afraid of me." I tried to be reassuring.

"Oh, I'm not!" she blurted. Her voice was surprisingly melodious.

"You're not?"

"No. I think you're wonderful." She fingered the neckline of her gown and I noticed that a thread of necklace disappeared beneath her bodice. A good luck charm of some sort?

"And why is that?" I hadn't anticipated her actually answering my questions.

She shrugged. "I liked what you did to my brother. Can you teach me to do that?"

Ah. I began to understand her desire to learn from me.

"The healing arts can be a powerful weapon."

She blinked and glared at me, her eyes losing the smile that had given them animation for a moment. Now, instead, they sparked with anger. There was a deep-set beauty that peeked out of those eyes for a moment. "I don't just want a weapon. I want to help people." She looked down at her hands and continued in a softer voice. "I know what you think. You think because I'm shy that I'm stupid, but I'm not. I've been practicing healing since I was a child. At first, I cared for the farm animals. Later, I tended to the servants. Eventually, the peasants would come to me for help. Then the war broke out and my father insisted that I had to come here and find a husband." She shivered. "I would very much like to learn from you, Lady Elainya."

There was an intensity in her tone that I found encouraging.

"There is a test that the Draska do, where we look deep into a person's soul and see where their heart truly lies. It does not hurt. Will you allow me to see if this is right for you?"

She nodded. "What do I need to do?"

"Just look at me and relax." I took her hand and was surprised by the transparency of the girl. She made no effort to resist; instead, she became as easy to read as a sunrise. I was shocked by the horrors she had seen. Her mother's death had been an escape, while her own life had continued in constant pain until she'd come to the castle and her father and brother had left her alone. The abuse the girl had borne was nothing compared to the vulnerability and desperate desire for love that I saw in her soul.

My attention was drawn by a faint sparkle. It was impossible, and yet I was sure. The girl had a small amount of Draska blood, even though she did not know it. I touched her abilities and was delighted to find that they showed the characteristic shape of a natural healer.

This was the apprentice the master had sent. I had expected someone threatening, dangerous, not this gentle soul.

I released her hand and nodded. "Yes, I think you should become my apprentice. Tell me, who was it who taught you to love healing?"

She pulled the necklace out of her bodice and held it up for me to see the shining sky-blue stone. "The same woman who gave me this. She was one of the maids who tended me as a child."

I looked at the familiar necklace in shock. My childhood friend Marla had such a necklace. She'd also had long flaxen hair and ivory skin, as had the maid, no doubt. I wondered idly if Trillia knew why she had none of her supposed mother's features. I looked again at the girl, seeing the vaguest hints of her heritage. If she had even the tiniest bit of Marla's talent, she could be a great help.

"Very well. I'll have quarters arranged for you near my own. We will begin your training in the morning."

She squealed in delight and hugged me. "Oh, thank you, Lady Elainya! I won't disappoint you, I promise."

At the cry, Laurel rushed in and pulled the girl into her arms, smiling at me over the gray-clad shoulder. She did not speak, but mouthed, *Thank you.*

I nodded and excused myself.

Chapter 12

Victims

Elainya

The next day the men returned from the coast and I saw the horror of the battle wounds for myself. After only two attacks, the raiders had left. Some said the enemies were unreasoning beasts. Others spoke of giants, while still others felt they were men. In the daylight, only the king's men were dead, the enemy apparently having suffered no losses, or else having removed their dead from the battleground.

Horrified, I went from patient to patient in the chapel, the only room able to hold so many. We cleared the pews and made pallets on the floor.

The wounds festered and the room stank of rotting flesh. The candles did little to clear the air and the weather turned overcast so that even this bastion of Light was dim.

"Whatever their weapons, they've poisoned the tips," I told Nian.

"I agree. I'd come to the same conclusion."

"What antidote do you have to the poison?"

Nian looked sadly at the men who lay wracked by pain. "There are none, Elainya."

Looking down at a young warrior not much older than Jauer, I summoned my power and reached out to destroy the poison. My power drained away—useless.

Startled, I tried again with a different victim, only to feel the power leached from my spirit as if the poison were retaliating. There was a taste to it, a dark earthy flavor that felt familiar. The drain on my power was coming from the Shadow Lord.

I returned to my chamber and retrieved my special vial. Nothing I tried made any difference.

Eventually, I summoned my master.

"Those men are sick," I ranted. "They need my help! Why are you blocking me?"

"They are killers, Elainya. You do not really want to heal them. They'll only return to the war. Let them die." With a cold breath, the master was gone, and no words of summoning would convince him to return.

How could he say that I didn't want to heal them? Of course I wanted to heal them! I remembered something Grandmother Nala used to say: Demons lie.

Desperate to help my patients, I asked Nian to help with the summoning, but he shook his head. "The master does not do the servant's bidding," he explained, and returned to caring for the dying wounded.

Miatra and Trillia were kept busy fetching and carrying, emptying bedpans, changing dressings, and running a constant series of unending errands.

For days, I moved between the men, trying various herbs and potions, succeeding only in trancing some to ease their pain before they died. Few remained conscious for long. Within a tenday, all were dead.

A sudden summer evening's storm surrounded the castle just as my last patient died. I raged outside to escape the stench and found myself in the midst of the wind. Inside it had whistled; without, it howled in tune with my anger.

I spun in a circle, staring up at the heavens. Why? I demanded of the unseen Light, knowing full well that it would not answer such as me.

Why? I screamed into the dark void of the heavens.

The world spun with me and the storm matched itself to my fever. Even the winds were within my grasp, but not the ability to heal those I'd tended so desperately.

I'd pushed myself to exhaustion, but I could not save even one.

Why not?

In a burst of fury, I focused my anger on a nearby tree.

A blast of lightning blinded me as the tree burst into flames, quickly doused by the pouring rain. I gasped and caught my breath, as the rain washed away the stench that had clung to me for days. The wind stopped.

I swallowed, horrified by what I'd done. With a deep breath, I willed the rain to stop. The moon emerged from behind the clouds and I stood in the moon shadow of the destroyed tree. I felt very small as I stood there dripping, my dress clinging to me, hampering my movement. I flipped a loose strand of hair out of my face and stared at the smoldering tree. The grasping shadows seemed to swirl about me.

"Isn't that power enough for you?" laughed the Shadow Lord as he appeared at my side.

"I want the power to heal the sick."

"You can—you have already used it."

"But the wounded—you drained the power from me every time I tried to help them. You killed them all."

There was a long silence. When the Shadow spoke, the tone was almost gentle. "Elainya, I can not let you heal them. This is a battle between the Light and myself. If you want to blame someone, blame the Light, not me. Tell the king to end the war. He has the power. Tell him to send a message of surrender with Nian to the front lines. That is the only way to stop the killing."

"You're saying those men were killed by the Light?"

"Did the Light shine to save them?"

I was so exhausted, the entire tenday felt like a dream. He couldn't be suggesting that we surrender, and yet he was. "And then what? Be ruled by those creatures? The king will not agree."

"They do not seek dominion over your people, just peaceful coexistence. Your king could offer them a home of their own—the Auroran forest for example."

"You would have us turn over the home of my ancestors to those monsters?" I was horrified.

"Your ancestors don't need the land anymore. The land is empty. A small price to pay to stop the killing, don't you think?"

I was stunned. Would I give up my ancestral home to stop the war?

"Didn't you say that you would give anything to stop the killing?" he pushed.

It bothered me that he seemed to be right. "Those creatures, are they shadow spirits as some say?"

The Shadow Lord laughed. "No, merely some friends of mine—as you are my friend, Elainya." A shadow brushed close to my hair and I felt chilled but stood my ground.

"So they are corporeal."

"Mostly."

"You don't give straight answers, do you?"

Laughter. "Would you expect me to? I've told you how to end the killing. Do try not to destroy any more trees, will you?"

I do not know why I went to meet with Reflect Rendel that evening. Perhaps I wanted his counsel. The anger still boiled within me, and I found myself pacing around his room.

"Useless!" I raged. "What good am I as a healer if I could not save even one of them?"

"You saved Viron."

"I should have been able to heal their wounds far easier than Viron's heart. If only I could fight the poison those creatures used! If I knew what it was, maybe I could find an antidote."

Reflect Rendel sipped his tea thoughtfully before he answered. "Lady Elainya, I know what the poison is, but you will not be pleased with the knowledge."

"You...know?"

He nodded. "Magic killed them. Shadow magic to be exact."

"How can that be? You're telling me that the attackers are magic users?" What he said made an eerie sort of sense. The Shadow Lord had said they were friends of his...like I was.

How much like me were they? Enough alike that our magic was the same? Enough alike that my magic could not counter theirs?

"Of a sort. My understanding is that they feed off the use of magic, turning it against those it is meant to save."

I shook my head. "No, that's not right. It was some form of poison. You're reaching for a spiritual answer because you do not have a physical one."

Reflect Rendel shrugged and went back to sipping his tea.

I sighed and sat down across from him. "Maybe you are right."

After a long silence, I forced myself to confide in the reflect. "Last night, outside the castle, I met a spirit. An ambassador of sorts. It spoke to me because I am Draska. It said that all they want is Aurora."

"The Draska forest is all that they want?" His tone dripped with sarcasm. He shook his head. "You know that land was given to the Draska by my master years ago?"

I did remember the stories. "Yes. It has always been a place of peace." But there were no more Draska, and the land was empty when Nian and I were not there.

"It was a good land, a rich reward for His special servants. But it is more than that. The waters there have given the Draska abilities beyond the normal range. They make the Draska what you are. The Shadow Lord is trying to put his own servants in that place of honor. It is a direct attack on my own dear master."

"So Light and Shadow are fighting and the people of this land are merely pawns in the midst of a battle, being slaughtered for no reason?" I was disgusted.

"Perhaps...or perhaps it is more than that."

Now he was just being vague. I frowned at him. "Can you heal these injuries?" I asked. I knew the answer, but I wanted him to acknowledge it.

"I have tried, but it is no use."

"So we are both powerless."

The reflect did not answer, but I noticed a tear in his eyes. My patients were now his charges—his to bury.

"There are no more Draska. That land is as useless as I am. Somehow, I will find a way to end this. I have to."

Whether prompted by his words, or some inner sense, I knew that the war was my fault. Somehow, I must find a way to end it. I left him to rest for the busy day he had ahead.

Relieved of my duties, I returned to my room. There was a small chest on my desk along with a note from Sir Reif, thanking me for my efforts on the part of his men. He echoed that the situation had been futile, but that my service was appreciated. Again, he professed his love.

I didn't even open the present. I called Miatra and asked her to return it for me. The girl looked exhausted, a worn-out shadow of my young friend. I hadn't seen Trillia all evening.

I lay down on my bed feeling guilty. Guilty for the girls' exhaustion, guilty for my inability to help, guilty even for the silly tree.

My heart held a deep dread that Rendel might be right. What if I was guilty of so much more?

Nian blamed me for the death of the Draska.

What had Nian once called me? A vile sourceress sent from the darkest pit, come to destroy the kingdom?

How was I going to stop the slaughter?

Chapter 13

Battlefront

Elainya

I sent word with the chamberlain that I wished a private audience with the king. Once ushered into the king's presence, I delivered the message the Shadow Lord had given me as clearly as I could.

"Who gave you this message, Lady Elainya?" he asked.

I'd argued with myself all night over how to answer that very predictable question. "My lord, the message was given to me by one who has helped you in the past. That is all I am allowed to say."

The king frowned deeply. "Were it my most trusted adviser who told me this, still I would not surrender any part of this kingdom to those creatures."

"I am merely the messenger. For what it is worth, I agree with your decision. I am sorry my abilities are not enough to heal the wounded."

"No one has tried harder than you have. Do not blame yourself."

But I did blame myself. If there was any way to help, I had to try. My only hope was if I could get to the wounded sooner, before the poison had a chance to invade their bodies. If I could clean the wounds, or perhaps amputate infected limbs...as horrific as the thought was, I knew I had to try.

I shuddered and presented my request to the king.

"When the troops return to the coast, I would like to go with them. Perhaps if I can get to the wounded sooner, I can be of help," I offered.

"You realize the danger?"

"If this continues, no place in the kingdom will be safe. I prefer to meet danger rather than wait for it."

He nodded approval. "Nian will be leaving with a regiment in the morning. You may accompany him if you wish."

"Thank you."

Nian

The girl left the king's presence and went straight to the stables. Nian followed, surprised by the turn in her focus. He found her next to Singe's offspring, whispering secrets to the animal.

"I've never seen you ride by choice," he said as he came up to them.

"I don't. But Reif felt this horse and I would get along."

"I'm sure you will."

She turned and he found himself struck by the challenge in her blue gaze. "I'm going with you tomorrow."

His protest was frozen by the ice in her eyes.

"Very well. And so you need a horse."

She nodded.

"And a weapon."

Elainya looked stunned. "I'm going as a healer."

"You're going to a battlefront." He motioned for one of the grooms to saddle Singe. "We'll take a ride to make sure you can handle the horse, and I'll teach you a few spells for protection."

He could see that she wanted to argue, but the protest stuck in her throat. With a visible swallow, she nodded.

Elainya

I did not sleep that evening. I left only one candle lit and spent the night arguing with my master over ways to heal the wounded. He would not agree to allow any intervention and declared my trip to the front a waste of time.

I packed the herbs and medicines I thought might be of use and dressed warmly for the early morning journey. As I sheathed my knife, I shuddered. Would I need it as a weapon today?

Just before dawn, I was startled by a knock. I drew the bolt and opened the door to find Reflect Rendel standing uncomfortably in the hallway. "I noticed the light in your room while I was out walking."

"Would you like to come in?" I asked, curious to know what would bring him to my door.

He shuddered. "Could we walk and talk?" Whatever it was, he wasn't desperate enough to enter my sanctuary.

I put out my light and wrapped the cloak Nian had given me around my shoulders, securing it with Drenil's brooch. The early morning was moonless. A distant glow proved that dawn would not be far off.

"You're up early," I said.

"Or late, as you are." The priest was silent for a moment before he continued. "Nian goes to the front."

"I'm going with him."

"Will you both be...." He took a deep breath and changed tactics. "I assume you intend to do everything in your power to help?"

"Of course."

"It is said that the battles were fierce when the Draska fought the invaders."

"I do not know."

"These creatures feed on magic, Elainya."

"What do you mean?"

"I'm not even sure I understand it myself. When you use your power, they will grow stronger. I just wanted you to be forewarned. Be careful, and watch what your magic causes."

"I know what you think about my abilities, but I would not aid war!"

"No...not intentionally. I'm probably wrong, but just watch the flow of the battle."

"I will," I replied, wondering what he thought I would see.

We walked into the courtyard together as the troops were gathering. Nian raised his eyebrows as he watched the priest blessing the troops. He sat astride Singe and I noticed he had collected my satchel and had strapped it to Ember's saddle. He motioned for me to mount.

Reflect Rendel looked as if he wanted to say something else, but instead he extended his hand in blessing toward us.

Nian chuckled. "Don't you think it a little late for that, Reflect?"

"It is never too late, my friend," Reflect Rendel smiled. "Be careful. We have yet to see what the past may bring to pass for you."

The reflect reached up to pat our horses and then stepped out of the way.

Nian grunted and shifted Singe's reigns. "Let's go," he called, and the troops moved as one.

The supply wagons creaked and rattled in time with the clanking weapons as we moved out into the morning mist. My heart was full of dread. As the day dawned, we rode toward Summerstown. I remembered this trip from my youth.

"I rode this path once with Drenil," I told Nian.

He grunted. "The Summer trek is a long tradition. When the battles were at a lull, the king and queen would go. I remember it was supposed to be great fun."

"Drenil had a horse that was so spirited—riding him was like dancing. Ember is a good horse, though." I patted the horse's neck and she flicked her ears at me.

"Singe is a war horse. He is reliable. I will have need of his strength today. Ember is not tested in battle. I expect you to stay out of the thick."

"Of course."

"The master will only allow you so much rebellion, you understand?"

I lowered my voice. "You believe he wishes us to lose this war?"

Nian shrugged. "He allows me more freedom for rebellion than he does you. Call it the reward of age."

"Or perhaps you have given up so he has no worry of what you may do," I said and slowed my horse so that Singe moved ahead of me. I did not feel like talking.

Reif joined us along the route but seemed even less inclined to speak than I was. He rode protectively near me, respecting the brooding silence that had drifted over us all.

We arrived at the encampment shortly before dark. I was stunned by the number of wounded.

"Do not leave camp," Nian ordered.

Ember was tied near the tent. She grazed uneasily as I prepared for battle, occasionally spooking at a sound only she could hear.

At sunset, the attack began.

By the light of our warriors' torches, I could follow only a bit of the battle, as I went from pallet to pallet trying to find some way to ease the pain of the dying. My abilities were drawing from my last reserves as I sought out some hint of the source of the poison. The rows of injured seemed endless. I was exhausted from the sleepless night and the long ride. My movements were almost automatic when I heard the scream behind me.

I whirled to face the creature—for creature it was. It screamed again with an eerily human voice coming from a shaggy, dark maw. It looked like night come to life, with glowing yellow eyes above flashing white fangs like stars in the abyss of mouth. It smiled at me and drove a huge sword through the patient I'd been tending, putting an end to the man's torment.

I realized that the tide of battle had shifted and that the camp had been overrun as I'd focused on the wounded. I started to reach for my knife and realized how useless it would be against that thing. It laughed as it noticed my movement and advanced towards me menacingly. I stepped backwards and summoned the power to defend myself. I raised my hand in the Draska warding gesture and the creature stopped. It cocked its head and moved forward more slowly. I stepped back again and tripped over one of my patients.

I sat down hard and the creature lunged. In a blur, Singe trampled through the ward, stepping over my patients. Nian's spirit sword sliced through the creature and it disappeared in a haze of foul-smelling smoke.

"Are you hurt?" he asked.

I shook my head and he was gone, back into the fight. I noticed his form flashing around the tent full of wounded where I made my stand. I called a protection spell into place and held the tent safe as the battle raged around us.

Ember cried in fear but did not fight to run away, perhaps sensing the fragile protection that I offered.

Nian stayed close to my tent and fought the attackers fiercely. I noticed a creature sneaking up on him as he fought a group of the foes. Without thinking, I drew my dagger and flung it into the creature's neck. In an instant, all that remained was my dagger lying on the ground. I called it back to myself, stunned at the realization that I had killed.

Dawn came at last, and the creatures were gone. I allowed the spell to dissipate and collapsed in exhaustion. Nian found me lying across the corpse of one of my patients who had not survived the night.

"Elainya!" he gasped at my blood-soaked clothing as he roused me from sleep.

"Not mine..." I whispered, gesturing at the wounded around me. "I'm just tired."

"Yes, of course." He didn't look reassured as he lifted me and carried me into a small tent to one side of the camp. "Sleep now. You've done well."

I remembered nothing else for hours. I awoke to the smell of death and barely made it outside the tent before I threw up. Nian was seated by a fire, staring at the sinking sun. He looked ancient as he sipped from his flask of ale. He handed it to me without a word and I drank deeply to settle my stomach.

The ale helped. I did not feel my power drain away as Nala had always warned would happen from strong drink. Perhaps Nian was right. Perhaps he was right about who we were, who we had become.

I shook my head, realizing that I was being philosophical as a way to avoid the horror of what I'd seen. What I'd become.

"Will they be back?" The question was forced from my lips. I did not want to know the answer. I wanted to pretend it would not matter.

Nian only nodded. "I've got to get you out of here," he said. "I helped last night...."

"Not enough. This is no place for a woman."

"What do you mean, not enough? I warded the entire tent."

He glared at me. "And yet there are still wounded in the tent. What does it matter if you protect them? They're already poisoned. I'm sure they'd rather die cleanly than screaming for days. You did nothing except risk your life."

"My life is mine to risk. Besides, the Shadow Lord has made it plain that I'm not allowed to die. I'm sure he'll find a way to protect his investment." I took another drink from his flask and held it out to him. "I'm staying. There has to be something else I can try."

Nian ripped the flask from my hand and took a long drink before corking it and returning it to his pack. He stared into my eyes for a long moment and I watched his expression change from anger to hope and then back to something else, something desperate.

He took a deep breath and said, "Elainya, you were the focus of the battle." His voice was soft, but clear. He turned away and looked at the dirt in front of where he sat, digging trenches with the toe of his boot. "They wanted you. I've seldom seen them that organized. The entire battle centered on you."

He turned back to me, and rested a hand on my arm. "I am afraid for your safety. I should not have brought you here."

He looked to where the sun was setting. "Curse this ancient body of mine, I fell asleep and have only just wakened. I'd intended to have you out of here before dark."

I followed his gaze. Was he right? Had I made it worse? The sun was already dipping below the horizon; a mere segment of warmth remained.

What had the reflect said?

There was no time to leave. "They'll catch us on the road," I pointed out.

"You used a warding spell last night. Can you do it again?"

"Yes."

Nian seemed thoughtful. "Perhaps we can use you to our advantage."

I hadn't eaten in over a day and there was no time to break my fast. The ale sent a burning haze through my blood. Desperation fueled a sense of reckless abandon.

I missed Dren. My peace-loving husband. I couldn't imagine what he would have done in this situation.

But Dren was dead. I so desperately wished that I was as well. Then maybe I would not cause any more harm.

Would the Shadow Lord continue to protect me?

"What can I do?" I looked to Nian. He understood war as I never would.

"Ride with me in the battle. Keep your area of warding as wide as possible. I know where one of their leaders watches the battle from. We can take the battle to him."

It was reckless. I'd be in the middle of the worst part of the fighting. With Nian.

We could both be killed.

It was a good plan. I nodded my acceptance.

He rested his hand on my shoulder in encouragement and stood up. He removed his cape and reached a hand out to help me up. I could see his plan in my mind as I stood.

Nian's heart was full of fury. I'd never seen a Draska that angry before. Then I remembered the tree. His mind was full of hunger for killing.

The ale and desperation mixed in my blood, pushing away the weariness. I looked at the wounded around me and the image of the death he wished to deal to our enemy no longer horrified me.

Yes, we would do great damage together, protecting each other with our power.

The Shadow Lord wanted us to be a team? We were. He wanted me to turn from my Draska heritage and embrace his ways? I would.

He would not be pleased with the result.

I removed my cloak and drew the light sword Nian had insisted I bring. He nodded in approval and lifted me onto Singe's neck before leaping up behind me.

As the sun set, the attackers returned but were faced with a dangerous moving target. Everywhere we went, the air was thick with the stench of their dying. Yet no matter how many we killed, they seemed to come on thicker. They focused on us, seemed drawn to us. My shielding kept them from approaching. The spell was hard to maintain, but I fed it with the hatred I felt towards them for the harm they'd caused. Every echoing cry of our wounded fed my anger. Yes, our people would die, but so would the enemy. If I could not save my charges, I would destroy their attackers.

Shortly before dawn, the enemy horde let out a unified scream and turned and fled. Nian laughed the hysterical laugh of the exhausted and reigned Singe in near the surf.

We could see the little black forms swarming into boats and putting out to sea. Soon, the beach was empty of the creatures and the sun was rising.

Throughout the night, I'd felt Nian's presence in my mind. We'd thought and moved and fought as one. Now we entered the surf together and washed the blood and stench from our clothing. I sat on a piece of driftwood and wrung the salt water from my hair.

Nian sat beside me, and I was stunned by the camaraderie I felt with him. "Where do you really come from?" I asked.

His presence was gone from my mind in an instant. I gasped at the suddenly broken bond and almost lost my balance.

He caught me and steadied me on the log. I looked up into gray eyes lined by years of agony. Anguish was written in the lines of his face. "My past is as painful as your own. You may enjoy thinking on it, but I prefer to forget." He turned and walked away, leaving me shivering in the early morning sun.

I stared out over the empty ocean and wondered at the creatures' retreat. At last, I felt my appetite returning and walked the distance back to camp, where the scent of food made me dizzy.

My cape lay trampled where I'd left it, but I picked it up and wrapped myself in it anyway. I found the clasp and was amazed that it was undamaged. How had I been so careless as to drop it?

Dazed, I went to the fire and received a plate of food from an exhausted squire. Tasteless, the food nevertheless filled some of the emptiness inside me. A tired-looking captain sat beside me. "I'd heard that the Draska were fierce fighters. I'm glad I lived to see it for myself. Thank you for your help, Lady Elainya."

"The Draska were a peaceful people."

He looked at me in disbelief. "I see. Well, thank you anyway."

"You're welcome. Have we met?"

He smiled. "No. I'm Captain Bertrand. I hear we have a mutual acquaintance."

"That would be the lovely Lady Eavyn," I said.

"How much has she told you?"

"Oh, she is the picture of discretion. But I have certain gifts...."

"Discretion? Eavyn?" He laughed. "You have a sense of humor."

"Do you love her?" I asked abruptly.

He looked down. "I am a soldier. A soldier cannot love one such as her."

"Ah, but she does love you."

His eyes brightened as he looked up at me. "She does?"

"And you love her," I said.

"What of it?"

"Come to me when this war is over, and we'll see what we can make of it," I said, as Nian sat down heavily beside me.

"They've gone. The attacks are over for now. We will return to the castle today."

I could only nod. All of my energy was spent. I barely remembered the trip back to the castle. Ember had survived the battle. With a shudder, I determined never to put her at risk like that again.

I accepted Miatra's help getting into bed.

I dreamed that Drenil lay with me that night, but even in my dreams, I slept.

Chapter 14

Summer

Elainya

Summer's heat attacked the castle with a fiery vengeance. I tended my overflowing herbs with care, thankfully dipping water from the barrels Nian had placed in the corners of the garden to ease the task. If there was a way to make a job easier, Nian would find it.

As summer wore on, my skin burned and then tanned to an unladylike shade of brown. The sun seemed to shine on my garden with unusual ferocity, making the lighting harsh and grating to my eyes. My eyes refused to adjust and I was forced to carry a handkerchief just for wiping away the tears.

One exceptionally hot day, Terror lounged in the shade of an overgrown fennel plant, not deigning to bat the wispy tendrils. His tiny cat-voice was developing into an intelligible thought-speak, but the only word he projected was *hot*.

After I passed him for the third time, to be greeted again with *hot* and an idle glance, I dropped a dipper full of water on his head. He startled to his feet and sneezed the water out of his nose, glaring at me with baleful blue eyes. *Hot AND wet*, he projected.

With a laugh, I went back to watering the more fragile of the plants. I closed my eyes against the ever-present glare only to find the light still blinding, even through my eyelids.

A slight movement in the brush caught my eye. I looked up to see Cyndace quietly watching me. She smiled. "I wanted to thank you."

I walked over to where she stood in the shade and sat down.

"Come sit by me," I said and smiled, glad of the diversion and more than a little curious about the girl. "I sent a young man after you the other day with a pot."

Concern showed in her frown. "Claude should have brought you the new one already."

"Oh, I have it. I wasn't asking about the pot, but about your opinion of the young man."

She was silent for a moment. She sat next to me and sighed. "Lady Elainya, I have met Jauer before. He's entertained my brothers in the marketplace."

"Some people think he is disfigured."

"He is far from disfigured."

"I've been keeping my eyes out for a suitable bride for him. I've been wondering if you might find him acceptable."

Cyndace harrumphed. "Do you think he'd really marry a commoner? I mean, he is so handsome, and he does have a place at the castle. Perhaps he could marry one of the servant girls."

"I'm sure I could convince one of the servants to marry him, if you aren't interested."

Cyndace quickly shook her head. "I'm interested...."

"So, what will I tell Jauer when I see him next?"

There was a hint of a smile in her voice. "Tell him the potter's daughter has no dowry."

I chuckled. "Maybe we can arrange for you to have that as well, my dear."

She treated me to a quick hug. "I'd better get back to work. I'm supposed to be gathering fresh clay."

"I suspect any you find today will be already baked," I said as she bounded off into the woods in search of supplies for her father.

When I was done with my gardening, I was as wet as the cat, the sweat dripping off my skin and soaking the thin fabric of my gown. I plucked it away from my bodice and wrinkled my nose at the smell. How I longed to be in Aurora, where I could plunge into the lake. A deep breath felt like molasses, and I found myself dizzy with exhaustion. Time to be done.

My basket was full of mint, parsley, and red raspberry leaves. Some were for the cooks, but most would go into the daily concoction I brewed for the nauseated queen. We hadn't discussed her condition yet, but I felt certain a new heir was on the way.

I carried my gathering back into the castle, pausing for a moment to lean against the cold stone wall beside the staircase. Nian came out of his workroom and frowned.

"It is unwise for you to work in the sun, Elainya. You should try working at dusk. I think you'll find your vision is better suited to shadow." He noted the cat beside me. "Like your young friend, you will be able to see better then." He twiddled his fingers towards Terror, who hissed and dashed up the stairs. "Your cat hates me."

I raised an eyebrow. "Perhaps he's smarter than I thought he was."

Nian stared at me in silence for a moment. Oddly, I felt as if the jibe had hurt his feelings, but that was ridiculous.

"Maybe your skills will be enough to treat your sunburn, but don't ignore the heat stroke." He turned and went back into his room. I felt a wave of cool air escape as he slammed the door. How did he manage to have a room that was not hot?

My rooms, when I entered, were even warmer than normal. I leaned against the outer wall only to find it had absorbed the oppressive heat. Was there no escape? I slipped off my sandals and reveled in the comparatively cool stone of the floor. In exhaustion, I sank to the stone to let some of the heat leach out of my skin.

Miatra came in at that point. "Elainya?" I heard the worry in her voice.

"I'm fine. It is just cooler down here. Can you ask one of the pages to bring up a pail of water?"

"Of course!"

Terror sat on my desk, staring down at me in disdain. He licked a paw.

"I'm hot, all right?"

He sniffed in acknowledgment.

"Yes, I know. I stink. I'll take a bath as soon as I get some water."

His ears twitched and he flicked his paw.

I rolled over and stared at him. "You're trying to tell me something."

His furry eyes closed. *Mmmmore water*, whispered in my head.

"You're thirsty?" I looked for his water dish, but it was full.

You.

"Oh, you want ME to drink water? Yes, I know. Nian said the same thing."

The cat's ears flattened.

"You hurt his feelings, you know. He seems to like animals."

Cold.

"In this heat, cold would be a blessing." I sat up and wrapped my arms around my knees, leaning back against the wooden chest at the end of my bed. I already missed the coolness of the stone. Perhaps I really was suffering from heat stroke. There was a tea I should brew and then try to chill to have on hand for patients, but I couldn't remember the ingredients.

Trillia came in and glanced from me to the cat before sitting beside me on the stone floor. "The air drags my energy away with each breath." She sighed, leaning her head back on the chest.

The cat leapt onto the top of the chest and put a paw on my shoulder. *Home?* he thought.

"Terror wants to go home. Probably to the mountains," I translated for Trillia.

She looked at the cat thoughtfully. "Maybe he means your home. Aurora would be wonderful today."

I shivered, remembering my last visit to Aurora. Still, Nian wouldn't have to come. Trillia was learning quickly. Trillia and I were more than capable of protecting ourselves and Miatra.

Miatra came in carrying the water; it sloshed onto her gown as she stopped and stared at Trillia. A flicker of a frown crossed her face and was quickly hidden. "I got the water myself. The pages all seem to have vanished."

"It's the heat. Makes everyone except you lazy," I muttered. "Miatra, come sit. You shouldn't be carrying that bucket."

She set it down in the corner and shrugged. "It isn't that heavy."

"I'm thinking about going to Aurora. Would you like to come?"

Her eyes flickered to Trillia and then back to mine. "I don't think so."

Interesting. Did Miatra have a problem with Trillia? The girl's eyes were closed, her head leaned back; she hadn't moved since Miatra came in. It wouldn't do to have these two fighting.

"I'd like it if we three could spend some time together planning what to do when the next set of wounded arrive."

Trillia didn't move. "There's nothing to do, Elainya. Just call the grave diggers. From the moment they are nicked with those poisoned weapons, they are dead. It would be better to slit their throats on the battle field, but my father doesn't see it that way."

"That is no attitude for a healer!" Miatra spat.

"It's honest and it's kind." Trillia's voice was a determined blast of cold that would have frozen lesser foe than Miatra.

I interrupted before Miatra could reply. Definitely some tension between these two.

"Enough. You see why we should plan? Besides, the pool at Aurora will be cool even today. Miatra, you're coming with us. I'll pack both of our bags while you go and get some food from the kitchen. Trillia, get your things for an overnight stay. We'll take horses."

Miatra looked at me in protest, but stopped when her eyes met mine. "Yes, my lady," she muttered, and left.

Trillia laughed at the barb and slowly pulled herself to her feet. "I like the idea."

"It's a dangerous trip. Have you been practicing the defensive spells I taught you?"

She smiled brightly. "Yes. Do you think there will be a chance for me to use them?" She reminded me of a young boy eager for his first hunt.

"Hopefully not."

She sighed. "I've been practicing, but trancing a dog is not very satisfying. I'd rather use my brother."

I raised an eyebrow.

"Well, you do," she said and flounced out.

I laughed and set about gathering the bedding and clothing we'd need.

***

Nian

Nian's eyes opened as the girls stopped talking. He wondered how long it would take Elainya to realize he could hear conversations through his chimney? He'd long ago warded the opening so that only the heat from his chamber rose into hers, not the sound. Foolish girl. She would run away to Aurora again, would she? Maybe it was time for another lesson. If nothing else, it would not do to have her wandering the country alone.

He packed his bags and went to take leave of the king. Let the girl have her respite. He'd see to her safety.

Elainya

When I arrived at the stable with the bickering girls in tow, Ember and two other horses stood already saddled. A quick glance into the pasture confirmed that Singe was gone. How had Nian learned of our plans?

"Did one of you ask the stable master to prepare horses?"

Both girls shook their heads.

"Did either of you tell Lord Nian we were leaving?"

Blank stares were their only response. No, they looked too confused to be lying.

He couldn't be reading my mind without me knowing, could he? By the Light, if I caught him snooping around the lake, I'd blind his eyes. Dirty old man.

"Well, someone seems to have gotten our horses ready. In this heat, I'm not going to worry about who it was." I tied my bundle onto the back of Ember's saddle while the girls did the same. A stable hand rushed out to help us mount. We dutifully sat sidesaddle and allowed him to fuss.

"It's a hot day, ladies. Take it easy on the poor beasts. Make sure you stop to give them water. Don't push them too hard."

"We'll take care of them."

Terror jumped into my lap and settled himself, unsettling Ember. I patted the horse's mane and projected an image of the meadow outside of Aurora into her mind. Her head came up with a snort and she pranced away from the stable hand, clearly eager to be on her way. The others followed, picking up on Ember's excitement. Once we were outside the prying eyes of the castle, I paused and switched to riding astride, hiking up my skirts in a most unladylike and cooler fashion. The girls followed suit with some timidity.

"Alright, Ember. You know where to go. We'll just hold on." I laughed as the three horses galloped straight and true down the road to Aurora. We made good time, meeting no one on the way, the heat keeping even the bandits ensconced in whatever cave of coolness they could find.

We dropped our belongings in my parents' hut and led the horses out to the meadow. I could see no sign of Nian or Singe. Perhaps I was wrong. Perhaps he'd gone on a different errand.

While the horses ate contentedly in the shade and sipped from the stream, the girls and I stripped down to our shifts and plunged into the cold water of the stream-fed pool. It felt heavenly to let the icy water whisk away the stench. Miatra produced some rose-scented soap and we lathered each other, pulling our dresses into the water to wash as well. We lay them on the stone ledge to dry while we continued playing. I lay in the water and let my hair fan out around me. The wet shift was clingy, but comfortable.

Even here, there was no breeze, the warm air oppressive on our faces as we kept them above water to breathe.

Where had Nian gotten to? I lay on my back and floated there, searching the shadows carefully. There was a hint of movement behind a bush, but that could be nothing more than a bird. Whatever it was did not have Nian's intelligence, the presence seeming more animal.

I let the water cover my ears and the silence echo, my heart slow, the heat evaporate into the cool water. For a moment, all was peaceful, the temperature was perfect, the healing water of Aurora reinvigorated my soul. The light played across the water, less harsh than it had been at Sun's Font.

The girls were making a vague attempt to get along, I noted. They washed each other's hair. Miatra had brought a brush and they sat in the shallows taking turns brushing and braiding, trading gentle jibes. Perhaps the heat had left them too tired to argue. Miatra's dark hair and complexion contrasted nicely with Trillia's almost white-blonde hair. Her pale skin was reddened from the sun but did not seem to be burning. They were slathering some form of cream on their faces. Probably aloe. Miatra had thought to bring that as well.

Miatra tired of the water first and climbed out to dry off. I lay back in the water again, reveling in the peace.

A piercing scream tore through the forest. I flipped upright and floundered in the water, disoriented.

When I blinked the water out of my eyes, I saw Miatra held captive in the arm of an unkempt ruffian with a knife to her throat. I glanced at Trillia and noted her stillness. Her eyes flicked over the forest—searching for others, perhaps?

He nodded at me. "You—witch. I've got archers in the brush. If anything happens to me, they'll skewer you before you can find them."

My senses weren't showing me any others, but I hadn't noticed him, either. Heat stroke. I should have used my abilities to deal with it. Trillia shook her head slightly. I must teach the girl thought-speech. Silly that I'd taught my cat before my apprentice.

Where was the cat? Would he be able to find the others?

Terror?

There was no answer. Lazy beast—probably asleep in the shade.

I turned back to the brigand. "I'm not going to hurt you. What do you want?"

He tightened his grip on Miatra. "Maybe I have what I want already."

"If you did, you'd have vanished into the forest. Besides, you know I'm not going to let you leave with the girl. So why don't you tell me what you really want?"

"Those fine horses, for a start."

I glanced to where the horses grazed peacefully in the shade.

"If I let you take the horses, you'll leave the girl in the clearing—unharmed?"

"Yes."

I was treading water and swimming slowly, my shift a drag. Could I get closer to him?

Abruptly, his eyes rolled up into his head. He shoved Miatra away and clutched at his throat. He tried to grab for the girl, but she ducked away, screaming.

I dove under the water and emerged near her. "Get down!"

No arrows emerged from the forest. Trillia had not moved, but I noticed she was trembling. "It's over," she said softly. "He was alone."

Swimming to her side, I climbed out, touching her shoulder. She looked at me with fear in her eyes. "His mind was so dark."

"A brute."

"He was alone. I checked."

"How could you be sure?"

"There were no lines from him to any others."

Enigmatic, but brilliant. "Well done. Did you trance him?"

"I—I think so?"

It wouldn't do to have the beast awaken. He'd be in a bad mood when he did. She was still young, her power poorly controlled. I moved to where the stinking, sweaty male lay on the ground and reached out to make sure he was unconscious. No sign of life greeted my probing. I gasped and knelt down beside him, my shift nearly dry already in the heat.

No breath escaped his lips. I touched his forehead with the tips of my fingers and felt—nothing. "Trillia, he's dead."

"Is he?" Her voice was flat as if she'd just noticed a dead spider.

Miatra was fumbling with her dress, the laces tangling in her hands. I stood and put my arms around her. "You're not hurt. Just breathe for a second. None of us is hurt."

"He's dead."

"Not likely to hurt you, then."

"SHE killed him."

"Trillia was afraid for you. She acted without thinking."

Trillia stood and shook out her gray dress, putting it on with a graceful minimum of movement.

"Don't try to tell me that was healer magic, Lady Elainya," Miatra whispered.

"You'd rather I let him take you and the horses?" Trillia snorted. "You've never been raped. If you had been, you'd be glad he is dead."

"I'm grateful, but.... It was so sudden."

"He didn't even have time to slit your stupid throat as he fell." Trillia tied her laces with a gentle flourish. "Elainya, thank you for bringing us here. That swim felt...wonderful."

"Trillia, you just killed a man," I said.

"Yes. I did." With a scrunched nose, she grabbed his shoulders and dragged the body into the forest, returning to wash her hands in the stream. "Do you think wild animals will dispose of the body or should we bury him?"

I finished helping Miatra and pulled my own dress on, leaving the laces loose. "We should bury him. I don't want a rotting carcass this close to Aurora or this pool, but I'm not sure what we have to bury him with."

Nian stepped out of the forest, his expression impossible for me to interpret. "I'll take care of the body for you, ladies. There is a cool meal of fruit and cheese waiting for you in your cottage."

"Where were you hiding?" I glared at him. Maybe it hadn't been Trillia after all.

"I am unclear what happened, but I heard a scream and came to help—just in time to clean up the mess, it seems."

"I can help," I said, but his expression turned fierce.

"No. Dealing with the dead is my specialty, not yours." He looked at Trillia. "That was well done, young lady. I am impressed."

She straightened and flipped her long blond braid over her shoulder. "I have an excellent teacher."

Nian turned to me and nodded. "Yes. Surprisingly so."

I led a shaking Miatra back to the hut, seeing her safely tucked into a corner.

Trillia seemed to have forgotten the event. She'd found Terror in a patch of sunshine and held the laconic cat in her lap. I leaned against the wall, feeling the sunset draining the heat of the day. The slight evening breeze carried a wisp of foul-smelling smoke.

Nian was burning the body.

***

Nian

Pity the master would not accept Trillia, but he seemed unaware of the talents of these young descendants of the Draska. Why? Elainya could have killed the man as easily as Trillia had, but her scruples interfered.

Maybe it was the heat stroke. The question remained in his mind, though: how had Elainya gotten heat stroke and why had her abilities not sufficed to heal herself before her girls were endangered?

She should have protected the girls.

He tossed the pouch of coins he'd retrieved from the brigand into the air and then returned it to his belt. There were too many of them in the forests these days. Next time he would hire one that was either lighter or more intelligent.

Chapter 15

Proposals

Elainya

Nian devoted most of his peacetime to Jauer—and then to his magic.

I was happy to be ignored.

My time was filled with patients and those seeking matches. When I was free, I sewed or walked with the ladies—or sent back Sir Reif's gifts. Each day, I found a letter, flowers, or some trinket on my desk.

It had become a light-hearted game between us. When we met in the corridors, he was always the gentleman. If it were not for the darkness I'd seen in Trillia's mind, I might have softened toward him.

Miatra laughed at seeing one she feared behave like a love-lorn suitor. She had become my constant companion. Eagerly she helped me gather herbs—more eager to write the new label than to gather.

On her birthday, I presented her with her own pen and ink along with a stack of paper. Each day, she would sit at the desk and laboriously copy a passage from a book. This copy she would bring to me and listen intently as I read to her.

The special glow about Queen Laurel appeared in early summer. I said nothing, but each morning, I arose early, brewed
a special tea of mint and berry leaves, and had Miatra deliver it
to the queen.

By midsummer, the queen sought me out in my chambers.
"Lady Elainya, is it true?"

"That you are with child? You have the glow about you. Even
better, I can assure you the child is a boy."

Her eyes glistened with happy tears. "How can you be sure?"

I shrugged and gestured at the room. "Tricks of the trade,
my lady."

"What do I need to do?"

"Nothing special. Take afternoon walks, but do not overex-
ert yourself. Be careful in this heat. Enjoy your time. If you have
pains or complaints, I want you to send for me immediately.
The rest will come quite naturally. Has the tea helped?"

She smiled. "Yes."

"Good. Now I have a concern." I gestured for her to sit in
my chair and I sat on the bed, leaning close so we would not be
overheard. "This child will be heir to your husband's throne."

She nodded. "You think my brother will be displeased."

"Jeiwan will have a rival. Do you have anywhere you could
stay for a few months?"

"My cousin is Lady of West Ridge. We were close as children.
She would keep my secret."

"Good. Before you begin to show, you should go there. I will
come to West Ridge before you are due and see you safely home
with the child. I'd like Trillia to go with you to care for you."

She smiled. "We are of one mind." She took my hand and smiled.
"I owe you much for what you have done with her and for me."

"Good, because I have a favor to ask of you, my lady."

"After what you have done, I would be hard pressed to ignore your request."

"There is a young Captain Bertrand in your husband's forces. He has fought bravely during this war. If you could mention his heroism to the king, I would be grateful."

Laurel looked at me in confusion. "To what end? Do you fancy him?"

"No, my lady, but I have a match in mind for him. As part of his elevated position, you could offer him the hand of Lady Eavyn."

"I thought you had Jeiwan in mind for Eavyn."

"I did, however I would not burden Eavyn with such as he."

"You don't see any hope for my nephew?"

"There is always hope, or so Reflect Rendel keeps telling me."

She nodded and paused to think. "You must know something about Lady Eavyn's wishes in this matter."

"You will see it in her eyes, should the king grant my request."

The queen smiled as she left, off to arrange for Lady Eavyn's happiness.

I visited with Reflect Rendel almost every evening but declined to attend further services. Since the battle, few commented on the source of my abilities, but I was widely accepted as a healer. By fighting at the front, I had become a hero.

The queen left to visit her cousin, and there was no talk of her condition. She had managed to keep her secret.

On a rare hot autumn night with no moon, Rendel and I chose to walk along the castle walls and enjoy the view of the bright stars. I felt myself renewed and refreshed by the darkness.

The reflect seemed to be aging with the worry of the war. Where just a few months ago he had seemed energetic, he now seemed frail. He often spoke to me about his master, how the Light would speak to him and tell him things. After I realized that he accepted me as I was, I opened up to Reflect Rendel and we had great debates over which of our masters was the more reliable. Philosophy and religion came together in our talks. He seemed to enjoy the intellectual discussions.

Our talks soothed my spirit. I was able to voice my concerns to him and then defend my actions. If I could convince Reflect Rendel that I was not a servant of darkness, I would feel vindicated. Of course, I never did convince him, but he remained my friend and this gave me some consolation.

"Elainya, I need to speak with you about something important," he said.

"Of course, Reflect."

"I have taken the time to get to know you. I've searched your heart, learned to understand you. I do not claim to know all that has passed in your life, but I know the source of your powers."

I stopped walking and leaned against the stone wall, letting the jagged edges of the warm stone cut into my back. "Yes, you do, but have you ever known me to do ill to our people?" I asked in challenge.

"Not intentionally." He raced on in his comments, clearly unsettled by his need to speak plainly. "The Draska died because their own magic turned on them. By using shadow magic, they gave power to the minions of the Shadow Lord who have been attacking us."

"You're wrong. Nian and I drove off the invaders with shadow magic."

"The Draska did not intend to draw the invaders closer to our shores, but they did, just as your own magic has caused more than one attack. I fear what this lull may mean."

"What if all it means is that they are defeated?"

"I do not believe that is so. I fear you have made our situation much worse."

Enraged, I turned on the old man. "You're insane. I would say moonstruck if there were a moon. How can you have spent so much time with me and then say that I could be responsible for these killings...the poisonings! How dare you?"

He paled, but continued. "I do dare, and I have a dare for you, Elainya. As you are my friend, treat your next patient without using magic."

"Why?"

He shrugged. "To prove me wrong. I know that if you treat this next patient with magic, he will die, and you will unleash a storm of attacks that can not be stilled."

"He?"

"That is all my master has told me."

"And if I do not use magic and the attacks continue?"

"Then I will have been wrong and I will tell you so."

"And what if you are wrong and he will die without my magic as Viron would have?"

"I am not wrong, Elainya, but if I were, his death would be upon my head, not yours. This patient wants to die."

"That is no comfort at all. How will you know whether I use magic or not?"

"I ask for your word. No matter what else you may be, Elainya, your honor is without blemish."

"How can you know who my next patient will be?"

He shrugged. "How do I know anything? How did I know that you were coming on the day we met?"

I could not deny that the Light often spoke through its own, much as my master spoke to me. Perhaps Reflect Rendel did know something about my next patient.

"Very well, you have my word."

The next morning, I sat near the window slit embroidering a tiny blue rose onto the sleeve of a gown. The peaceful moment was shattered as the castle rocked beneath me. The jars rattled and then settled back onto their shelves. For a moment, Miatra and I merely stared at each other in shock—both of us having leapt to our feet.

I turned to lay the gown on my chair and Miatra gasped.

From the doorway, Nian's voice was faint. "Lady Elainya, I am glad we have a proper healer."

Turning, I stared at the more than slightly singed magician.

Recovering my wits, I helped him lie down on the cot I kept in my room for patients.

When I touched him, my hands burned with the residue of power. I pulled my hands away and looked deeply into his gray eyes. "Nian, this was done by magic."

He sighed and winced at the pain in his lungs. "My own, I fear...."

"For what purpose?"

He glanced meaningfully at Miatra.

"Miatra, I will need Aloe—not the sweet we make for the queen, but the pure. Fetch me some fresh from the plot beside the oak trees. Quickly. Also —" I felt the pain of Nian's wounds and rushed on before I could reconsider. "The witch's bane. You remember where it was; bring me the root. Hurry."

As she left, Nian sighed. "The king has need of a new weapon...."

"I don't think this is what he had in mind."

"Of that, I am certain."

"Nian, why did it have to be you?" I whispered.

"Perhaps because the king had only one magician?" He tried to smile and failed as the pain increased.

"You don't understand. The reflect blames us for the war. He challenged me to treat my next patient without magic. If the war continues, he will agree that the Draska are not at fault. He could do much to end the fear people have of us."

"You gave your word?" he winced.

"Yes."

His tight pained expression flickered through anger and then back to agony.

"I thought I'd trained you better than that."

"He spoke a prophecy and said that if I used magic to heal you, you would die. Nian, I can't risk you, but I don't know what to do."

His hand on mine sent shivers of pain through me, but I did not pull away. "Elainya, you and I both know this is bad. I'm not so badly hurt that I don't know I'm dying. Magic or no magic, it will make no difference. You need to know the rest of my bargain with the Shadow Lord because it will make your decision easier." He paused for breath.

"I won't let you die."

The anger returned. His voice was a harsh whisper I had to lean close to hear. "You will! It is my wish, woman. Have you been my friend these few months and not seen that I hate life? Life itself is painful for me. My deal with our master involved my right to die after I had trained another Draska to take my place as his servant. You are that replacement. I've lived a full life. Let me rest now, Elainya." He gasped as the pain became stronger.

Miatra returned and helped as I tended Nian. She thought very highly of him and feared for his safely ...yet her fear was distracting me.

"Child, go see to the magician's office. Make certain the fires are out and then try to set things to rights."

Nian started to protest, but I quieted him with a gentle hand. "Let her be, my friend. She will have the proper respect—and I am certain Jauer will help her. He was not with you, was he?"

"No."

"Good. He would have been killed."

Nian nodded sadly.

Thus, alone with my patient, I ran my hands gently over the burns on his face and arms. His pain seared my hands.

"The power continues."

He nodded. His eyes had lost their piercing power—he was fading. "You had her bring witch's bane root."

"Yes. You were right that it will not kill us, but the root will drain your power and stop the damage from getting any worse."

"When I die, know that you have my gratitude, Elainya." I looked away from the tenderness in his pain-wracked eyes.

"You are not going to die." I set water boiling over the fire in preparation for the herbs Miatra was fetching.

Nian tried to argue, but the attempt only aggravated the pain.

Frustrated, I glared at him. "The only magic I need for you is a healer's trance," I muttered.

With a shrug, he lapsed into unconsciousness, trancing himself. Sleep would spare him the pain of my ministrations. I was stunned at how easily the trance had come on him. It took practice to learn to trance oneself. I'd known others who could accomplish the feat, but it was uncommon. Dren could have done it.

I applied the juice of the aloe to his burns.

I ground oak bark and soothing herbs together with a mortar and pestle. The herbs would ease the pain—the oak would fight the power that still burned his skin. I mixed more aloe with the baneroot brew and sprinkled the mixture on the wounds. Moving him was hard work, but I managed to bind his injuries with bandages soaked in aloe. I hoped this would be strong enough to still even Nian's considerable powers.

These preparations finished, I returned to my sewing to wait.

Always, waiting was the hardest. I stitched and watched. Nian passed from unconsciousness into sleep, but his sleep was not peaceful, for he fought his own magic. Pain burned into his mind, even as his body sought to heal itself. As his pain eased, I began to hope that he might survive.

The instant his eyes opened, I knelt at his side.

He breathed deeply and then glanced at me. "How long?"

"The sun is nearly set."

"Ah." The pain was less now, but his mind and body were strained.

I began changing his bandages. "You make a fairly easy patient once you're tranced. Where did you learn to do that?"

"The trance has proven helpful on several occasions. I seem to have a talent for injuring myself."

"Every magician I have ever known has had that talent—though usually it is not this severe." I thought of how Drenil's mind had resisted the trance the first time. He'd broken his thumb with the pestle while grinding herbs. He'd had to learn how to trance himself, my power not being strong enough to overcome his natural resistance.

"I believe that if one is going to make a mistake, one should do it in grand style," Nian smiled weakly.

"Style you have." As I sprinkled more powder onto the new salve, he winced.

"Lady Elainya, my life's power drains from me." His eyes caught mine and I understood his question.

I gently brushed his gray hair from his forehead. "You will not die, Nian, on my life—you will not die."

He pulled away from my touch, something that would have been a grand gesture if he had more strength. "That is not my question." He nodded to the herbs I held in my hand.

"It is your own power that fights you. It must be quieted for you to be healed. I don't know how long you will be powerless, but you will live."

It took no power to read the desire in his eyes. "I don't care whether you want to or not, you're going to live. You haven't given me a choice and I won't give you the choice either."

I watched him rage at the inevitability of my decision, and then he accepted it. "Elainya, you need to be wary." His eyes glanced around the room.

I caught his meaning and closed the door to the hallway.

"You have enemies here?"

"Is there anyone who does not?"

"No," I smiled, thinking of Jeiwan. "I will stay beside you until your power returns—or I will call Jauer if you doubt my friendship or my abilities."

He shook his head. "I trust you."

"It will not be an easy recovery."

He sighed and relaxed. "So my head is telling me. Very well, I trust you. I am glad you are here, Elainya." His eyes closed and he returned to the healer's trance. I sensed the effort draining the last of his reserves.

I could heal his wounds, but treating the wounds would not heal the patient.

As I wound the last of the new bandages around his left hand, the chamberlain entered the room, followed by the king. I stood and bowed carefully as the king inspected my rooms for the first time.

"Please, Lady, tend to your patient. Formality is impractical at the moment."

"Thank you, my lord," I nodded and knelt beside Nian to finish tightening the bandages.

"Do you need anything?"

I looked up at the king as I spoke. "More cloth for bandages—or someone to clean these. Miatra is tending to Lord Nian's chambers."

"I do not envy the girl the task," said the chamberlain.

My expression must have revealed my confusion.

"The explosion which injured Nian also burnt anything in his room to ash."

I shook my head. "He is a very powerful magician."

The king smiled. "I know. My father trusted Lord Nian with his life as I do. Now, I fear my request has been too much for him."

"He will recover, my lord, but it will take time."

"How long?"

"He will not be able to move for several days. After that, he may not be himself for many tendays."

The king frowned. "Did he tell you how he was injured?"

"Yes."

"The barbarians are attacking the East shores again. The raids are sporadic, but given your success at Summerstown, Sir Reif felt that perhaps our magician could find a way to succeed where his own warriors had failed."

"My king, I fear this battle must be fought without the help of a magician. The entire race of the Draska was not enough to stop the invasions. We won only one battle, and that in tandem. What did Reif think one magician could do?"

The king looked confused for an instant as he pondered what I'd said. At last, he shrugged. "Heal him, Lady Elainya."

"I will, my lord."

After the king left, I sat down at my sewing to watch over my patient.

Miatra awakened me sometime after the moon had set. I had fallen asleep sitting next to the window slit, my sewing still in my hand, my head against the stone wall.

"Leave me, Brenna, I must think," I mumbled.

"Elainya, it is Miatra."

I opened my eyes and squinted at her through the smoky orange haze the untended torches had made of my room. "I was asleep."

"Yes."

I glanced towards Nian. "Has he stirred?"

"I've only just come in."

"Thank you for waking me. You should get some sleep, child."

"Shouldn't you go to bed? I could watch over him for you."

"I will, soon. I should tend the magician for a while longer, though. You go on."

"Call me when you want me to stand watch." She sighed with exasperation and left.

Nian seemed so peaceful. I left my needlework and adjusted the furs which covered him. I would not heal him for the king, I would heal Nian for myself. Few people could understand my sad times—but Nian had once lost someone he loved—and I knew he understood. I needed his friendship. Besides, when Nian died, the Draska would die.

Despite his age, Nian was strong. I still had hopes of finding a wife for him, someone young enough to carry on the race. We'd have to forego the bonding ceremony so that she could outlive him, but that seemed a small price to pay. I'd watched Trillia when he was near and wondered if she might not find his status appealing despite his age. She did seem fond of him, and she was undoubtedly of Draska descent.

I knew eventually, I should also have a child, but I wasn't ready for that choice yet.

A loud knock at my door startled me from my musings.

I opened the door to find Drenil's spirit standing there looking sheepish. I motioned him inside quickly. "Quiet! Have you no respect? I thought ghosts were supposed to be quiet."

He grabbed me in his arms and turned me around as if I were a rag doll. "Elainya, I'm here! Don't chide me for being eager to see you. It has been so long!"

I laughed and held onto him—feeling his youth—his strength. At last, I looked into the eyes I saw in my heart day and night—the pale blue that glinted like the sun on the sea at sunset. Every move he made stirred with magic and power. I whispered, "Oh, spirit! Have some pity on me...you will drive me mad."

He ran a hand through his short brown hair and seemed thoughtful—then he grabbed me again. "I can't help it, my Elainya. I am bound to you. I long for these moments when we can be together...."

I felt hot tears burning my cheeks. "This you say to me! I must live alone here—would you have me kill myself and join you?" I reached towards the tapestries that hid my medicines.

He grabbed my hand with the strength that I remembered so well. "No! Elainya, my sweet, magical Elainya, no. Just live—and let me walk with you in your dreams."

"Am I dreaming now?"

"No, but you were thinking of me, so I came."

"Drenil, why did you use the door?"

"You were with a patient...I wanted to give you the chance to avoid me if you wanted to."

"That's ridiculous. I'm bound to you, you know that."

"I could release you. Would you love this one?" he gestured to Nian.

"I love only you." I touched his beardless face tenderly. "Never will I love another."

He sighed. "My sweet, what have I done to us? You must have a child, or the Draska will die with you."

"There were children who survived the plague. I want to find their children's children. Some of those have gifts."

"You have already found two of them."

"Jauer? You're sure?"

"Yes."

"Trillia?"

"Yes." He seemed thoughtful for a moment and then sighed again. "What have I done to us?"

"Was it poison we took?"

"Like your patient, our magic turned on us. It was not poison."

Drenil held me close for a long moment before drawing me towards the bed. His link with me was so strong, I could feel his touch. "I wish I could have given you a child," he sighed as we lay down together.

"So do I," I whispered. The rest was lost in a blur as we did our best to pretend that he was with me in body as well as in spirit.

Nian did not rouse from his uneasy slumber.

In the distance, I heard soft music. "I must go now—but I made this for you." He placed a delicate silver rose in my hand, the match of the one I'd been embroidering.

"My love..." I began, but he was gone.

I awoke with dawn streaming through the window, stinging my eyes. My back ached from sitting up all night and I was hungry. A sharp pain in my right hand focused my attention.

My sewing lay in a heap on the floor—dropped as my hand clutched a bright silver rose.

I stared at it in shock. So lovely—so delicate! Only one silversmith I knew could create such a piece—and he had died many years ago. I held it to my heart and cried.

"Lady Elainya?" It was not the first time that weak voice had called to me.

I turned to see Nian trying to rise.

"No, lie down. Forgive me—I dreamed..." I placed the rose on my desk and helped to ease him back onto his cot.

"Your sleep was troubled, Elainya."

"Yes."

"You spoke to a spirit."

"I am sorry I woke you." I touched his skin and smiled. "The burning is gone."

"You called for Drenil."

I felt a blush creep up my neck and turned away. "Yes. I saw him in my dreams. He will be in my heart until I die—and beyond."

"And you would not be free?"

"No."

He smiled weakly. "You will break many men's hearts."

I unwrapped his bandages.

There was a knock at the door. "Come in," I called.

Sir Reif entered and glared at the two of us.

"How is our wise man?" he asked, adding a sarcastic emphasis to the "wise" that I did not like.

"He is much better, but he cannot deal with visitors. What is it that you need?"

He smiled charmingly. "I have come to call on you, Elainya."

"I am with a patient."

"Surely, you have some time. Let your maid watch him."

"Sir Reif, I am very busy."

"Elainya, my darling, how can you treat me this way?"

My nerves could not abide him. "Leave," I said simply, but the word was an order, and he left.

My hands were not gentle at their work and Nian grasped them suddenly. As I felt his pain, I was ashamed. "Forgive me, Nian, but that man torments me so."

"I need no power to see that. Be careful, he is a dangerous man."

"I am a dangerous woman."

He released my hands. "This also I know."

"I'm sorry, Nian," I said with a sigh, and resumed my work with more gentleness. Someone had washed the bandages and put them in the aloe bath I had made. I sprinkled more of the powder on his wounds and then replaced the bandages.

"Could you eat?" I asked hopefully.

Nian made a face. "Gruel? If you're going to kill me, I wish you'd do it quickly."

I laughed. "I know something that will give you strength." I went to my hidden medicines and pulled forth a jug of herbed ale.

I poured a large cup of it and helped him to drink it—and then refilled it. The powerful relaxant eased him into a natural sleep.

So we continued for three days. I left his side only for matters of decency.

Terror lounged on my desk, watching Nian as if he expected my patient to attack me. At one point, Nian moaned in his sleep and the cat hissed.

"Shh. Stop that," I said shooing him back from my patient. "What's wrong with you?"

The cat glanced from Nian to me and whispered, *Ghost*, into my mind.

"You leave him alone," I said.

Terror hissed and flounced off to find somewhere else to sleep until the wizard recovered.

One day as I changed Nian's bandages, I felt a slight stirring in his power. I did not put any powder on his wounds.

He sat up when I finished, feeling much stronger. "How much longer, Elainya?"

"You could go for a walk today."

He smiled eagerly. "And when will my power return?"

"You have tired of my company so soon?"

"Not your company—but this room. How is my laboratory, by the way?"

"Miatra and Jauer tell me that it is almost restored. They have been hard at work replacing what could be replaced."

He seemed lost in thought for a moment. "I remember an explosion—and then everything turned to dust."

"That is how it was described to me."

"It was not bad at first," he said.

"No, the burns continued to grow after you came to me."

"Yes. I understand. So you drained my power with herbs. You didn't answer my question."

I looked deeply into my friend's eyes, and let the truth come through in my words. "Nian, I'm sorry. With my own magic, maybe I could restore yours. Without using magic, I don't know if you'll get much stronger than you are now."

His eyes closed and he whispered a curse against the Shadow Lord. "You should have let me burn, Elainya," he muttered.

"Why is life such a burden for you?" I asked.

He glared at me and I saw anger in his eyes. "A child like you could never understand. Never mind." He wrapped his emotions away deep inside himself and his eyes cleared. "You said we could go for a walk?"

It was the first of many walks we would take together.

Our walks soothed us both. The king's land was beautiful, and we rambled the forest throughout most of late fall and early winter. I used my need to watch over Nian as an excuse to avoid my meetings with Reflect Rendel. Sadly, while Nian's body recovered, his power stirred feebly and then died.

Jauer felt Nian's torment deeply. I saw much of the boy during this time and began to speak with him of Cyndace.

The two of them met on several occasions and we started the arrangements for their wedding the following spring. Cyndace was concerned with her lack of dowry, and I began searching for the best present for the young couple.

Each night, Drenil came to me in my dreams. His vitality seemed to grow, taunting me. His presence reminded me of what I could not have. A maddening ache formed in my heart that occasionally spilled over into my waking moments. Only Nian knew of my torment.

Drenil loved to talk about my matchmaking efforts. He chuckled over the troubles I was having getting all the arrangements set for Jauer's wedding. The potter wanted the entire village to attend, while Jauer and Cyndace favored a more private ceremony. The dreams became my only solace. Soon, they began to invade my waking hours as they had when I'd first risen from my years-long sleep. Sometimes they took the form of daydreams, other times they became even more powerful memory trances.

Secretly I hoped to slip into a trance and find myself back with Dren forever. I knew it could not be, but the trances felt more real than these cooling days.

During one of my walks with Nian, we were intercepted by Reflect Rendel. "Elainya, have you heard the news? The attacks have ceased. There have been no attacks anywhere along the coast since Nian's injury."

"I know." I had been trying to ignore that aspect of Nian's recovery.

"Be strong, Elainya." He turned to Nian and placed a hand on his shoulder in a gesture of comfort I'd never have thought possible, given the men's professions. "Your life is not over yet, my friend. The best is yet to be. Remember, the Shadow Lord is not the only source of power."

Nian grumbled his thanks for the man's concern.

With a smile, Reflect Rendel turned his attention back to me. "So, you have arranged another wedding for me. You're keeping me busy. When will I have the honor of assisting at your wedding, Elainya?"

I was horrified by his comment. "The only man I will ever love is dead, Reflect. You've heard me speak of him often enough."

Reflect Rendel merely smiled and turned towards the castle. As he did, he leaned towards me and whispered, "Ah...but some spirits are more dead than others, eh?"

I stared after him. Did he know of my waking dreams?

As soon as he was out of sight, Nian frowned. "I do believe the good reflect is losing his mind." With a shake of his head, he changed the subject. "So, did you have a pleasant visit with Drenil last night? You look as if you did not sleep well."

"Yes, and no. I can't take much more of this, Nian. The dreams are so very real. How do you explain the gifts he has given me?" My fingers brushed the clasp of my cloak.

"Perhaps Drenil had finished them before he died? Wedding presents? Hidden for years and now he's giving them to you?"

"I don't know. One of them was a match to a pattern I was sewing. How could he have known? Was he this real when you spoke with him?"

Nian looked thoughtfully around the forest. "Drenil's presence has always seemed very real to me. He is a powerful young man, or spirit, or whatever you want to call him. Why does this trouble you? His visits seem pleasant when you speak of them. Why can't you accept the situation?"

Angrily, I answered, "Don't you see? I need a real husband, not some spirit."

Nian was quiet for a moment. As we walked, he seemed to reach a decision. His words seemed offhand, and yet there was an intensity in him that alerted me that he had something of import that he wished to say. "Drenil spoke with me a few days ago and was quite pleasant. He asked for a favor."

"What kind of favor?"

"As Lord of Aurora, I have more property at my disposal than I know what to do with. He felt I should give one of the better huts to the potter's daughter, Cyndace. He said you could explain why."

I laughed with glee. "Of course! How perfect. Then Cyndace will have her dowry for the wedding. She and Jauer will have their own home. They belong in Aurora, the first of the new Draska."

Nian smiled at my reaction. He nodded in agreement. "Jauer does belong in Aurora. Perhaps someday, the city will be alive again."

"Would Lord Nian also be so good as to grant me a home there?" I mocked.

"Of course, provided you help me re-populate it with Draska."

I paused. His gaze was on the forest. Surely he hadn't meant what that sounded like. There were other descendants of our people, others like Jauer. Maybe that was what he meant.

"I'm not sure how to find the children."

"You could marry again. I've noticed that Sir Reif is interested in you. He wouldn't expect you to love him."

I gasped and gripped his arm, forcing him to meet my eyes and see the horror that suggestion gave me. "I have a husband already! Besides, can you see Reif living happily in Aurora?"

"No, but that's not my point. Apparently, even the good reflect does not have a problem with your marrying again. You could be free of the past." His lips trembled as if he were unsure of what expression to allow on his face.

Tears coursed down my cheeks. "I don't want to be free! Don't you understand? I want to be Drenil's wife in more than my dreams."

Nian held me in his arms and let me cry out the frustrations I felt. "You are his wife, little one, a truer wife than any man could wish for, but he is dead. A widow is allowed to marry again. For the sake of our people, you need to have children."

"There are no decent fathers available."

He whispered, "I also would not expect you to love me."

I pushed him away in shock. "I will never marry again!" I screamed. I walked back to the castle, alone with my anger.

Lady Eavyn was waiting for me when I returned. Her long red curls hung loose as she paced my room.

"Lady Elainya, you look terrible!" she said.

"Thank you," I snapped as I sat down at my desk.

She started at my tone and paused.

"I'm well enough to talk—come sit with me." I motioned her to a chair.

"I wanted to thank you. Captain Bertrand has been made a lord, and we are to be wed on the morrow."

How sudden. How rash. How like Eavyn. "What a lovely day for you." I tried to sound encouraging and failed. Fortunately, the bride was too caught up in wonder to notice.

"Were you this nervous before your wedding?"

I frowned. "I'm rather tired right now, child. I would like to forget my wedding, but I can't. You see, my husband died on our wedding night."

"Oh."

I forced a weak smile in response to her nervous green eyes. "Go on, rest. You'll have a lovely wedding. I will drink to your health."

She pouted, but she went.

As she left, I could feel the strain that had grown within me for days threatening to devour me whole. I glanced out the window slit to see the late afternoon sun slipping behind the trees. Perhaps a solitary walk would heal me.

As long as I could keep from blasting any trees.

Out of habit, I picked up my gathering basket. My aloe supply was severely depleted.

The meadow was cool as it drifted towards midwinter sleep. The world was at peace with itself. No ghosts stood here, and even as I thought this—I regretted it.

If only Drenil and I could wander the woods as we had when we were younger.

"Every time you are tired, I find you here," he would laugh.

The remembered laughter brought a smile to my face. Like an echo of the past, I followed the wisp of memory into my garden.

"It is so beautiful—I love this place." I whispered to the spirit.

"And you are even more beautiful when you are here." Ah, I could hear his voice, almost feel his breath. I turned, and the years fell away. He was there.

It was a dream, but more. It took so little to enter the memory trance, I felt it slip over me and did not resist.

"Oh—I am far from beautiful now. Everyone keeps telling me how terrible I look."

"What? You stand there with the sun gleaming on your hair, mischief in your eyes, and magic all around you, and you say you are not beautiful?" He forced me to meet his eyes. "You are beautiful, my sweet, magical Elainya. Never forget that." The pull of Drenil's presence was too great to resist.

I wanted this to be real. I let it be real, let it consume me.

"Oh, stop. I need to get this planting done." I gestured toward the oak grove.

Dren smiled. "I'll help you. You're planting more aloe?"

"Someday I may need it—especially if there is a war."

"True, I suppose."

"I want to plant it by these oak trees so it will grow strong and powerful."

"Why would you need that much power in aloe?"

"In case I ever need to heal a magician."

He had laughed. "Don't worry about me, Elainya."

The aloe at the foot of the tree was huge. These plants had lived many years, growing as I'd slept. The trance wavered. I forced myself to return to the memory.

I spread fresh oak leaves in my basket and drew my small dagger to cut through the thick skin of the plant. I remembered the day he'd given me that dagger.

"Why would I need a new knife?" I had asked.

"I've made a stronger one for you—for your gathering. It is very sharp."

"Thank you—but you spend too much of your time making me these lovely things!"

The gold inlay work on the dagger was delicate and he had set a blue jewel in the hilt. As I attached the sheath to my belt and drew the dagger, I noticed a gentle glow and looked at Drenil curiously. "Magic?"

He smiled. "It will stay sharp—may it never fail you, Elainya."

I slashed through the thick aloe easily and placed the slimy leaves in my basket. Still, the dagger glowed with the warmth of his spell.

As I wiped it clean with a leaf, I sighed.

"You seem so sad, my love."

"I was trying to imagine how I should ever live without you beside me."

He laughed. "We shall always be together."

"I've never been without you. We've played together, cried together, grown together—could it ever be possible for one of us to live alone?"

"No, my love, but there will be no need."

"I have seen the way the king looks at me."

"You are not of his class."

"I know that look, Drenil. He may not approve of our match."

"Oh, Elainya," he sighed and held me close to calm my fears. "You and I will always be together. It is our choice. We choose to be together."

"Lady Elainya?" The voice threatened to penetrate my trance. I clutched Dren tightly.

His embrace was more than I could bear. "Would you have me join you in death?"

"Elainya, what are you talking about?"

"Will this dagger you have given me serve in my time of deepest need? You said that it was not a weapon, but it is, Drenil. At heart, it will always be a weapon, just like this magic!" I held the small dagger and stared into the deep blue jewel. Death would be quicker and less painful than life. Death was peaceful...I knew him well.

Strong hands held my wrists and removed the dagger from my hands. "Elainya!"

I looked deeply into sad eyes and cried out. "Drenil, I can't—I can't go on this way!"

"Oh, Elainya," he sighed and held me close to him.

When the memory trance broke, the sun was below the horizon and the sky was streaked with color.

I watched the clouds grow thicker and sighed. "It is so peaceful here."

"Yes, it is," Nian said. His voice was soft, tentative. Gentle.

Eighty years passed in an instant and I sat up. "Nian?"

He looked deeply into my eyes and nodded. "It is over, then."

"Memory trance?" I remembered then. I'd been sad, and the memory had felt so close. I'd allowed myself to drift off into a trance so that I could be close to Dren for just a moment.

Nian's eyes were sad. "It seems the past is more pleasing to you than the present." He handed me my dagger. "Perhaps you do begin to understand me after all, Elainya." I could not know what had caused Nian's pain, but I did see the depths of torment that were possible on this side of death. "I did not mean to upset you with my offer. I was out of line. Please forgive me."

"I need time to think about that offer before I give you an answer. The stress...I reacted too quickly."

"Take all the time you need."

I changed the subject, reaching to forget what had happened. "I need to travel to tend to a special patient, and I need to leave before the harsh storms begin. I could use pleasant company on the journey."

"You have an evil gleam in your eye."

"I'll tell you as soon as I can, but for now it is a secret. Perhaps the change of scenery will help you."

The evening after Lady Eavyn's marriage, we left for West Ridge. Terror was only too happy to stay with Miatra.

I was eager to be on my way, feeling the child's due date nearing. We led our horses out of the stable, and I found myself at ease with Nian's company.

"I think we can get several hours' journey behind us before sunset," Nian said.

"If you're sure you're strong enough to stay in the saddle," I teased.

"Such lack of faith...." He trailed off as a shadow loomed over us.

"Where are you off to, Elainya?"

I looked up sharply into Reif's face. He seemed a bit unsteady on his horse. "I'm off to treat a patient."

"You should not travel without a guardian. Meaning no disrespect, Lord Nian, but you are hardly strong enough to protect the lady from harm."

Nian looked steadily into Reif's eyes. "She has little need of protection. I merely give her company on her journey."

"Company is it?" Reif swayed and I could see he'd had too much ale. "For that she needs a man who's still young enough to...er...entertain her."

I smiled up at Reif. "When you find someone suitable, please send him to me." Feigning oblivion, I turned back to Nian and suppressed a giggle as Reif rode away. "So, you think I am in no danger?"

"Oh, you are in danger enough, but the Shadow Lord will protect you."

"Will he, indeed?" I wondered. If Rendel was right, my refusal to use magic could endanger that protection.

We rode westward quickly, forcing Singe and Ember into a breakneck pace.

Nian fumed at the necessity of fastening a sword to Singe's saddle. Try as he might, he had not regained the strength for even simple spells. The spirit sword was far beyond his ability.

As we paused to water the horses, Nian pulled his cloak around himself and glared at me curiously. "So, why are we riding into the jaws of winter with such urgency?"

I smiled. "I promised to deliver Queen Laurel's baby personally."

"And the master allowed this?"

"What, for me to deliver the baby?"

"You know what I mean. You had a hand in the conception of the child or you wouldn't know when to expect its arrival. I thought the Shadow Lord was pleased with Jeiwan's designation as heir."

"Apparently he changed his mind." The thought hadn't occurred to me, and now I wished it hadn't.

"Perhaps he is humoring you."

"The child will be heir to the kingdom."

Nian stood and shook the first flakes of snow from his hair. "We'd best not keep the young king waiting, then." He retrieved the horses and adjusted Singe's saddle.

I bent over to pick up my cloak and found myself jerked backward harshly, a dagger dangerously close to my throat. "I'll be taking those horses," a rough voice said from behind me.

Nian turned slowly, and I watched his hand move toward where he would usually draw his spirit sword and stop. Anger flared in his eyes, but his voice was calm. "I don't think you want to make the lady angry."

"I'm not planning on making her angry, but I'll make her dead if you don't step away from the horses."

I calmed my breathing and gathered my power to force the knife away from my throat. "Hey, what're you doing?" I'd learned control from my dealings with Jeiwan, and I forced myself to gently move the man backward. He stumbled over a log and released his hold on me. As I turned, he saw whom he'd attacked, and paled.

"You're that witch everyone's talking about. You and the wizard. Aw, I wouldn't harm you two. Don't kill me, please?"

Nian glared at him, and the man scurried into the forest. "Brigands get thicker in the woods every year," he muttered, but I could see the pain in his eyes. He'd been powerless to protect me, and he didn't like the feeling.

He helped me mount Ember and leapt onto Singe's back. We rode through the night in silence. The next day, we arrived at West Ridge, eagerly awaited.

Chapter 16

Delivery

Elainya

The final ride into West Ridge was easy as the terrain drained the run-off of the early winter snows into the western sea. The queen's cousin and her husband kept a neat castle with modest, defensible barns and strong walls. I could see why Laurel had thought of this place when she sought a safe haven for her pregnancy. The walls were well guarded, yet no one challenged us as we approached the gate. It was opened on well-oiled hinges by a stable boy who bowed and reached up to assist me in dismounting.

Another lad stood by, ready to take Singe's reins from Nian. "We will see to your horses, Lord Nian." His tone was quietly confident and, while respectful, it lacked the fear I had so often noted in people dealing with the court's wise man.

"Thank you. And will you see to our packs as well?" Nian asked.

"I will see that they are taken to your rooms." He turned to me. "You have been expected, Lady Elainya." With a graceful motion, he gestured toward a side door into the court where Trillia's gray-clad form blended into the stone. She stepped away from the wall and came to meet us in the empty courtyard as the boys left with our horses. The girl glanced at Nian and then turned to me. "I've cared for my aunt just as you asked, Lady Elainya. She is strong, with no complications."

I let my hand rest on her shoulder and looked into the pale gray eyes. "And you? How are you?"

"I am well." She looked up, her confident face as close to a smile as ever passed her lips.

I gestured around the empty yard. "Quiet here. Were we expected by anyone else?"

"The queen has asked for you every day." She glanced at Nian. "We are honored to have you here as well, my lord."

I noticed the respect in her eyes.

His reply was lost as the lady of the house emerged from a large door across the yard in a bustle of skirts and shawls. The woman resembled an older version of Eavyn as she burst into the yard. "Trillia." She stopped to catch her breath. "Thank you for greeting my guests! Sorry for my delay, I was in the kitchen discussing the preparations for dinner! I find myself at wits end trying to get my cousin to eat properly."

Trillia took in a slight breath and seemed to exude calm. I patted her arm to reassure her that I would not be misled by this flurry of worry. Laurel could not have a more devoted caregiver than Trillia.

I nodded to our hostess. "You must be Lady Magreta. Thank you for sheltering our good queen in this time." Her dress was of a dark forest green velvet without so much as a speck of dust to mar the surface. Her hair was perfectly coiffed, the rich red adorned with a smattering of green stones that matched the gown. Her brow was clean, unmarred by even a hint of perspiration. While I sensed no harm from her, I was equally certain she had not been near a kitchen fire this day. "I would like to see the queen and let her know I have come."

She smiled brightly and looped her arm through Nian's, startling him into accompanying her to the main entrance of the castle. I smiled brightly and twiddled my fingers at him in farewell as she led him away, babbling about the honor of having a person of his reputation in her home. "Are you hungry, Lord Nian? My husband is always hungry, and we've a fine feast prepared."

Trillia blew her breath out. "She's harmless, you know, but she hates Draska. She's been at the queen to send a messenger to say you needn't come."

"Has she really? And I take it your aunt did not see fit to mention that you are my apprentice?"

Trillia's mouth twitched, but the smile remained hidden in her eyes. "She seems to have forgotten to mention that detail. Don't worry about my aunt's health, my lady. She is fine. I've made sure she ate exactly as you instructed." She led me into the family wing of the castle and up a set of stairs to a room set in one west-facing wall. The sound of the ocean created a soothing ambiance, excellent for the mother-to-be.

The queen stood near a window-slit that overlooked the ocean. She'd tied back the thick tapestry and seemed to be drinking in the sea air. As she turned, her face lit up and she waddled across the room, impeded by the full-term size of her belly. "I knew you'd come!" The arms that embraced me were stronger than I remembered. She had blossomed in this peaceful retreat. "You've come just in time!" She ran a hand lovingly over her stomach. "He has been restless all day."

The room was brightly lit and tended by ladies I'd never met. One in particular seemed venerable, with long white hair held in a tightly braided bun. The queen called her over to meet me. "Lady Elainya, this is Elen. She was my own nursemaid and has come to help with the babe."

"It is a pleasure to meet you, Elen."

The woman glared at me with open hatred. Her ancient eyes squinted. "I know you," her voice rasped. Her lips moved silently over nearly toothless gums. "Witch! What evil has brought you back from the grave? You'll not touch the child!"

I froze, unsure how to respond.

Laurel intervened. "Elen! This woman is my trusted friend. You will not speak to her in that manner."

The woman licked her lips and moved closer to me. She peered up into my face, and reached one hand up to touch my cheek. Was it possible she might indeed be old enough to remember me? "As you wish, my lady." Her words whistled through missing teeth, but her sharp eyes met mine. "Elainya. I was only a girl when I spread flowers outside your grave." She left the room still muttering.

Laurel was shocked. "I apologize, Lady Elainya, she's never behaved like that before. It must be her age, but I assure you, she will not harm the child." Her brow furrowed. "Trillia, have you seen any sign of age addling Elen's wits?"

"No. Although she does serve Magreta and you know there are no friends of the Draska here."

"Other than ourselves, you mean," Laurel corrected.

I intervened to calm their fears. "I've no doubt the child will be safe with her. He will need a fiery protector, and she seems perfect." Elen? There had been a girl at court, a child of six that I'd often held on my knee. She'd played with my jewelry and I'd braided her hair. Could it be? She'd been the daughter of some minor noble. I'd found her charming and bright. What had life done to her?

I shook off the reverie and began a cursory check of the preparations that had been made for the delivery. The clothing for the baby lay spread on a table. Each piece had been lovingly embroidered, sewn from the finest flannels and soft woven cloth. This child would be spoiled before he was an hour old.

Clean linens lay folded in readiness for the unavoidable mess of childbirth. No doubt the kitchen was full of water already warmed for his first bath.

Queen Laurel laughed as I reviewed the preparations. "I'm past ready to have him. It has been an easy pregnancy, but..." she gestured to her rather large stomach, "he is a little much to carry. You are certain the child is a boy?"

"Yes, and you're not to worry for either of you. I'm sorry to be so late in coming. I'd hoped to be here several tendays ago, but I had an unexpected patient."

"I've had news sent to me from the castle when my messengers could slip out on other rounds. How is Lord Nian?"

"He came with me. In some ways he is recovered, in others it is hard to say."

She lowered her voice to a whisper. "Is it true he has lost his magic?"

So, the news had traveled this far. "Misplaced, perhaps, but he will find it again in time, I'm sure." Could there be a safe place left for him anywhere in the kingdom? If those who envied his position knew he was weak, they might take the opportunity of this journey to be rid of the king's Draska.

Laurel nodded. "He has been a faithful servant to my husband, despite my brother's dislike. I hope he will serve my son as well."

"Yes, I'm certain he will." I helped her to sit on the edge of her raised bed, and then lifted her legs so the slightly swollen feet would ache less. "You should rest. I suspect the babe will come tomorrow. Do you need anything to help you sleep?"

"Only your assurance that all will be well."

"I promise you, he will be perfect. You will ride with me in early Spring to take him to his father." I did not mention the source of my certainty, as it seemed not to have occurred to her.

Trillia tucked the covers around her aunt. "I'll make sure a light supper is sent up for you. Rest a bit now, and then I'll read to you."

"You are too good to me, niece."

"It is you who have been good to me. I will see that Lady Elainya is taken care of before I return."

We left the room together, shutting the door easily. I noted the guard stationed unobtrusively down the hall. "Good to see that precautions are being taken."

"My father would be most displeased to learn of the queen's condition," she allowed a tiny smile to pass her lips. "It will be a joy to see Jeiwan displaced."

I felt my eyebrows lifting. "So you do smile when there is something worth smiling about."

"I don't know how you managed this, Elainya, but I am grateful. When I think of Jeiwan as king..." she shivered. "No, nothing could be worse than that."

"The Shadow Lord is capable of good. It is all in how the power is used."

She nodded and led me to the dining hall where we joined Nian at a table overflowing with an abundance of food. I laughed. "How much did the good lady think you could eat?"

He frowned. "I have no idea. I feel like I'm being stuffed for the slaughter. That woman is a contradiction. I don't need my power to sense that she hates Draska and yet she drips good will from every honeyed phrase."

Trillia disappeared on other errands as I sat next to Nian and picked up a small baked root dripping with butter. "Her cook certainly knows the way around a kitchen."

"Better than our dear Lady Magreta. I'd wager she's never been inside one," he said.

"No, I don't think so either."

"So, why the lie when we arrived?"

"I'm not sure. Maybe she wanted to hide what she'd been doing? Maybe she was uncomfortable, lying to be polite?"

"You realize that makes no sense." He sliced a rare piece off the roast in front of him and placed it on a plate.

The plate was snatched out of his hand even as he handed it to me. I turned to look into the laughing eyes of Reflect Rendel. "Oh, it makes more sense than you think, my dark friend." He plopped the plate down across the table from me and sat down heavily. "You see, our hostess was in conference with me, begging me to intervene and convince the queen that she needed a different midwife."

My mind tried to adjust to his presence, and refused. I'd seen him last at Eavyn's wedding. He must have ridden fast to beat us here.

"Had you two told me you were coming, we could have traveled together."

I swallowed the last of the root, and reached for another plate. "Wouldn't that have damaged your reputation? Being seen traveling with us?"

He laughed. "They're sheltered here in West Ridge. Do them good to relax their fears a bit. You are a brilliant healer. I doubt your master will be well served by your deeds over the next few days, but that is your affair, not mine."

"Actually," I glanced at Nian and he shrugged for me to continue. "My master does not object."

There was silence at the table. Reflect Rendel put his knife down and looked into my eyes. "Tell me you had nothing to do with this child's conception, Elainya." His gaze was intense.

"I have never lied to you, Reflect."

The light faded from his eyes as he stood. "What have you done?"

Nian frowned. "There's no need to make a scene, Reflect. Sit down."

He shook his head in shock. "No. I'm sorry, but I must study this out. I'd been so happy, now I find that my enemy has had a hand in this most blessed event. Could it be there was hope for Jeiwan after all?" He left his barely touched plate and dashed out of the room.

With a shrug, Nian retrieved the abandoned food. "Wasteful. Simply wasteful." He took a bite of the meat. "The man is insane, Elainya."

I looked after the reflect's retreating form and wondered.

Elen sat in a corner of the hall, tending a weak fire. Evening had come upon the castle and all had gone to sleep, leaving us alone.

"You are the daughter of Jethan and Marista, aren't you?" I asked.

"Yes."

"I used to braid your hair when you were a little girl." I touched the gray bun tenderly. "How have you come to hate me so much?"

The ancient face looked into my eyes and tears appeared. "You killed yourself."

"No, Elen, I simply went away. Perhaps it was selfish of me, but I wanted a life with Drenil. I wanted happiness."

"I used to feed your cat." She stared into the fire for a while.

When she continued, her voice was hoarse. "The king died the next morning. Had you waited, you would have had your freedom. As it was, you were gone before the plagues came that killed the Draska. The kingdom was plunged into turmoil. The new king was weak. My father died in the early battles, my mother followed him shortly out of sorrow. I became an orphan."

"You cannot blame me for that."

"I don't. But I've lived for many years while you slept in your daydream of love. I've seen the world die around me, seen the Shadow Lord and his minions destroy the Draska. I watched

Aurora fall into ruins. I'm an old woman, but a wise one now. Nian serves the Shadow Lord and I hate him, as I hate you. Keep your hands off the child, Elainya, or I will tell them all who you are."

"They'll think it merely the ravings of an old woman. It'll do you no good."

"All that you touch has the stench of your master upon it. Leave the babe alone."

I started to point out that without me there would be no child, but thought better of it, remembering the reflect's reaction.

"Very well. Stand beside me as I assist with the delivery. Your hands will draw him from the womb. You will cut the cord and bathe him. I will tend only to the queen."

Elen nodded her acceptance of the arrangement. Satisfied, she led me to my room for the evening. I noticed that she made the warding symbol of Light as she turned away. For the first time in many months, I felt unclean.

Nian

The days without his powers blurred together. At first, he'd still been able to project himself into Elainya's dreams, but now even those stolen moments were gone. He tried to find joy in the coming of the new baby, but everything melted into meaninglessness. He was a useless old man, relegated to sitting by the fire and watching the world go by.

He'd been helpless to save Elainya when the brigands attacked. Thankfully she was now strong enough to care for herself, provided she didn't let the Reflect talk her into doing anything else stupid.

He wondered how long the master would make him suffer in weakness before he was allowed to die.

***

Elainya

As predicted, the queen's pains began the day after our arrival. It was a slow labor, but easier than some I'd witnessed, in part due to the slowness. The babe came in the evening. Trillia wiped her aunt's forehead with a cool cloth while I helped her push. As agreed, I did not touch the infant, leaving Elen to pull the screaming creature forth into the world. She bundled him away quickly for his bath and a visit with the reflect. Queen Laurel was exhausted. I helped her maids clean up the mess and brew the mother's tea from the placenta. I added enough herbs that she drank without protest. "My baby?"

"The prince is visiting the reflect and will be back momentarily."

"He is well?"

"Perfect, my lady. Does he have a name?"

"I want his father to name him."

"And he didn't pick a name yet?"

"No. He was afraid to curse the birth by too much bravado. I think he may choose to name him for Cydril, the last strong king our realm has had."

"Cydril?"

"Yes. He was a friend to the Draska, in a day when your people were still plentiful. Some people say his death was related to the destruction of the Draska."

"True, but we should discuss that another time, when you are not so tired."

She smiled at me warmly. "My cousin is wrong about your people, Elainya. I'm glad you were here for me."

I patted her hand gently and tucked the warm covers around her. As I left, Elen returned with the blinking babe, screaming for his first meal. She held him carefully away from me, as if expecting me to reach across and do him harm.

I held my hands up in a gesture of innocence. "You have nothing to fear from me, Elen." In my heart, I wondered if I had not already done harm to the child.

Cydril. May he be unlike his namesake in every way.

As I fell into my bed, I heard the shadows laughing.

At breakfast the next morning, I found myself seated next to Reflect Rendel. We sat aside from the regular castle company, most of whom kept looking at the good reflect in awe, presumably for sitting so close to me.

"You've kept your word to me," he began.

"I'm still having difficulty believing that the attacks stopped because of it, however."

"I know. Ultimately, that makes all the difference...your belief, I mean. Nian must be free to choose what he believes as well."

"What does it matter? He's powerless. I've tried to pretend his power will return on its own, but I doubt it."

"Which is why you must heal him."

The reflect's eyes met mine for a long moment before he looked away.

I was stunned. "You asked me not to heal him. You made me swear I would not. You said he would die if I did."

"At that time, he would have. Now it is time to heal him. He has a choice to make, several in fact, and he'll need his freedom to make them."

"And if the attacks resume? By your theory, more people will die."

The reflect met my gaze with one of sadness. He said nothing before returning his gaze to his food.

I cracked the shell on my boiled egg and began peeling it thoughtfully. "Has your master mentioned to you how dangerous that procedure will be?"

"He has only said that you will succeed."

"Well, that's some comfort, I suppose. I just hope my master agrees."

He chuckled. "Nian is no use to him as he is."

I thought for a long moment, staring at the fragile shell as I slipped it off the creamy white egg. Nian's power was hidden inside him. How deep would I have to go? I placed the egg carefully on Reflect Rendel's plate and stood. "I've preparations to make. Thank you."

My first thought was to ensure the well-being of the queen and the baby. The queen was recovering quickly, so I asked to speak with Elen about the child.

"He is well, thank you." Her voice was curt.

She'd met me in the anteroom to the queen's chamber. We were alone. Brilliantly colored tapestries adorned the walls. I walked to one that showed a tranquil meadow full of dew-gathering maidens. "I would ask a favor of you, Elen."

"Of me?"

I smiled wryly. "I need help with some very special arrangements. All that is to be said is that I am working with a patient. You may have noticed that Lord Nian is not well."

Her eyes clouded. "It makes no difference to me."

"But you will keep your word, and if keeping your word means that I may return to the land of the dead, all the better, don't you think?"

"I will do whatever you ask," she answered too quickly.

"I thought you might," I said, wincing at the disgust in her tone. "I'll require an inner room with no windows, several days' worth of food and water, a jug of ale, and some herbs from your stores. The door will need to be strongly shut and guarded. No one may enter or leave the room for three days. If we do not emerge in that time, you may enter and bury us both. Can you arrange that?"

"I've buried you once already. Be wary—I may do it more efficiently the second time." There was a faint mirth to soften the harshness of her words.

"I could ask for no better promise."

"You would risk yourself to heal Lord Nian?"

"Yes. How long will it take you to gather what I need?"

"Which herbs will you require?"

I pulled the list from my pouch and read the words to her before placing it in her withered hands.

"A few days, Lady, to gather and arrange all that you require."

"Good, the queen will be strong enough to do without me by then. I will place her in your care at that time."

Elen bowed slightly and went into the queen's inner chamber. I looked at the gaily clad ladies in the tapestry and wondered if I should ever feel so free again.

On Midweek afternoon, Elen came to me. "All is as you have requested, Lady." She led me to the chamber and I inspected the herbs for potency. "Have you some young men to guard the door?"

"They will come when I send for them."

"Very good. I will return shortly."

My deep blue gown seemed to hinder my footsteps as I searched the castle for Nian. He'd been more distant of late, but with winter winds howling outside the castle he could not hide for long. I found him near the fire in the great room, watching the servants go about the evening meal preparation. I stood over him for a moment unacknowledged. His pain had caused a deep depression that worried me more than his powerlessness.

"Nian, I have kept my bargain with the reflect."

"True."

"Do you think the attacks were caused by our use of magic?" He shook his head. "How could they be?"

"Reflect Rendel now feels that it is time for us to choose whether we will continue to use our magic and cause further harm, or whether we will forswear the…evil of our ways."

His chuckle was without mirth. "I suppose I will choose to live without magic then, as he has left me with no choice."

"He's said that the choice must be freely made and has given me leave of my promise so that I may attempt to heal you."

His eyes snapped up, meeting mine with a fierce hunger. "When?"

"Now, if you will come with me."

He followed me eagerly to the tiny room and I motioned for him to sit on the cot. I worked on the floor beside the cot so he could see what I did. I turned the aloe to a fine juice to which I added many herbs and then diluted it with the ale.

Nian looked troubled as I finished the medicine.

"I think the worst part of this is still to come—am I right?"

"This will either restore your power or kill you," I said.

Elen entered then. "The men are come as you requested, Lady."

"Thank you, Elen. Remember—no one is to enter this room for three days. After sunset on Kuladay, they may enter."

"It will be as you have requested." She bowed and closed the door. I drew the bolt across it and found myself leaning against that solidity for just a moment.

Nian looked at me closely. "You are afraid."

"I've had more nightmares. I may not be strong enough for this, but I'm the only healer around."

"I wouldn't trust anyone else."

"Nian, you should consider this: you are healthy now. If we leave it at this... a person can live without magic."

His eyes grew angry. "No, I understand what you are saying, but no. If you can, restore me or kill me. If I die—I do not care. I am already dead."

I looked away. "I had to ask."

"I know."

He watched as I filled two silver goblets with the potion. "You will also be drinking the potion? You did not tell me you would be in danger."

"It is decided." I drained my cup in one gulp. "There is more for me in death than in life, but I will not leave you like this—so either way, we go on. Drink."

I handed him the cup and he drank.

The power within me grew as the herbs flowed through my blood.

Nian lay on the cot Elen had provided as the potion took effect. He was still weak, and the herbs had a draining effect on his resistance. I knelt next to him and touched his forehead, placing him into the deepest level of healing trance. Beyond thought, beyond feeling, his body drank the power that overflowed from me. His own power was there, beneath the level of conscious control, dormant. Gently, I let the overflow replenish his strength, but it was not enough. Slowly, my own body sank deeper into a healer's trance. I could not break free without killing Nian, so I gave in to it, joining him in the trance. Then his power awakened and grasped at the source of strength, drinking deeply from my failing reserves. His power was so much stronger than my own that I could not pull away. I felt myself overcome by his strength and I rejoiced that I might yet escape the Shadow Lord in death.

The demon wouldn't let us die like this, would he? Surely he'd intervene at the last possible moment and save us.

Nian held his mind far from me, and yet there was a tenderness which stopped him from draining the last of my energy. A fleeting scent, a taste of emotion crept through the walls of his mind, and I was startled by the depth of his love for me, like to honey, sweet but with the power to entrap. There was no time for love. The healing required my complete concentration.

Sometime in the second night, the torches burned out. The room filled with a furious, fierce darkness.

Chapter 17

The Trap is Sprung

Elainya

I awoke to darkness. I was on my knees, my head on Nian's arm. He lay on the cot, sleeping. I could feel the health in him, both in body and soul.

There was not enough energy left in me to move. Instead, I listened to the gentle sound of his breathing.

Nian stirred. His hand stroked my hair gently. "Elainya?"

"Yes?"

"Are we alive?"

"Yes."

"Is it over?"

"Yes."

He tried to get up and fell back onto the cot. "Are you sure?"

"Yes." I stretched lazily. "Just move slowly—and don't try to use any power for a while. I think we've both strained ourselves."

"Should you open the door?"

I laughed. "If I could move, I would, but I can't, so I won't."

We laughed until the guards broke in the door.

They took one look at us and called for Elen.

She entered the room quickly and helped me regain my unsteady footing. "You seem to have survived," she said, a sardonic smile twisting her thin lips.

"Maybe," I whispered.

With only a chuckle, she gently led me to my own chambers and tucked me into bed, where I fell into a deep sleep, guarded by Trillia.

When I opened my eyes, the queen herself put a bowl of gruel in my hand.

I sat up and put the bowl beside me on the bed. "My lady—you look so worried!"

"Elen did not tell me what you had done until a day had passed. She said you'd made her swear to guard your privacy. When you didn't come to the door, I thought you were dead."

"I made a mistake—Nian's condition was worse than I thought. I had only just come out of a healer's trance at the appointed time."

"You could have opened the door."

I thought to smile, but found my muscles would not accomodate me. "The hard part would have been finding the door."

She looked at me in confusion.

"Never mind. I will be fine. How is Nian?"

"He seemed quite well. He was looking for you earlier."

I laughed. "It is rare that the patient feels better than the healer... but sometimes it works that way. What else has been happening?"

"You have slept for days. We received word that the attacks have resumed on the Eastern Coast. Several villages have been destroyed. The king has sent an escort to bring me home. He worries with me being so close to the shore, even though they've never attacked the West before."

"He may have a point. When do we leave?"

"Lord Nian insists upon leaving today. We are to follow with the escort on the morrow. There is a break in the storms."

"You said Nian is preparing to leave?"

"Yes, if he hasn't left already."

"By your leave, my lady, I must speak with him." I leapt out of bed on shaky legs and pulled a gown loosely over my shift. I did not bother with the laces but raced from the room. My recent contact with Nian had left a faint sense of his presence in my mind like a tiny thread between us. I knew I would find him in the stables.

"Where are you going?" I demanded as I entered. He attached the last of his gear to Singe's saddle.

Confusion and frustration fought for control of his eyes. Confusion won. "Elainya, the attacks on the coast resumed three days ago, north of Summer's Castle. It may be just a coincidence, but I have to know. I will get Jauer and we will move ahead of the troops. If I can find a way, I will stop the fighting."

"The reflect was right."

"Maybe. I must see for myself."

"Nian, has it all been a trap? Maybe the Shadow Lord has been putting us in a position to use our magic? What if...could he have planned this so many years ago?"

"I'm not sure time means anything to him, Elainya. Maybe time itself is irrelevant."

"I should come with you. If the reflect is right, we're the only reason they can attack the kingdom. If we were gone, they'd be gone."

"According to Reflect Rendel, peace would reign if we simply ceased to use magic. Come with the queen and see her safely home. I'll be back as quickly as I can." Nian climbed onto Singe's back.

Our eyes met and I was reminded of the love he hid for me.

Nian glanced away.

"Be careful," I said.

"I'll try not to get myself killed." He spoke softly to Singe and the horse threw itself into a gallop.

I wandered unhindered back to my room to find one of the queen's ladies packing my things. I removed my outer dress, ate a few bites of the now-solid gruel, and fell into a dreamless sleep.

The trip to the castle was uneventful, if cold. I wrapped my cloak around me tightly and checked often to make sure the queen and the baby were warm. Elen and Trillia traveled with us, so I need not have worried.

The trip was a blur. I'd barely entered the courtyard when Miatra met me. She helped me from Ember's back and supported me into my rooms. I fell into bed where I slept fitfully, dreaming of the trip and Reflect Rendel's accusatory glare boring into my back.

Terror lay on my feet, daring anyone to disturb my rest.

The next morning found my head clearer and my strength somewhat restored. Miatra greeted me.

"Sir Reif has been worried about your absence."

"No doubt. Miatra—pick a gown for me to wear, please."

I combed and braided my hair while she rummaged through my clothes, at last returning with a soft gray gown and a blue and gold woven belt. I put them on almost without thinking and walked the short distance to Nian's chamber.

His door was open, but his things were in disarray. He had come and gone quickly.

I turned to see the chamberlain coming towards me. "Lady Elainya, the king requests your presence."

Now what had I done?

I followed him to the throne room and he announced me.

The king was alone, save for a few guards. "Lady Elainya, you do not look well."

"I am recovering."

"I do not pretend to understand your magic, but you have restored Lord Nian to health and I thank you."

"I have done nothing beyond what I promised."

"That is true." He paused. "I have a proposition to present to you."

"Yes, my king?"

"You have no father."

"No."

"You have no guardian."

"I do not need one, my lord." I did not bother to point out that I was a century beyond the age where I should need a guardian.

"In such a case, when the lady in question is also the match-maker, a suitor finds himself in an unusual position."

"As you say, my king."

"Lady Elainya, a suitor has asked my permission to marry you."

I paused. I tapped each finger against my side. I breathed. Then I exploded. "May I remind my king that I am not a ward of this court, nor am I bound to this court as anything other than a healer?"

"I am aware of that, Lady Elainya. I also owe you a great debt for the heir you have brought me with your return."

I paused. "Then...."

"I am asking you if you wish to marry Sir Reif or not?"

"Not, my lord."

"May I ask why? Is there another you wish?"

"Your majesty, I am married...or I was. We were young. On our wedding night, my husband died. Even though my period of mourning is over, I am disinclined to marry again. Should I choose to marry, I am considering an offer I've received from Lord Nian."

The king's eyebrows raised, but then he laughed. "I wish you both happiness, then. My young wife has restored my own youth. May it be so for Nian. I will explain to Sir Reif your refusal when he returns from the front."

He shifted on his throne and leaned toward me. "There is another matter I wish you to bear witness to. Wait with me a moment."

Reflect Rendel entered with the queen. In her arms, she held the precious heir to the kingdom. I watched the glow in the king's eyes and thought the child had also had a part in restoring his youth.

"As of now, Jeiwan is no longer heir to this throne. However, should something happen to me, my son will need a guardian." He turned to his wife. "Would you agree, my dear, that your brother would not be a wise choice?"

Laurel shook her head. "No, Reif will not be pleased at this turn. He does not know of the child yet. He left with the troops before I arrived."

"Reflect, I have it in mind to appoint Lord Nian as regent. Do you have any objections to this?"

"None, my lord. I think you have made a wise choice."

I was surprised by the reflect's approval, but did not speak. "Very well, then it is decided. I will go with the second wave of troops to the front, but first I want to enjoy my son." The king rose and took the child from Laurel. He left the room quickly, cooing to the baby in a most un-royal fashion.

I returned to my room and was pleased to find myself alone. Drawing the bolt on my door, I summoned my master.

The shadows in the room swirled, slowly taking on the handsome form he chose when he was being charming.

"You've been using me to feed your war."

"No, I've been allowing you to heal the sick."

"You would never allow such good unless it brought more suffering. I see that now."

The Shadow Lord's smile darkened the room.

The anger that had been muted by exhaustion finally boiled over. "I renounce you and your powers! I will never use them again—kill me or torment me if you wish. I don't care anymore.

You've destroyed all I love and now you've used me to bring evil upon this kingdom." The images of the dying wounded echoed through my head and I knew I would be sick. "I hate myself for being your servant."

His voice was surprisingly quiet. "You will beg me to restore your power, but I will not. Remember, I have it in my ability to take Drenil from you."

"You've already done that."

"No, but I will."

"Go ahead. I pray never to see you again."

"Use caution, my servant, you may get your wish." He vanished in a rush of wind that blew the covering aside from my window. The room was filled with bright hazy sunlight from the winter's early setting sun.

I stared around the room in awe until a pounding knock on the door disturbed me.

"Who is it?" I called, mindful of the sudden weakness I felt. My powers were definitely gone.

"Cyndace. Lady Elainya, I need your help!"

I opened the door.

"Why, child—what is the haste?"

"My brother is very sick. Please, Lady—help—please...."

I gathered a supply of my herbs as Cyndace told me she had seen her brother eating mushrooms earlier.

We collected Ember from the stables and rode double.

"How are your wedding plans?" I asked to distract her.

"I've been stitching the lovely fabric you gave me. I'm glad you are here to make Claude well again."

"How can you be sure I can heal him?" I asked.

"Because you are Elainya," she whispered.

I glanced back into her trusting eyes and hoped I would have the skill to help the boy.

Cyndace led me toward a small hut. I noticed the kiln outside and remembered Eryn saying he'd only lost two children.

The boy lay on a cot in a dark corner of the room. Carefully, I ran my hands over his body—and felt nothing. There was no stirring in my powers at all. I took a mixture of bitter herbs and ale and convinced him to drink. "Get me some straw," I told the girl. I'd just spread it beside him when he threw up all that he had eaten that day, including some unhealthy-looking mush-rooms. I gave him something to counteract the poison still in his system and left him to sleep quietly.

Perhaps the Shadow Lord was wrong. Perhaps I could con-tinue in this life without my powers.

I indulged in a short walk with Cyndace. "Lady Elainya," she said at last.

"What is it?"

"Thank you...for what you did for Claude...and for helping me find Jauer...."

I motioned her to silence. "You love him?"

"Very much."

"Did you know that Jauer has Draska blood?"

"I've thought he must."

"How will you feel being a mother of the next generation of Draska?"

"I would be proud to raise children to be like you."

"See that you raise them wiser than I have been. I've made terrible mistakes in my life."

Her protest was interrupted by the rattle of armor and the rush of horses' hooves approaching. I cringed, seeing the king's forces going into battle to face the unknown enemy. They'd be heading to Summer's Castle.

We stepped to the side of the road, almost into the woods. The horsed knights led the way, followed by the supply wagons. I noticed that Reflect Rendel was accompanying the troops this time. The foot soldiers brought up the rear. The attacks must have been bad for the king to send such a force. My mind was filled with worried thoughts of Nian and Jauer being the first to the battle scene when I was grabbed from behind by strong arms.

Cyndace managed only a small squeal before her mouth was as firmly covered as mine. I tried to turn and see our attackers, but my arms only twisted tighter. I kicked my assailant, who cursed rudely in my ear. Tired and unable to reach my dagger, I was overcome by his strength. Unable to resist, I gathered my wits and was surprised when I was turned and brought face to face with Reif.

The army having passed, he allowed me to speak. My first thought was for Cyndace. "Let the girl go," I ordered, wishing I had some power to put into my words.

"No, I want to take her with us. She knows you haven't come with me willingly. Until we can finish our arrangements, she'll have to stay with us. I'm sure Jeiwan will find some way to entertain her. Unless you have changed your mind and decided to accept my marriage proposal?" he said, a dirty leer bending his features.

I fought down my rage and managed to answer quietly. "Eventually, you will have to untie me," I whispered.

"True."

"I will kill you."

He laughed. "Fiery, aren't you? We'll see."

Reif and Jeiwan saw to it that we were tightly gagged and wrapped in sacks. I felt myself lifted over a horse and jolted into motion.

The sounds of the army grew louder and then were all around me. I felt myself lifted and dropped heavily onto a hard, rocking surface. Unable to see, I noted that it was cooler. We must be inside something, something moving. I smelled cheese and dried meat, mixed with the sour smell of ale. A supply wagon. Scuffling sounds nearby let me know that Cyndace was still with me.

Unable to call for help, I tried to summon some of my power, but it was gone. I focused my mind on Nian and willed for him to hear my cry for help, but I had no way to know if the thoughts would reach his mind.

Familiar laughter and the freezing touch of the master's hand on my skin sent shivers up my spine. "You won't escape, you know, Elainya. I warned you not to disobey me. You've decided you don't want my power any more? Let me see how you enjoy living at the edge of the world with no one around except your lustful, violent husband." He laughed again, and I ceased to struggle. It wouldn't matter even if the bonds were removed. He would not allow me to escape.

Somehow, I fell asleep during the long ride to Summer's Castle. I awoke to the curious echoing of horses' hooves as we entered the courtyard. The chill in the air let me know it was night, or probably early morning, given the distance we had traveled. I heard grumbling and clanking as the men dismounted from their horses.

As the horses were led away, I heard Sir Reif giving orders that our wagon was to be left for his servants to unload. I tried to remember the layout of the castle from years past and to place where we were. The cart had seemed to go straight through the entrance and then veer to the right, which would put us near the kitchen entrance. That would make sense, given the strong odor of food in the wagon. Reif's voice was distant, but it carried well.

"Reflect Rendel, a word with you!"

He must be coming down off the stairs that led into the castle. If I remembered right, the chapel was to the left of the entrance hall, so he must be scurrying across the courtyard to catch up with the reflect.

"Glad tidings! After months of courtship, the Lady Elainya has agreed to marry me."

If I could move, or make a loud noise, or otherwise attract Reflect Rendel's attention, perhaps he could find a way to rescue us. In my struggles, I could not hear Reflect Rendel's reply.

"Well, you'll see it for yourself tomorrow afternoon. If all goes well, I'd like you to perform the ceremony. Afterwards I'll have a great feast to welcome my new bride. Elainya will arrive this evening and will most likely need to rest. She has not been well of late."

Again, I could not hear the reflect's soft voice.

"You'll have a whole day to see her before the ceremony. You can perform whatever blessings you feel are necessary at that time. Don't you think it unwise to bless a witch, though?"

Reif's laughter carried for a long moment and then I heard heavy footsteps approaching. There was a whoosh as a tarp was pulled from the cart. I felt myself lifted roughly, and I heard Cyndace squeak in protest.

"Hush," grated Jeiwan's voice.

Footsteps crunched on gravel and then echoed on stone. In a moment, I felt myself turning, and the motion became uneven. We were going up steps...narrow ones, to judge from the frequent bumps.

What was in the east wing of Summer's Castle above the kitchens? I remembered the main chambers were in the west wing. Servants' quarters, maybe.

Reif smelled of horse and sweat as he carried me down the enclosed hallway. He shifted my weight, and I heard a key turn in a lock. Roughly, I was deposited on a straw mattress. I felt the edge of the knife as he cut away the wrappings and bindings that held me.

Once he freed my head, I looked around at the empty room. Two mattresses, a chamber pot, bare stone walls, a torch in the holder high on the wall, myself, Cyndace, Jeiwan, and Reif were the only features. No windows, and the door looked depressingly sturdy.

Reif noticed my inventory of the room. "You are quite trapped, Elainya. I had worried about your using magic, but then I heard how exhausted you were after Nian's illness. Any idea when your powers might return?"

I sat on the mattress and looked deep into his eyes. "You'll be the first to know."

He laughed. "Such a woman!"

"Reflect Rendel knows I'd never marry you."

"Well, you'll have to convince him otherwise. You see, if anything goes wrong with the ceremony tomorrow, your little friend here will die. Jeiwan will be with her constantly."

I looked from Reif to Jeiwan and paused. There was something wavering on the boy's face. Cyndace, also untied, looked to have been roughly handled, so I doubted it was concern for the girl.

"And how will you explain why your bride must eat with her fingers?" I brushed my hands across the place where my dagger usually hung. Reif would know better than to return my eating dagger to me.

He reached into his cloak and casually pulled out the familiar jeweled hilt. "This? This is clearly a magical talisman, don't you agree? My bride will have to renounce such dark magic. I'll see that you have a plain one to eat with at table, but none other. I doubt you'll have the chance to kill me in a crowded banquet hall." He smiled thoughtfully as he put my knife back inside his cloak.

If I'd had a shred of magic, I could have called the knife into my hand, but I remained powerless. "You may be surprised by what I might do," I muttered.

He laughed. "Well, we'll see. Rest yourselves. In a few hours, I'll move you into more suitable quarters. I'll have my seamstress fit the gown to you in the morning. In the afternoon, you will be attended by the good Reflect Rendel. Afterwards, we will have a lovely wedding ceremony and a feast to celebrate."

"Aren't you supposed to be fighting a war?" I asked.

"If and when the enemy attacks, my men can deal with the raiders. I doubt there will be any attacks, however. Reflect Rendel mentioned something to me about the attacks being fed by magic. Now we've only two magicians in the kingdom, and one is powerless. That only leaves your friend Nian. He's lived a long and full life, and he left the castle so soon after his injury, there's no way to know what might befall him on the way. So, no, I don't think I'll need to worry about a war. But you must admit, it did give me an excellent opportunity to carry you off."

"Nian is stronger than you think."

"We'll see," Reif growled, and motioned Jeiwan towards the door.

"Jeiwan," I called, "do you want to go through with this? You'll have to spend the rest of your life looking over your shoulder."

He glanced at me briefly before leaving. Reif took the torch with him, leaving Cyndace and me alone in the dark.

The girl was remarkably calm while we stayed in that hole of a room. We slept little, hunger and nervousness keeping us awake. I tried to make some sort of pleasant conversation.

My voice sounded very loud in the utter blackness of the room. "He miscounted how many magicians there are."

Her voice was tiny. "I noticed."

"Jauer will find you. Just keep thinking about him. Sometimes love is the most powerful magic."

I felt her hand on my arm, frail but insistent. "Do you think Sir Reif will ever let me leave here?"

How was I to answer that? "Reif isn't a bright man. Eventually, he'll make a mistake. Just stay calm and watch for a chance to escape. If you get one, I want you to run. Don't wait for me. Once you are safe, I will be able to take care of myself, understand?"

"Yes."

In the darkness, I thought of Nian. Drenil and I had always been able to sense when anything was wrong with the other, but this was Nian. We'd become friends, but I couldn't be sure he could sense my danger, or even guess where I was, even after the closeness of what appeared to be my final spell. I'd need to think of another way to escape. Somehow being married to Nian didn't seem like such a bad proposition right now.

I was still thinking when Jeiwan and Reif came to take me to the family wing of the castle. The light and smoke made my eyes tear.

He chuckled as he tossed a traveling cloak to me. "The tearful bride," he said with a smile. "Remember to play the part well, my dearest. You've just come in from riding all day. You're tired and you need to rest. You'll abide no visitors tonight."

"Do you plan on feeding us?"

"I'll bring you food later. Jeiwan will bring something to Cyndace. She'll stay here until the ceremony. I'm sure Jeiwan can amuse her."

I glared at Reif and tried to find some suitable remark, but he cut me off. "Don't worry, I'll see that she's safe as long as you behave. Do you understand?"

"Yes." I stood up and wrapped the cloak around my shoulders.

There was no point in trying to talk to Reif. He was determined to go through with this ridiculous plan of his. Jeiwan, on the other hand, seemed unsure. "You know, Jeiwan, I had thought your manners were improving."

I caught one last glimpse of Cyndace looking at me confidently before she was left in the darkness. Jeiwan ignored the comment as he barred the door behind me. Now if only I had confidence in myself.

Trying to think of a way out of this that didn't involve magic was becoming more and more difficult by the moment. "Don't forget to feed her."

I followed Reif dutifully through the castle, searching for a familiar face anywhere, but I knew no one. Servants glanced at me, occasionally making the sign of the Light in my direction. I was certain they did not mean the gesture as a blessing. My reputation had spread farther than I realized. Perhaps Reif had encouraged the rumors to prevent anyone from speaking with me.

The bridal chamber was luxurious by comparison to the simple room I'd just left. I glanced around at the tapestries and focused my attention on the dressing table.

Reif only laughed. "I assure you, Elainya, I am not so stupid as to put anything within your reach that could be in the least bit harmful either to you or to myself."

The windows were covered by tapestries. The castle was built on a cliff overlooking the sea. Waves echoed throughout the chamber. "And what if I choose the only option you left open for your first wife?"

His eyes hardened. "Then you are not the woman I think you are. However, I think you'll find the windows are narrow in this room. Too narrow even for you to slip out of."

"Understand one thing," I said, "I would as easily kill myself as I would kill you. Either possibility seems more desirable to me than marriage. Surely you've heard that I am already married?"

"You are a widow."

I shrugged out of my cloak and tossed it towards the bed. I knew my rumpled state would only weaken the image I'd gone to such lengths with my wardrobe to create. "Just remember—my husband was a very powerful magician. He died during a spell so evil that his spirit has been bound to the earth. He haunts me. I doubt he will take kindly to you."

"I'm not afraid of shades or spirits, woman. You're the only source of danger to me, and I will be watching you very closely until you adapt to your changed circumstances. I have a lot to offer you. In time, you'll come to enjoy my company."

Now it was my turn to laugh.

He slapped me roughly and then turned to leave. "Remember the girl, Elainya. Don't make me angry again."

I sat in the now-dark room and listened to the ocean. I followed the sound, bumping my shin against the dressing table, and managed to uncover the thin slit that passed for a window. Reif was right, even I could not escape that way. Of course, if he didn't feed me, I might be able to eventually.

Pulling back the tapestries at least allowed some feeble moonlight into the room. Reif was right, however, that the wedding ceremony would leave me trapped. No one would aid me in leaving him. Surely, that was why Neelysella had chosen to throw herself off the cliff. Reif was also right that I was not of the same temperament as his first wife. Eventually, he'd leave me an opening and I'd kill him.

Frustrated, I sat on the bed. My face hurt, but I knew it wouldn't even bruise. He'd been careful. That was another thing he was right about: I should remember not to make him angry.

In the dim light, I noticed the wavering image of the spirit which slowly solidified into the form of Drenil. He looked around thoughtfully. "Where is this place?" he asked me.

It didn't surprise me that he knew my predicament. "The castle above Summerstown."

He sat next to me and put his arms around me, allowing me to relax briefly. "Don't worry, Elainya, I'll get you out of this," he whispered.

"And what are you going to do, my love? Despite what I told Reif, I know you can't help. Besides, the Shadow Lord has arranged this."

"I know. He's used us badly, but he won't get another opportunity to attack the kingdom. I'll see that Nian knows what's happened, if he doesn't know already. He'll see that Jauer stops practicing magic as well. There'll be no more attacks."

"Sir Reif plans to have Nian killed."

Drenil laughed. "Don't worry, Nian is more than a match for that buffoon. The Shadow Lord thought I couldn't find you, but he was mistaken. I'll tell Nian where you are. He'll be here before the wedding." Dren fingered a lock of my hair. "He's very fond of you."

The door opened, taking us both by surprise. Jeiwan entered, carrying a tray of bread, mixed cheeses and a candle. He looked at me and then his eyes focused on the image of Drenil.

"You really do consort with demons," he whispered.

"Not any more. Now I just consort with ghosts."

The boy put the tray down and paused. "Your ghost can't hurt us, we're mortal."

Drenil growled, but I put a restraining hand on his arm. "True, but he will probably make life quite miserable for your father."

"Definitely," Drenil added.

Jeiwan made the symbol of Light, but Dren only laughed.

The boy turned and fled, tripping as he struggled to shut the door.

Drenil held me close again before rising to leave. "Eat and then sleep, my love. Tomorrow will be a full day. Get ready for the ceremony, but keep your eyes open. If necessary, marry the brute. Once Cyndace is safe, Nian will come for you. You're already a widow. If you are forced to marry Reif, I swear it will be only a moment before you are a widow again." He vanished before I could reply.

Eating and sleeping made a lot of sense at that moment.

Chapter 18

Marriage

Elainya

The gown Reif had picked out for me was elaborate, probably left over from his first wedding. Embroidered with white on the white fabric, the train spread out behind me, making movement difficult. The sleeves were long and flowing, the neckline low and far more revealing than I liked. The overall effect was as entrapping as this marriage.

His servant girls fussed about with the belt and managed to take in some of the seams to make it fit better. They wove my hair around a thin gold circlet and then one of them darted forward and hung a golden emblem of Light around my neck. She jumped back as if expecting me to scream or melt away. When I did neither, she returned to finish straightening my gown.

Reif entered at noon and shooed them all out. Jeiwan was with him, looking more uncomfortable than ever. "I tell you, Father, there was a ghost here last night!"

Reif's eyes focused on the revealing bodice of the gown, but he spoke to his son. "A ghost can not harm me, boy. Be quiet."

"But Father...."

The look Reif turned on his son made the boy pale. "Just remember: if anything happens during the ceremony, I want you to kill the potter's girl."

Jeiwan nodded obediently, dashing my hopes that escape could be that easy.

Reif's gaze returned to me. "I've come to escort you to your meeting with Reflect Rendel. Remember, play your part well."

Having nothing to say, I placed my hand on his proffered arm. Silently, I hoped Drenil had been able to reach Nian. I could not see how much help that could be, however. Surely there were guards posted, and Nian was only one man. If he didn't dare use his power, there would not be much he and Jauer could do against Reif's men.

Reflect Rendel was kneeling at the altar when I entered. Silently, I knelt next to him. Reif remained at the back of the chapel.

"Sir Reif tells me that you have decided to marry him," the reflect said carefully.

"Yes," I replied.

"You know I can not perform the marriage ceremony for someone who serves a demon?"

"Yes." I could see he was suspicious. Reflect Rendel knew how rarely I would answer in monosyllables, and he knew my feelings about Reif.

"Have you renounced your service to that demon?"

"Absolutely."

Reflect Rendel's eyebrows shot up in surprise at the vehemence I put into that one word. I noticed the faint laugh from one of the shadows in the room.

It was then that I realized that Nian and Drenil's plan could not succeed. The Shadow Lord had already told me this was to be my punishment for turning from him. They had little chance against Reif, but none against a being that powerful. I shuddered.

"Are you cold, Elainya?" the reflect asked.

"No." The room seemed to grow a bit darker. Despite the holiness of the chapel, there were more shadows in the room than the afternoon could account for.

"Elainya, do you remember what I once told you about not being able to be too far from the Light?"

I nodded.

"Rely on the Light, Elainya," the priest said gently.

I looked at my hands in quiet thought, knowing in my heart that his words could not apply to me.

"Is it your will that this marriage takes place?" the reflect asked softly.

By the rustling in the back of the room, I knew that Reif had heard the question. I turned towards the back of the room and noticed that Jeiwan and Cyndace were standing outside the door. She looked frightened, but not injured. Someone had given her clean clothes.

I turned my attention back to Reflect Rendel. "Yes," I whispered.

He made the sign of the Light over me and then turned to Sir Reif.

"Where are your guests?" he asked.

"The ceremony is to be private," Reif explained and closed the door.

I was not ready to let Cyndace out of my sight, however. "But, my dear, I wanted Cyndace to stand with me."

Reif started to protest, but then noticed Reflect Rendel's curious expression. "Of course, anything for you, my love," my groom cooed.

He opened the door and had Cyndace come to my side. Jeiwan stood obediently beside his father, glancing at me nervously.

Reflect Rendel took his place on the step above us, and motioned Reif to kneel beside me. "Elainya, you will need to remove your ring," the reflect said.

I glanced down at my ring in surprise. Obediently, I reached to remove it and laughed when it turned out to be stuck.

Reif reached to help me. His touch was not gentle, but he was constrained by the nearness of Reflect Rendel. "Can't she simply wear that one?" he asked, impatience edging into his voice.

Reflect Rendel glanced towards the back of the chapel as if consulting a book of rules, and shook his head. "No, the ring must be removed. I've some oil, just a moment." He rustled around behind the altar for quite a while. Reif watched in amazement as the priest managed to knock over a small table, toppling an unlit candlestick and an empty gold chalice to the floor. The noise was so loud, I almost didn't hear the door open and shut quietly. Jeiwan did not take his eyes off me, as if expecting me to vanish. At least the boy had learned some respect.

Afraid to hope, I did not turn around. Reflect Rendel stood up triumphantly with the small vial of oil and righted the table.

He laughed as he placed the oil on my finger and slipped the ring off. "You need the extra blessing anyway, Elainya," he whispered. I watched as he put my precious ring in a pocket of his robe.

"Now, shall we begin?" he said and glanced meaningfully towards the back of the room.

I followed his gaze and saw Nian walking down the aisle, followed by Jauer. Reif reached instantly for his dagger but was stopped by Reflect Rendel. "This is the Light's house, sir. You will not spill blood here."

"That sorcerer has no right to set foot in a holy place," Reif sputtered.

Trillia was also there, slipping quietly into the room. Her movements were timid. Reif had not mentioned that she would be at the wedding. She sat near the back of the room, almost invisible with the gray stone walls behind her.

Was this how the girl had spent her youth? Hiding from her father's notice? She was clearly good at it.

Jauer reached his hand out towards Cyndace. She ran to him eagerly and he stood protectively in front of her. Jeiwan did not move from his place at his father's side.

Nian's eyes met mine and he sighed. "Actually, I have every right to be here, Sir Reif. Reflect Rendel sent for me."

The good reflect nodded. "Nian needs to speak before this marriage can continue. I will not allow Elainya to marry unless Nian gives her away."

I stood and turned to face Nian as he took my arm. I said nothing, waiting for him to explain whatever ruse he had planned.

He pulled me close to his side and wrapped an arm around me protectively. "Elainya can not marry because she is already married."

"Her husband is dead." Reif was losing patience.

"No, he's not." Nian's voice was weak as he turned to look at me. I was not prepared for the sadness in his eyes. "Elainya, surely you have to recognize some part of me," he whispered.

Reif started to protest, but Nian glanced at him and he was silent. The fierceness of that glance was almost as powerful as magic would have been.

Reflect Rendel nodded. "Lord Nian is as close to a father as you have, child, but I do not want him here as your father. You are his to give or keep as he chooses. My friend, it is time to tell her the truth."

"I didn't die, Elainya," he whispered. His wrinkled hand caressed my cheek tenderly before he continued. With a gasp, I realized what he was saying. "I woke up forty years ago. I tried to wake you, but no magic, no pleading could rouse you. I hadn't been gone long enough for the tale to be forgotten, so I created a past for myself. The Shadow Lord helped to ensure that I was well received though unrecognized at court, and I followed him. He promised that as long as I served him, I would eventually have a chance to be with you again."

He shrugged and his hands dropped to his side. "Once I grew old enough that I knew you would not want me, I tried to kill myself, but he would not allow it. He told me that I could only die after I had trained you in the use of shadow magic. That didn't seem like such a terrible thing at the time. We had sworn to serve him, so it made sense. Only once my chance finally came, you didn't let me die."

"But you were a spirit...." I whispered.

"I couldn't bear to be so close to you and never have the opportunity to be with you. Forgive me, my love, but the dream projections seemed like the obvious way for us to have time together. Once I realized that I was upsetting you, I tried to leave you alone, but I couldn't. I would never have held you to a marriage you didn't want if it hadn't been for this...." Nian looked at Reif and he seemed unable to think of a suitable description for my would-be husband.

Unable to contain myself any longer, I wrapped my arms around him and held him close. "You fool!" I fought tears of joy as I looked up into his eyes. "As if I would mind gray hair and wrinkles!" Now that I knew the truth, I couldn't see how I had been so blind as to miss the resemblance before.

He kissed me gently. "It has been so hard being this close to you and not being able to kiss you," he whispered. "Reflect, may I have that ring back?" he asked.

"Of course."

Nian placed the ring on my finger as he had so many years before. "Thus our hearts shall be entwined—my soul on fire for only thee," he whispered.

Sir Reif started to protest but was silenced as the room darkened and echoed with laughter. "At least you remember the words of your vow," the Shadow Lord said. He turned his attention to Reif, Jeiwan, and Reflect Rendel. "I bear a message. The king is dead."

Jeiwan's eyes widened. "Then I am king."

I noticed Trillia standing in shock, her hands pressed to her lips.

I shook my head. "No, you are not. I would have told you sooner, but as your prisoner, it didn't seem appropriate."

"We delivered the new heir to the castle only a few days ago," Nian explained.

Reflect Rendel smiled. "Yes, and the king spoke with me at length over the choice of a new regent. He chose you, Nian."

Nian's eyes revealed surprise, but he had no time for argument. The Shadow Lord laughed. "As I had planned. Now Nian can end this war. All I ask is Aurora, which you have the power to give me."

"I will not give you Aurora or any other part of this kingdom," Nian snapped.

Reif's hand was on his sword. "You claim my bride? Now you claim the kingdom? Even while your evil master stands in this holy place?" He turned to Rendel. "And you, Reflect, you do nothing?"

The reflect gestured at the walls. "The castle is yours, Sir. If there is evil here, it is by your invitation."

The Shadow Lord laughed. The noise level outside had been slowly increasing. Now it reached an unavoidable crescendo. A soldier rushed in and ran to Reif. "The castle is under attack! You must come, my lord!"

I could see Reif's pulse clearly in the veins of his neck and temple. He drew his sword. "You stand between me and all that I want, sorcerer. We will settle this."

Jeiwan also drew his sword and stood just to his father's left. I saw him then as the man he could have been, not as the boy I had felt so unworthy. His eyes shifted between Nian and the

Shadow Lord. He stood up straighter. "It would be wrong to let the kingdom become enslaved to a demon."

Jeiwan stepped toward me and Trillia screamed. "No!"

She'd stepped into the aisle and now held her hands out towards her father. "Please, Father, Jeiwan, stop. They have been good to me."

Reif did not even look at his daughter.

The Shadow Lord spoke into the echoes of her plea. "I need to speak with my servants, alone."

Reflect Rendel did not move. "You do not command me, demon. I acknowledge that you have been summoned, and that you have a right to speak to those in your power, but I think I'll stay and watch. Jauer, take Cyndace somewhere safe."

I was surprised that the master merely accepted the old reflect's wishes and allowed the young couple to leave unhindered.

Reif stepped forward, his sword at Nian's throat. "I will not be dismissed."

"You will not harm them!" Trillia shrieked as she ran down the aisle. She was in front of me suddenly, pushing me back and staring intently at her brother.

Half brother, some part of my brain whispered. Her other half was Draska.

Powerful, undeniable, and enraged.

With a wave of her hand, she used her power to disarm her father and brother.

Both Jeiwan and Reif fell to the ground, gasping for air, their hands clutching at their throats.

"Trillia, no!" I grabbed her shoulders and tried to turn her to face me.

She was stone.

She refused to move until the men's struggles ceased. Then she turned to me, composed and calm. "They have done enough harm. They will never hurt anyone again."

She glanced at the reflect and nodded. Her smile was a fragile thing, foreign to her lips. "I apologize for interfering, Reflect, but I could not allow my father or brother to further besmirch our family. Now if you'll excuse me, I have a castle to defend."

She turned to the Shadow Lord and bowed.

"Good day, my lord," she said into the stunned silence before turning and walking calmly from the room, taking the soldier who had come to summon Reif with her. After what he had witnessed, he wisely recognized his new ruler.

Before the doors closed, I could hear her issuing orders.

The Shadow Lord laughed. "Such a lovely girl." He turned back toward where Nian and I stood.

"You are reunited as I promised. I require one thing more of you. Give me Aurora and I will give you the rest of this land for your own. I and mine will leave you alone for the rest of your lives. Only this one thing I demand."

Nian and I exchanged a glance before he spoke up. "And what if we refuse?"

"Then you will both die, here and now. Choose."

"I would rather die than serve you for one more instant." I held tight to Nian. "No matter how pleasant the alternative might be."

Nian nodded.

The master seemed to rise up before us, terrible in his anger.

"Excuse me," interrupted Reflect Rendel, "but you seem to have forgotten to tell them all of their alternatives." He smiled almost apologetically as he looked at us. "Neither of you has ever listened to me. Repeatedly, I've told you that you are still free to serve my master."

In shock, my hand went to the emblem of Light that hung around my neck. "But... the Light would not be served by such as we...."

"Of course not," interjected the Shadow Lord. "Nian, you have no choice." His voice was ice. "Elainya has chosen to defy me."

I felt the pain begin and tried to run, but there was no hope of escape. The master's anger was burning my soul. He forced me to my knees and I screamed in agony.

Slowly I became aware of a cool hand holding my own. I turned pain-filled eyes toward the reflect. "That creature cannot harm one of the Light's servants," he whispered. "In the eyes of the Light, you are no more wicked than I was when I took my vows."

"You have no choice, Nian," the Shadow Lord repeated.

I focused my attention on the reflect and felt him pushing the pain further from me.

"Do you wish to serve darkness, Elainya?"

"No."

"Will you serve the Light?"

"I will." I gasped for air and continued. "I will serve the Light." In an instant, the pain abated. I stared at the reflect in amazement as I felt power return to me. His touch was soothing and healing to my soul.

"You see, that creature is not the only source of power."

Nian's expression was of a man lost. Unable to hear the conversation I was having with the reflect, his gaze had been traveling back and forth between the master and myself.

The Shadow Lord spoke tenderly to him. "I can offer you something else, Nian. Something you want most of all. I can make you young again." The master waved his arm and Nian transformed into the Drenil I remembered.

I stood up and we faced each other. He saw the renewed energy in my eyes and smiled, misunderstanding my joy. "Aurora is dead, Elainya. What use is fighting for it?"

I shook my head. "Dren, I'm free. The reflect is right. Aurora is ours. We can rebuild the Draska. We can teach our people to serve the Light."

I took Nian's hands, and let my new courage strengthen my words. He had to hear me. He had to understand. "I will not serve the Shadow Lord, and I love you regardless of your out-ward form. I would have you as my husband, but not as the slave of darkness."

The spirit drew closer. "Nian, the Light does not want you. It will strike you dead for what you have done. It is true, Light once loved the Draska. You have completed their destruction for me. The Light will accept your service only in death."

From the semblance of his younger self, an older, wiser Nian looked at me, and I saw his eyes drift to the reflect's.

The reflect nodded in encouragement.

Nian's voice was tender as he turned back to me. "Perhaps that is best. I will serve Light. In death or in life, let the Light choose."

The master's response was a low growl. I watched as Drenil's body aged to the man I'd known as Nian. The smooth features withered like drying fruit. The spark of his blue eyes faded to gray along with his hair. His cheeks eroded into hard lines, re-flecting the pain of his last forty years. Small wonder I had not recognized my own husband—he was no longer the innocent love of my youth.

Nor, for that matter, was I.

"You have chosen poorly," the Shadow Lord cursed as he disappeared.

Nian staggered and I caught him. The reflect reached out to him, and he grasped the reflect's arm, turning his faded gaze to the warm brown eyes of one who would be our friend. "So, does your Light want me dead?"

"Actually, my friend, you'll need a long life if you are to re-store the Draska."

"Restore?"

"You will find the children, and you will father more."

Nian shook his head in befuddlement at such a thought. We were interrupted by the sound of screams from the castle walls. The battle was going poorly.

"What of the battle?" I asked.

The reflect frowned. "I had thought it would end when you denounced him."

"Perhaps it would have if we were the only Draska," Nian's voice was weak.

He looked at me in fear. "Jauer," he said.

"Trillia." I shuddered.

"Reflect, bring Jauer and have him meet me on the east tower." As the priest rushed off, Nian grasped my hand. "It is as if I can hear our new master whispering to me."

I nodded. "His voice will take some getting used to."

"You think the Light will protect us through this?"

"I have no idea. We have to try."

We walked out into a blackness darker than any night I could remember. No stars shone overhead. Nian went back into the chapel, and returned with a torch. Together, we made our way toward the east wall. Nearby screams shredded the darkness. At the top of the tower we were joined by Jauer and the reflect. Against Jauer's wishes, Cyndace had come with them.

"Reflect, take the girl to safety," I urged. "This battle is ours."

"I will stand with you, and she does not look like she wishes to leave."

Cyndace wrapped her arms around Jauer's right arm and would not budge. With a sigh, Nian told Jauer of our decision. "I have shielded you from the Shadow Lord, but he will try to recruit you now that I have denounced him. He has much to offer, but the decision is yours alone."

Jauer nodded and waved towards the destruction below us, only visible in patches near the fires. "I want nothing to do with the creator of this abomination."

"Very well." Nian took a deep breath and then relaxed. With a voice louder than his frail form seemed capable of, he summoned the Lord of Darkness.

Nothing happened.

I looked at the surrounding darkness, listened to the screams from the battle below. "He is already here," I said.

Nian yelled over the battle. "Creatures of Darkness, your master is defeated. You have no servants here. We denounce you. Aurora is ours and will return to the ways of Light. You have no dominion here. Begone."

The creatures let out a scream and withdrew to one side of the beach but did not leave. Dawn crept slowly over the eastern sea. The moon appeared overhead and the day brightened until only the shadow before us remained.

The Shadow Lord seemed far from defeated. His smile was broad. "You may have escaped me, but I have set my desires on this kingdom and I will have it. If you will not open the door for me, then others will. It will only be a matter of time." The sun burst above the horizon and he vanished, only to reappear near his troops. With a swirl of shadow, they all disappeared, leaving only a solitary gray-clad figure standing where they had been.

Trillia turned and walked up the path to the castle, every stride full of confidence and purpose. I watched as she gathered the castle's defenders in her wake.

Reflect Rendel took a deep breath of the fresh sea air. "I suspect our welcome here is about to end."

Nian put his arm around me protectively. "I agree."

I shook my head. "Maybe I can talk to her. Warn her."

We climbed down from the tower to be greeted by Trillia. Her eyes were piercing in their intensity and there was no denying the darkness that empowered her. I stepped toward her, but she motioned me to a stop. "I will not hear what you have to say, Elainya. You have been good to me, and for that I will allow you to leave." She sent a servant to saddle horses while she led us down to the courtyard. Another servant rushed up with a bundle of provisions and my stolen clothing.

"My father was an evil man. I am sorry for what he did to you, but he will cause no further harm. As of today, the province of Summer is mine. I intend to see that it is managed fairly and justly." She turned to Nian. "But we will not be tied to your infant king and the whims of his Draska guardians."

Rendel nodded. "I understand your concerns, but these have stood with me against the darkness today. You would do well to stand with us, not in opposition."

Trillia shook her head and a look of sadness passed over her face that did not extend to her eyes. "My men witnessed your collusion with these Draska, Reflect. They witnessed the death of my father and brother at their hands even as I tried to stop the conflict."

I was stunned. "But..."

She cut me off. "No. I will hear no more. You are all to leave my lands and not return. I offer you safe passage this once only. If Draska are found on my land again, you will be killed."

The girl that I had once thought weak turned and walked away, her people following, clearly enchanted by their new queen.

Nian mounted Singe and pulled me up to ride in front of him. I felt ridiculous riding away in the entangling wedding gown.

We did not speak during the first part of the journey. At midday, we stopped and Nian set about preparing a meal.

Reflect Rendel laughed as he watched me trying to walk in the confining gown.

"It seems a shame for you to be dressed so and not have a wedding," he said.

"I'm happy enough having escaped." I looked at Nian—at Dren—startled again that I had missed the resemblance for so long. "Besides, I am already married." I smiled tentatively and Nian returned the gaze.

Then he paused and looked at the reflect. "I think we should renew our vows, and make a few changes."

The reflect nodded. "A wedding would save having to explain to the court that you were already married," he pointed out. "You could leave the past and move into your future."

I looked at Jauer and Cyndace. "We'd be honored to share in your wedding as well. We could have a dual wedding."

"I want a Draska bonding," Jauer said, looking hopefully at his bride.

She nodded, and I felt compelled to explain. "You realize that when the Draska bond, their spirits become linked. When one dies, so does the other."

The girl nodded and took Jauer's hand in hers. "I would not want to live without him."

I looked at Nian. I understood the feeling well. And we were bonded. Had been all this time. The Shadow Lord had spoken some truth. My life was tied to Nian's, for however long we had left. We would make things right.

"We will rebuild Aurora," Jauer said. "We'll find any others with Draska blood and bring them home."

Nian nodded. "The Shadow Lord's purpose was to take Aurora. We must reclaim it, restore our people. Raise our children to revere the Light."

"So they will not make the same mistakes we made," I said.

Reflect Rendel nodded. "The darkness is not gone. Night hides while it is day, but returns at sunset. You must make certain that your children will be strong enough to resist the darkness when it returns."

With Nian's arm around me, I looked at the young couple and hoped, by the Light, to live long enough to see the bright future they would build.

Acknowledgments

There's no way I can thank everyone who has helped along this journey. I will surely forget someone, and if I named you all, this book would be too large to lift! Thank you in particular to my fabulous beta readers: Barbara, Michael, Suzy, and Donna.

To the many writers who have offered support and encouragement over the years from Compuserve and AOL's Books and Writer's forum, thank you. You've been friends and goads. To the fabulous writers of SectionSixx...thank you. You are brilliant, creative individuals. Elise, thank you for staying with me.

Martin, I'm sorry I didn't finish this on time.

To my family, my husband and my children...thank you. You have been beyond supportive. You've been patient and understanding and you bring me food. I love you all.

I had fabulous teachers at Santa Clara University. Thanks to Dr. Cory Wade for believing in me and helping me believe in fairies.

Margie Lawson—thanks for being an amazing teacher.

Lori Patrick, thank you for editing my work. Over. And. Over.

And to Dreamer: you were there when I started this journey. Thanks for reading to the end.

If you enjoyed this book, please consider leaving a review on Goodreads and the site where you purchased it.

Connect with me online at **Deleyna.com**. I'd love to hear from you!

Sign up for my newsletter to be the first to know when my next book comes out.

Also by Deleyna Marr:

A single gunshot shattered Dana's perfect life. Now she's starting over with a new life, new rules and an old flame to chase all her demons away. But Dana's demons have other ideas. They want her—and her sisters—at any cost.

www.ingramcontent.com/pod-product-compliance
Lightning Source LLC
Chambersburg PA
CBHW031109030726
47496CB00002BA/459